BORN TO BE HIS BRIDE?

It is said that Braden MacAllister, English baron and proud Highland warrior, can fell an enemy with a single blow—and a woman with a single kiss. But not Maggie, it seems. For the fire-haired beauty, determined to end the long-running feud that rages between their clan and its common foe, is immune to Braden's attempts to stop her foolishness. But stop her he will, once he gets the meddling minx alone ... and favors her with a passionate caress and an irresistible kiss.

No matter how she trembles beneath Braden's sensuous touch ... he has given his heart to none. But dare she dream that by assuring peace for her clan she may also be claiming the most magnificent Highlander for herself?

KINLEY MACGREGOR

Claiming the Highlander

An Avon Romantic Treasure

AVON BOOKS
An Imprint of HarperCollinsPublishers

AVON BOOKS
An Imprint of HarperCollins*Publishers*
10 East 53rd Street
New York, New York 10022-5299

Copyright © 2002 by Sherrilyn Kenyon
ISBN: 0-7394-2382-7

To Monique, who couldn't wait to read Braden's story; Nancy for all the sage advice and laughs; Lyssa for all the hard work and valuable insights; my friends who kept me sane during the insanity: Rickey, Celeste, Valerie, and Cheryl.

As always, to my boys: Cabal, Madaug and Ian; my mother; and most especially, to my own hero, Ken, who taught me to believe in everlasting love when I was sure it had long forsaken me. You gave me wings to fly and the freedom I needed to explore my boundaries. Thank you.

A special thanks to my contest winners who named the various characters of the book:

Pat Gamberi: Aisleen

Fatin: Ceana

Leslie Hiatt: Lochlan

And most of all to you, the reader. May love and happiness always be yours.

Chapter 1

London, during the reign of Henry II

Handsome as sin and more dangerous than the devil himself, Braden MacAllister had but one affliction in life.

He adored all women.

At a score and five years, he had claimed more hearts than anyone could count and charmed more women than there were stars in the heavens. It was said that on the hour of his birth, the midwife had been enthralled by the newborn's playful air. The woman, who had helped bring over three score wee bairns into the world, had instantly proclaimed Braden a bane to any lass foolish enough to give her heart over to one such as he.

For the boy had the devil in him. 'Twas plain for any to see.

Braden himself didn't know why women fascinated him so. He only knew that he adored them all—young, old, single or married, beautiful or plain. It mattered not, for each woman possessed a special flame within her that he found irresistible, and in return, women were fascinated by him.

Wherever he went, feminine heads came together with gasps and giggles as they relayed his reputation to each other. Those who knew his bedroom skills firsthand lorded it over those who only knew him by rumor.

Braden always responded to the women he met with a roguish smile. Never was he too busy to stop along the way to pass a moment or two with a willing female.

Indeed, he lived for the sensual. Lived for the sound of soft, feminine sighs of pleasure whispered in his ear as he reveled in the giving of pleasure to his lover. He could never consider himself well sated until his partner had found her own satisfaction at least three or four times.

And Braden loved to be well sated.

His family claimed it was a terrible addiction he had.

For his life, he didn't know what it was about women that captivated him so. Perhaps it was the smell of them, the feel of their soft, supple limbs sliding against his naked skin.

Nay, he decided, 'twas the *taste* of women he loved best.

And right now he was surrounded by three women who were vying for his attention.

The Ghent sisters.

Well, only two of them were still from Ghent; the other, Piety, had married Rufus of Nottingham the winter past. And though Braden liked the old earl a great deal, it really was a shame for such a vibrant young woman to be shackled to a man thrice her age. Especially when said man spent more time tending his hawks and hounds than he did doting on his beautiful bride.

Piety, in great contradiction to her name, had been making advances toward him ever since his arrival in England three months past to visit with his brother and swear homage for his English lands to King Henry II.

Ever one to avoid unpleasantness with the English when he could, Braden had deftly side-stepped the young woman's seductive contrivances and machinations.

When he had received a letter earlier that day from Rufus requesting his presence to talk over some Scottish lands the earl was thinking of selling, Braden had thought little of it. Until he had arrived to find the three women in residence while the earl and his brothers had departed that very morning for France.

Braden's first inclination had been to leave. But what mere mortal man could refuse such fruits of heaven when they were literally laid bare before him?

It was certainly more temptation than Braden could resist. Not that it took much in the way of temptation for a hedonist such as he.

If the women were content to seduce him, then he was certainly content to be seduced.

The three women pushed him down on the bed and were starting to make free use of his body for their pleasure. Delighted to let the ladies have their way with him, Braden relaxed and simply enjoyed what they offered.

"Milord," Patience purred as she dropped his dark blue surcoat to the floor. "Tell us again how you slew the Kilgarigon Dragon."

Prudence tugged at his right boot until she bared his stockinged foot. "I prefer the tale of how you dispatched that highwayman on your way to London."

Piety slid her hands over his thighs to the back of his hips. "And I prefer this tail, right here," she said as she grabbed two handfuls of his buttocks.

"Ah, ladies, ladies," he sighed contentedly. "Where shall I begin?"

Lifting her kirtle to gift him with a luscious view of her bare bottom, Piety moved to straddle his waist. She wiggled her hips suggestively against his, then settled the yellow material down around her. She peeled back a portion of her kirtle to expose the curvaceous swell of her well-rounded bosom.

"Why not begin here?" she said, brushing her hand over the top of her left breast.

"Aye, that looks like a fine place to start," Braden said huskily.

But before he could oblige the countess, the door to the room burst open.

"Piety!" came the outraged bellow.

Braden propped himself up on his elbows to see Rufus standing in the doorway, his lips grim. The earl's face was redder than the embers of the fire, which made his well-trimmed white beard all the more apparent.

Braden growled low in his throat. Couldn't a man have a moment's worth of fun without some angry father, husband or brother rushing in and demanding his blood?

Well, if you'd marry the woman first, brother, you'd not have that problem. Braden flinched at Sin's familiar words in his head.

Och now, what did his brother know of it? Sin spent just as much time avoiding holy matrimony as Braden did.

Piety scooted off his lap with an indignant shriek while the other two women made haste for a nearby corner. The light of the chamber's fire and tallow candles highlighted their quivering shadows against the wall.

Braden sighed in regret. Well, it had certainly been fun while it lasted.

What was it with husbands who couldn't be trusted to go out of the country when they said they would?

One would think a man would have more respect than to barge into his wife's chambers without being announced. Why, such a thing was downright rude.

"How dare you!" Rufus snarled as he stormed into his wife's chambers.

Piety met Rufus in the center of the room, hands on her hips. "How dare *you*!" she shouted as she moved to confront her irate husband.

She caught Rufus by the surcoat as he made for the bed and swung him about to face her. "You tell me you're leaving, only to return the minute I have a little fun. I'm beginning to think you lie to me just so you can come home and spear whatever man I've caught!"

Braden cocked his brow at her words. Just how many men had the countess caught?

Rufus narrowed his glare on his wife. "Woman, I swear, if not for your father's wealth and the fact that I know he'd be a mortal enemy, I'd have thrown you out the first week of our marriage or beat you until you couldn't stand."

"Well, then, 'tis a good thing I come to this marriage well connected, isn't it?" She gestured to where Braden was still lying on the bed. "You know, I'm beginning to suspect that you like to skewer young men just for spite."

Rufus puffed his chest out in anger. "I'd have no cause to skewer him if he hadn't skewered you first!"

If only I'd gotten that far, Braden thought regretfully. Unfortunately, the earl had atrocious timing. In truth, he had yet even to kiss the lass.

Braden rose slowly from the bed. "Perhaps I should be going."

"Perhaps you should be dying," Rufus said as he pushed past his wife.

Having found himself in a similar situation on more than one occasion, Braden knew the best course of action was not to panic. Indeed, cool rationale would save his head from being separated from his shoulders.

And the last thing he wanted was to die on English soil. If he had to die, then by all that was holy, 'twould be with Scottish soil beneath his feet.

And preferably with a Scottish lass moaning in his ear.

"If it's just the same to you, Rufus, I'd rather wait a few more years before I meet my maker."

"Then you should have kept your hands away from my wife."

Actually, Braden was the one who'd been fondled, but right now didn't seem like the time to point that out. Not to mention the fact it would be less than gentlemanly to compromise the lady any further.

For all her brashness, Braden did, in fact, like Piety, and the last thing he wanted was for her to be harmed in any way.

Piety took refuge with her sisters in the corner while Rufus unsheathed his sword.

Braden assessed his opponent.

As the youngest of five boys, Braden had been a warrior since he could first clasp a sword in his hand. In all the years of his life, only his brothers had ever been able to stand toe to toe with him in war. And the foolish Sassenach before him would prove a poor match for his skill.

Though he'd never shirked from killing men in battle, it didn't suit Braden to draw blood over so trivial a matter. A woman was not worth a man's life.

Now, if he could only convince the earl of that fact.

Braden spread his arms wide. "Now be reasonable, Rufus. You don't really want to fight me."

"Not fight you, you backward Highland barbarian? After what you were doing? I'll see you in hell where you belong, you primitive, unholy dog."

Braden stifled his laughter. How charming. Insults. Too bad the man hadn't had more practice. Braden's elder brothers could well tutor him in ways to draw blood with the tongue.

"Can we not be mature about this?" Braden asked the earl.

"Mature, you boiled-brained fustilarian?" Rufus choked.

Then, without warning, Rufus lunged with the sword.

Braden sidestepped him easily enough, but since the point of the sword whistled just inches away from his throat, he decided it was definitely time he parted company with the earl.

"Come, now, Rufus," Braden said in an effort to distract the man from the fact he was inching toward the open doors of the balcony. "You know you're no match for me. I could fight a dozen men such as yourself."

Rufus pulled back with a speculative smile. " 'Tis good then, that I brought my three brothers."

Said brothers chose *just* that moment to enter the room and unsheath their swords.

You just had to say that, didn't you? Braden thought wryly.

Braden paused as he summed up his new opposition. None of them could possibly be younger than two score. Still, by the way they held their swords, he could see these were trained knights and not dandies out to pay scutage to their English king for their service. These men had battled much and still trained for war.

Not that it truly mattered, for he wasn't afraid of mere knights. There would never be a day when such could ever lay low a Highlander. But Braden wasn't a fool, and four trained knights against one half-dressed, unarmed Highlander were not the odds on which he was used to wagering.

He decided to play to the earl's good English breeding. "These odds really aren't very sporting."

"Neither is cuckolding."

Well, so much for sport.

Again Rufus lunged. Braden grabbed a pillow from the bed and deflected the blade with it. Jumping to the bed, he rolled across the mattress as Rufus brought the sword down for his shoulder. Rufus's blade missed by a hair and tangled with the drapes of the bed.

Braden came to his feet on the opposite side and glanced to where the earl's brothers were moving in.

"Braden!"

Dropping the pillow, he turned to see Prudence in her corner, holding his sword. Kissing the hilt of it, she tossed it to him.

Braden caught it by the hilt and thanked her an instant before one of the earl's brothers charged him.

He deflected the man's blow with ease and twisted out of the corner. Before he could make his way to the balcony, he was set upon by all of them at once.

Braden made a good showing, but with one boot on and one boot off, his hop-along stance made it rather difficult to keep up. Damn the English for their strange clothing. At home, he'd never been bothered by these uncomfortable boots, or so many other articles of clothing.

To think they called his beloved Scots brethren backward. At least in the Highlands a man knew how to dress for convenience and health.

And, most importantly, for unexpected trysts.

As they fought, the earl lost his balance and

stumbled, giving Braden the chance he needed to escape without shedding English blood.

Twisting against the wall, Braden cut the cord to the chandelier.

The earl and his brothers dashed apart as it crashed down, scattering tapers about the room.

While they rushed about stamping out the small fires, Braden ran to where the three women were huddled in the corner. He grabbed his supertunic from Patience, his boot from Prudence, and his cloak from Piety.

"Adieu, my fair ladies," he said with a smile, touching Piety lightly on the cheek in a gentle caress. "If you ever venture to Scotland . . ." He looked at the men who were heading back toward him. "Leave the husbands at home."

With that, he rushed through the open door to the balcony and jumped gracefully to the courtyard below.

He gazed up at the balcony to see the three women looking down at him.

"Remember us fondly," Prudence called as she waved her hand delicately.

"Always, my loves," he said, smiling.

Braden blew them a quick kiss, then pulled on his boot and made for the stable. He had little time to make his exit before the earl and his brothers would be after him. Not that he was afraid of them; far from it. He really could have killed them all, but therein lay the problem. He refused to kill a man over a dalliance.

Women were fun. They were his raison d'être.

However, no woman was worth his life, nor would he ever take the life of another man over a woman.

That was one harsh lesson he'd learned years ago.

Besides, 'twas time he headed home. These Englishwomen were enjoyable for a time, but in the end it was the Highland lasses he craved the most. What with their gentle, lilting voices and bright smiles, they were the gems of the earth and it was time he returned to them and their open arms.

As well as other things they were only too happy to open for him.

Braden smiled at the thought.

With the speed of a trained warrior, he saddled his horse and was out of the stable before the earl could make his way out of the keep. Indeed, Braden was through the gate before the man reached the yard.

He had one quick stop left before he was free. But then he was northern-bound.

"Lay on, Deamhan," he said to his black stallion. "Let's see what other trouble we can find along the way, shall we?"

Chapter 2

Kilgarigon, Scotland
Three weeks later

Lochlan MacAllister was a practical man. A reasonable man, according to most. As the leader of his clan, he had to be. But this . . . this beat all he had ever seen in his score and eight years of living.

No woman in Kilgarigon would bed or feed her man until Lochlan agreed to end the feud with Robby MacDouglas!

He was still reeling from the unreasonable request. The women were mad. All of them. But none more so than Maggie ingen Blar.

In fact, he himself was ready to go and throttle the women's ringleader.

And he wasn't the only one. The men of his

clan were fast passing the point of charity, and already he had heard rumors of them going after Maggie themselves. Indeed, every morning he half expected to find her poor, rotting carcass nailed to the front door of his keep or hanging from the merlons.

Frustrated, he looked across his clean, elegant great hall to where his younger brother Ewan sat at the table sawing at a piece of beef Lochlan had attempted to cook a short time ago. In truth, he would have been better off salting and frying up his leather boots. For surely the leather couldn't have tasted worse than the meat.

If not for the seriousness of his predicament, Lochlan would laugh at the sight of Ewan trying to keep his long shanks beneath the table. There were few men in the clan who came close to Ewan's six-foot-six height. And though Ewan's body was lean, it was muscled well enough to make even the stoutest gulp in fear.

But it was more than the man's size that frightened most, 'twas also his fierce demeanor. Ewan rarely smiled. In fact, Ewan avoided most people entirely and seldom ventured from the cave in the hills he called home.

Yet for all his moodiness, Ewan possessed an ability to see straight into the heart of a matter and call it by its name. It was for that reason Lochlan had summoned him from his hermitage.

"What am I going to do?" he asked Ewan.

Ewan attempted to chew the meat, but he

looked more like a cow with cud than the warrior Lochlan knew him to be. "Learn to cook, lest you starve."

"Ewan," he growled. "I am in earnest."

"So am I," Ewan mumbled as he pushed his wooden trencher away, then took a gulp of ale to rinse the fetid taste of charred beef from his mouth. "You can't go on eating like this or you'll never last another week."

"Ewan . . ."

His brother ignored his warning tone. "It seems to me there is an easy solution to this."

"And that is?"

"Go into the kirk yard, toss Maggie ingen Blar over your shoulder, take her out of there and force her to cook us a meal that's edible."

Lochlan sighed. "You think I haven't thought of that? But she's on holy ground. I'll not violate that sanctity."

Ewan rose slowly from the table. "Then I'll do it. Satan's throne would freeze before *I* let another woman make a mockery of me."

"True enough," a familiar voice broke into their conversation. "That's why the good Lord put *me* on this earth."

Lochlan turned to see his youngest brother, Braden, standing in the doorway of the hall.

Braden's black hair was tousled as if he'd ridden hard. He wore his black and green plaid haphazardly over his left shoulder and his look was as mischievous as ever.

For the first time in a fortnight, Lochlan laughed. "Well, well, the prodigal son has returned," he said as he crossed the room to greet his ever-errant and irreverent brother.

As soon as he drew even with Braden, Lochlan caught sight of the man in the shadows who stood quietly behind his baby brother. The smile froze on his face as he stopped dead in his tracks.

Nay, it couldn't be . . .

But it was.

Lochlan blinked in disbelief.

It had been years since he'd last seen his half-brother Sin. Even as a child, Sin had been more serious than Ewan and filled with more hatred than Lochlan could fathom.

When Sin had been sent against his will to the English king their father so detested, the youth had sworn never again to set foot north of Hadrian's Wall.

Lochlan couldn't imagine what had happened to cause Sin to change his mind, but he was certainly glad he had, for he loved his older brother and had missed him greatly.

Sin still had those piercing, mirthless black eyes that seemed to see straight into the soul. He had the same black hair as Ewan and Braden, and surprisingly enough, he wore it long like a Highlander, not short like the English.

But his clothes were another matter entirely. His black surcoat, mail, hose and boots were all

English. And oddly enough, they bore no markings on them whatsoever.

"What's this?" Lochlan asked, recovering from his surprise. "You've returned from England with a guest?" He extended his arm to Sin, who stared at it a full minute before shaking it.

Lochlan clapped him on the back. " 'Tis good to see you, my *bráthair*. It's been far too long."

Sin's taut features softened a degree, and it was only then Lochlan realized just how uncertain Sin had been of his reception.

"I was afraid to let Braden come alone," Sin said as he removed his arm from Lochlan's. "After the number of close calls he had in England, I feared he'd never make it home before some poor husband or father speared him."

Ewan gave a shout as he recognized Sin. Crossing the room, he grabbed him up into a bear hug.

Sin bristled in the hold. "Put me down, you big, ugly *úbaidh*!"

"So," Ewan said as he set Sin back on his feet. "You do remember your heritage. With those clothes on your back, I wasn't sure if you were my big brother come home, or another of Braden's conquests."

As always, Braden took the ribbing in stride, but Sin's look turned murderous.

"Speaking of conquests," Braden inserted, "where are the women? I've yet to see a single one since I crossed into MacAllister lands."

"Nay!" Ewan gasped as he turned to face Braden. "Can it be Braden's made it a whole hour without a woman? Quick, Lochlan, send for a healer afore he collapses from the stress of celibacy."

Braden clucked his tongue. "Now, that's no joking matter. It's not good for a man to go too long without a woman. His juices back up and before you know it, he turns into a soured, ill-tempered beastie."

Braden's eyes widened as he regarded Ewan. "So *that's* what happened to you! Come," he said, draping an arm over Ewan's shoulders. "We'd best find you a woman quickly before you get any worse."

His lips curling into a grimace, Ewan knocked Braden's arm off his shoulder. "Would you stop with your foolishness?" He turned to Sin. "You'd best take him back to England before *I* run him through."

Lochlan ignored their almost routine bantering. Ewan and Braden couldn't communicate with each other unless they were exchanging insults.

Lochlan looked to Sin. "I'm glad you came home. 'Tis been far too long since you last ventured to the Highlands."

Sin nodded. "You, Kieran, Braden and Ewan are all I ever missed from this godforsaken place. No offense, but I much prefer English luxury to this rough existence."

"Spoken like a true Sassenach," Ewan said, his lip curled in repugnance.

Sin's eyes narrowed at the insult.

"Enough," Lochlan intervened before Sin could respond. Sin had never been the type one taunted with impunity, and the last thing he wanted was any more blood spilled between his brothers.

Regardless of the past, and all the words spoken in anger, Sin was always welcome in his home.

"There will be no insults here," Lochlan said to Ewan, his voice stern. "At least not against Sin. Braden, on the other hand, you may feel free to attack."

"Och, now," Braden bristled, "where's your brotherly love?"

Lochlan smiled devilishly. "That *is* my brotherly love. Notice I have yet to taunt you."

"Aye, but I'm sure it's nothing more than an oversight." Braden turned and looked expectantly about the hall.

Even before Braden spoke the words, Lochlan knew what was on his mind. This was the only time in his memory that Braden had returned home without an entire army of women running out to greet him, elbowing each other in an effort to gift his younger brother with food and other things they were only too happy to offer.

"Where are the serving maids with something for us to eat?" Braden asked.

Lochlan opened his mouth to explain, but Ewan stopped him.

"Nay, please let me be the one who tells him." Ewan's blue eyes twinkled in rare humor.

"Very well," Lochlan said. "If it gives you pleasure."

"Aye, that it surely does." Beaming in satisfaction, Ewan turned to Braden. "You remember Anghus and Aidan's little sister, Maggie ingen Blar?"

Braden frowned. "The little hellion with red hair, freckles and buck teeth? How could I *ever* forget her?"

The harsh words set Lochlan aback. He'd never in his life heard his brother describe a woman as anything save beautiful, and Maggie was anything other than bucktoothed.

Hellion, on the other hand, he would gladly concede.

"I don't recall her having buck teeth," Lochlan said.

"That's because she never *bit* you with them," Braden responded. "Me, on the other hand, she seemed to love to attack. Never knew why."

"Must have been your charming personality," Sin said dryly.

Ewan threw his hands up and stepped in front of Braden. "Do you mind? I'd like to stay on the point." He glared meaningfully first at Lochlan, then at Sin.

"Seize the moment," Lochlan said.

"Thank you." Ewan placed a hand on each of Braden's shoulders so as to savor his reaction. "Anyway, Maggie, whether she has buck teeth or not"—he glared at Lochlan in warning, before turning back to face Braden—"has led all the lasses into hiding."

Braden's frown deepened. "Hiding from what?"

"From us wicked, lustful men."

Braden stared blankly at Ewan as the full, horrific impact of the words dawned on him. "Surely you jest."

Braden looked to Lochlan for verification. "He jests?"

"Nay," Lochlan sighed. "He's telling the truth. It seems the women have decided that I must put a stop to the feud against the MacDouglas or else they'll serve us no more."

"In *any* capacity," Ewan added for effect.

Braden's face actually paled as he stepped away from Ewan. He reached out and grabbed a handful of Sin's cloak. "By Satan's hairy toes, Sin, it appears I've died and gone to hell."

Sin snorted. "Guess again, little brother. 'Tis too cold here to be hell."

Braden shook his head in disbelief, then a dark look came over him as he faced Lochlan. "All right, *laird*, what did you do to the women to get them so riled?"

"Me?" Lochlan asked, stunned by Braden's assumption that he had done anything to the

women. "I did nothing. Why, I've tried everything I can think of to make them see reason. I've
threatened and cajoled. Hell, I even tried seducing Maggie myself, but—"

Braden's derisive snort interrupted him. "Well,
there's half your problem. I can assure you, order-
ing a woman to lift her skirts isn't the way to get
her into your bed."

Lochlan felt his jaw drop in indignation. "I beg
your pardon, I have more subtlety than that."

"The devil you do. You forget, I've seen your
clumsy attempts at seduction firsthand."

"Clumsy? Why, I've had more women than
you, you whelp."

Braden cocked one arrogant, taunting brow.

"Well," Lochlan conceded after reflecting on
the matter for a second. He doubted if a Saracen
sheikh with a harem could claim more women
than Braden. "Maybe not more than you, but certainly more than Ewan."

"That's not saying much," Braden inserted.
"My left boot has had more women than Ewan."

"Hey, now," Ewan snarled. "You'd best be
keeping your insults directed at the brother who
tolerates you. I'll not take kindly to such."

Ignoring him, Braden draped an arm over
Lochlan's shoulders and pulled him close, as if
about to impart some great secret. "Now, listen to
me, my dearest brother who tolerates me. You are
laird to a powerful clan. 'Tis not your feeble at-

tempts that seduce women so much as your title and fair face."

"My what?" Lochlan asked, offended by his condescending tone.

" 'Tis true," Braden continued. "There's not a woman among them who wouldn't love to lay claim to a night with a laird. Is that not right, Sin?"

"Why ask me? Am I a woman to know these things?"

"Well . . ." Braden paused.

Whatever thought he had, he must have reconsidered, for he quickly returned to Lochlan. "As I was saying, your title and face are all you need."

"Aye, well, neither impressed Maggie. She dispatched me in record time. At this point, she's left me with no alternative that I can see. If they aren't out by midday tomorrow, I'm leading a raiding party against the kirk and dragging them out by force."

Braden released him. "You don't want to be doing that. They're women, Lochlan. *Our* women."

"You think I don't know that? Our mother is in there with them. But what choice do I have?"

A speculative look came over Braden's face. Lochlan could almost see the workings of his mind. Good, Braden was always a mastermind when it came to dealing with women.

"I can think of another choice," Braden said. "What say you, I talk sense into the wench and get the women back where they belong—in the kitchens and in our beds?"

Lochlan considered it. If Braden could end this peacefully, then it was certainly worth a try. He didn't like the thought of hurting one of their women any more than Braden did.

Perhaps his brother *could* succeed where he had failed. Braden had always been good at settling hot-blooded issues peacefully.

There had only been one time when he had failed. Lochlan winced at the memory.

There had been enough tragedy in their family. The last thing he wanted was to add anything more. He would give Braden a chance to talk the women out.

But only one. He couldn't afford any more than that.

"Very well. But know this: At the rate Maggie's going, my men will either storm the kirk on their own, or they'll toss me out on my arse and elect a new laird."

"Women," Sin muttered. "I can't believe they'd construct this rebellion against you while you have a feud to contend with. The last thing you need are your men distracted by women's foolery while they have lands to protect."

"Aye," Braden agreed. "I'm surprised the Mac-Douglas isn't taking advantage of this mutiny."

Lochlan glanced out the window in the direction of the kirk. In spite of his anger, he did take a moment to savor the amusement he felt over the bit of news he'd received. "I'm sure he would have, had his own women not done the same thing to his clan."

"What?" Braden asked.

"It's true," Lochlan continued. "His own wife has joined them. I received word of it just three days ago. The Lady MacDouglas has made a laughingstock of her husband."

"Is he willing to talk peace, then?" Sin asked.

"Nay. Even if we could agree to terms, neither of us dares it. If we concede to the women over this, then they'll think they have power over us and anytime there's a matter they don't like, they might very well hie themselves into hiding again. I shudder to think of the consequences. Can you imagine?"

"Aye," Braden said with a wicked smile. "It could be amusing."

Lochlan glared at him.

"Well, it could," Braden said, dismissing Lochlan's ire.

He swept a confident look over the three of them. "For years the lot of you have mocked me over the fact that no woman can resist me. Well, now, my brothers, you shall be grateful to me for my gift."

Braden's look had never been more cocksure. "Come and bear witness to how quickly I end this matter. I'll wager it'll be less than a quarter hour before I have Maggie feeding from my hand."

"I'll take the wager," Ewan said. "Especially after the way I saw Maggie send Lochlan packing. It'll do you good to fail."

"Me, fail?" Braden asked in disbelief. "Hah! There's no woman alive immune to me."

"For once, I hope you're right," Lochlan said. "I can't afford for you to lose this wager."

"Then come and see my most tender triumph."

Ewan clapped Lochlan on the back. "I don't know about you, but this is one confrontation I canna wait to see."

Chapter 3

Braden MacAllister could very well mark the end of all her grand plans.

Maggie ingen Blar froze at the window of the kirk as she saw the small group of men headed her way. If ever the four riders of the Apocalypse appeared in the flesh, it would be in the form of the four men gasconading down the road toward the small kirk where she and the other women had taken refuge.

It would be any other woman's dream to have four such sinfully handsome men headed toward her, knowing she was the one they sought with such determination.

For Maggie, it was a waking nightmare.

The handsome Lochlan she'd expected to see again. Standing six-foot-four, he was one of the tallest men of the clan. His fair hair looked as if it had literally been spun from gold. And when it came to his features, she doubted if the angels in heaven could compete with the gentle sculpted face or dimpled smile that had made many a maid sigh.

But there was no smile in place today. Only a grim, lethal stare.

Lochlan's younger brother Ewan stood two inches taller and possessed broad shoulders and a deadly swagger that made the men of the clan scurry at his approach. His darkly handsome face had rendered many a woman mute. But it was his dangerous countenance that kept any woman from pursuing him.

Most women were as afraid of him as were the men.

The third man stood between their heights and was dressed as an Englishman, and she knew him not at all. Still, he possessed that same lethal aura of all the MacAllister brothers, and his confident stride held a captivating, seductive quality to it. He reminded her of a dangerous dark beast pursuing his prey.

And the fourth . . .

He was the one her eyes feasted on, for she knew Braden MacAllister well. A friend to her older brothers, he had come often to her home while she was growing up.

Like some lovesick mooncalf, Maggie had adored him always.

Would there ever come a time in her life when

the very sight of him wouldn't quicken her breath? Make her heart beat out of control?

All of the MacAllister brothers were handsome, but there was something special about Braden. Something about him that was truly irresistible.

His wavy black hair fell just past his muscular shoulders and Maggie could easily recall the scent of elderberries that clung to the silken strands. Not that she knew for certain his hair felt like silk. 'Twas merely the sheen of it that suggested it would be wondrous to brush her hand through the long, dark locks.

He had a high forehead with finely arched black brows that lifted up when he laughed. And he laughed often. It was a deep, throaty sound that filled the air with music and warmth.

And his lips . . .

Full and well shaped, they were the kind of lips a woman went to bed at night dreaming of kissing. Or better yet, the kind of lips that could kiss a woman senseless.

Or so she had been told.

Unfortunately, Maggie had never known the pleasure of those lips herself. Braden had always viewed her as a pesky child, even though only three and a half years separated them in age.

Ever since she'd turned twelve, she had tried to get him to notice her, even to the point of biting him once when he failed to look her way. Yet she seemed to be the only woman alive he truly had no interest in.

Her brother Anghus had told her it was Braden's loyalty to her brothers that kept him from looking twice at her, but inside she suspected it was more than that. Maggie wasn't a fool.

She had never been the type of woman men pursued for anything other than a hot meal or advice on how to attract some *other* female.

As her twin brother Ian so often said, she was a good, reliable friend; the kind of woman a man could turn to for advice and never worry about her judging him.

At best, she was passably attractive, not a beauty by any stretch of even the most accomplished imagination.

But what she wouldn't give to have the courage or beauty to make Braden notice her for just an instant. To be the one woman who could tame the wild wind.

However, today was not the day to try and gain his notice. In fact, today was the worst possible day she could *ever* see him. For in her heart, she knew he was the one man who could sneak past her defenses.

And today she couldn't afford to lose. Not even to him.

Nay, she must keep the handsome warrior at arm's length. That is, if any woman could keep a man like him at arm's length.

While Maggie watched Braden's approach,

Pegeen came up behind her, asking about blankets.

Though she heard her friend's question plainly enough, Maggie couldn't speak. Her entire being was fixated on the most handsome Highlander ever to live.

Braden walked toward her sanctuary with a confident, masculine swagger that turned every maid's head. The wind blew against his ebony hair, stirring strands of it about his chiseled face. He moved with his left hand on his sword, his shoulders thrown back in pride.

The hem of his black and green plaid slapped against the tanned, well-muscled flesh of his thighs. Thighs that moved sinuously with each step that brought him closer to her.

Mo chreach! he was gorgeous.

Raw, untamed masculine sensuality and attitude bled from every pore of his body.

Braden was a man comfortable with himself and assured of his place in the world. He'd never been one to follow the dictates of others, but rather he had always walked his own path, consequences be damned.

Today he seemed even more confident than he had the last time she had seen him.

He was up to something, she realized with a start. She could see it in the firm set of his jaw, in the sharpness of his gaze. There was an unmasked determination about him. He had a goal.

And in an instant she knew what he was about. *"Och, balgaire le sùilibh mear!"* she said beneath her breath.

"What dog with lustful eyes?" Pegeen asked from her right.

"The one headed our way," Maggie snarled, angered over the fact that his walk *did* affect her.

And even worse, she wasn't keeping him at arm's length!

Pegeen stood on her tiptoes to look out the window. "Oh, bother me," she whispered. "There be four of them for sure. Handsome all."

Maggie glared at the approaching group. "They say the devil himself is a handsome man, and I'd sooner meet with him than Braden MacAllister."

"The devil ne'er saw a day he could rival a MacAllister for looks," Pegeen whispered. "My, my, that Braden be the one for sure."

A dreamy smile curved her lips.

Only a year older than Maggie, the attractive, raven-haired Pegeen had married four winters past, but she still had a roving eye that drifted toward any bonny man. And right now both of Pegeen's eyes were fastened on Braden, and they were larger than platters.

"Oh, to have my Ross look like that one," Pegeen said dreamily. "You can rest assured, if he did I'd not be hiding in here with you right now. But rather I'd be in my home giving him the—"

"Pegeen!" Maggie chided. "You're inside a kirk."

Pegeen waved her words aside with her hand. "The good Lord knows I mean no harm with my thoughts. I'm merely speaking the truth, and well He knows it."

Maggie barely heard Pegeen's words, for her attention had now shifted to the other women who were coming out of various buildings to peer over the walls at the men. Even from her distance, she could hear the breathless sighs and giggles of the women as they admired various parts of the men coming toward them.

"Braden's home!" several of them shouted.

"Mary, how's my hair look? Think you Braden will notice it?"

"Saints, that man gets bonnier with every year!"

"That man's got the finest backside the good Lord ever saw fit to put on a man. Now if we could just get a good, strong wind to blow, we could be in for quite a wondrous sight!"

Maggie ground her teeth in anger as a plethora of such comments filled her ears.

Leave it to the laird to summon the one man home who could spoil her plan. She should have expected this. Indeed, she should have planned for it. But the idea had seemed so flawless, and with Braden gone she hadn't thought about his possible effect on her senses.

Until now.

Her vision turning dark, Maggie gathered her skirts and headed out of the kirk to confront the devil before he came too close.

She reached the gate at about the same moment Braden did. She snatched open the door to see him standing there with his arm uplifted as if to knock.

"Maggie, my love," he said, his face breaking into one of those wonderful, charming dimpled smiles that could make any woman weak in the knees.

Or worse, weak in the head.

His eyes shone with his confidence. Aye, the man knew he was irresistible.

But worse was the fact that she knew it as well.

"You're just the woman I was coming to see."

"I can imagine that," she said, her voice icy even though there was a treacherous part of her that thrilled at his words.

His gaze became daring, probing, as he boldly assessed her body from the top of her head, which reached right to his shoulders, all the way down to the bottom of her skirt.

"Och, Lochlan," he said to his brother, "you failed to tell me what a bonny lass she'd become over the last year. Why, I doubt if there's a maid in all of Kilgarigon who could come near to such beauty."

Lochlan said nothing in response.

In spite of her best intentions, Maggie's heart

leapt at his words. She'd yearned all her life to hear such from a man, and especially from Braden.

Unfortunately, though, she knew it for the mere flattery it was. There wasn't a bit of truth to it.

Lifting her chin, she met his bold look levelly. "You must think me lacking in the head to fall to your honeyed words, Braden MacAllister."

"Ah!" his brother Ewan said from behind him. "You were wrong about her teeth, Braden. She's not bucktoothed at all."

Turning his head to glare at his brother over his shoulder, Braden elbowed the giant in his gut.

"Bucktoothed?" she asked, offended by the mere thought. That was probably the *only* insult one of her brothers had never hurled at her. And why would they? Her teeth were as straight as anyone's teeth could ever be.

Braden's stern glare melted as he flashed one of those devil-may-care smiles her way. "I never said you were bucktoothed."

"Aye, you did. I heard it as well," the Englishman said.

"Nay," Braden said between clenched teeth as his malevolent stare went to the Englishman in turn. "I said no such thing."

Braden took a step toward her and lifted her hand in his.

Maggie steeled herself as the contact sent chills along her arms. She could feel the rough calluses on his hand, the raw power of the man who was as much a fierce warrior as he was a woman's downfall.

She watched, mesmerized, as he lifted her hand to his lips and placed a kiss just over her knuckles. His lips were feather-light against her flesh. And as he moved those lips in a slow, searing circle around the back of her hand, he looked up at her with such bedroom eyes that for an instant she lost herself to the desire playing havoc with her senses.

At that moment, the terrible, treacherous part of her wanted to feel those lips against her own. She wanted to feel his strong arms wrap around her body and draw her close to his delectable heat.

Oh, heaven help her, she was as susceptible to him as all the other women were.

Braden ran his tongue over her flesh in a tender caress that both startled and titillated her before he gently nipped her skin with his teeth and moved her hand to rest just over his heart, which beat strongly beneath her palm.

It was all she could do not to close her eyes and moan in pleasure as his thumb toyed with her palm, sending wave after wave of heat through her.

"They misheard me, my love." He all but purred the words at her.

Her body all but melted as she stared into eyes that were warm, inviting. A rich greenish brown,

Braden's eyes could compel a woman to forget everything else in the world.

Get hold of yourself, Maggie! The devil'll take the rest of your loved ones if you yield to his charms.

Though it was one of the hardest things she'd ever done, she narrowed her gaze on him as she forced her wanton thoughts to the back of her mind.

She had to get control of the situation or all would be lost.

"Let me guess," she said coldly, removing her hand from his grasp before she succumbed any more to his masterful touch. "Did you perchance say I was sweet-toothed? Or pearl-toothed, perhaps?" Maggie noted the stunned look he quickly hid. She was on to him for sure, and he knew it.

She took a moment to savor her victory.

But a moment was all she had, for in the next minute a scream rent the air.

"Maggie, come quick!"

She left the front gate open and rushed through the kirk yard toward the back gate, where the scream had originated. She reached the small courtyard in time to see one of the women, Bridget, being accosted by her bear of a husband. The man fairly dwarfed the petite blonde, who was doing her best to resist being pulled out the gate.

There were several women standing about, but none moved to help. Maggie couldn't understand how they could just stand there and do nothing.

"I've had enough of this, woman," Fergus said as he twisted his grip on Bridget's arm.

"Nay, Fergus, I'll not go home with you." Bridget tried to loosen his grip, but he held fast.

"I'll be taking no more disobedience from you," he snarled, then backhanded her.

Bridget fell away, sobbing, but the grip on her arm kept her from hitting the ground. Fergus snatched at her, hauling her once more toward the gate.

Maggie shrieked in outrage. Without thought to her own safety, she launched herself at the oaf and knocked him away from Bridget.

Releasing Bridget, who instantly crumpled to the ground, Fergus stumbled back only a few steps. Maggie, on the other hand, collided with his massive chest and fell backward, hitting the ground dazed as if she had just bounced off a wall.

She quickly pushed herself to her feet and moved to face the man, who stood a full head and shoulders above her. Her own shoulder throbbed and her heart pounded in fear. The man really was tall. Much, much taller than she. And about twice as wide.

Still, Maggie would never stand by and watch someone be hurt. Not if she stood even a tiny chance of helping. "You leave her be," Maggie warned.

Fergus drew back to hit her.

Maggie tensed in expectation of the blow, but

before his hand could make contact with her face, his arm was grabbed and he was spun about.

Braden held Fergus by the front of his saffron shirt, and the fury on Braden's face would have quelled an ogre's wrath. "If you want to take issue with the women, Fergus, you'll have to come through me to do it. I'll not have you abuse a woman in such a fashion so long as I breathe."

Fergus curled his lip as he shoved Braden away from him. "Bridget be my wife. I'll do with her as I please." He made a move for Bridget, who was now on the ground crying uncontrollably while Pegeen and two others held on to her.

Braden and the Englishman stepped between the two of them. Their spines rigid, it was obvious they were ready to fight Fergus if he made another move toward his wife.

"You should take better care of your wife," Braden said. "If you treated her more kindly, she probably wouldn't have locked herself up with the others."

Fergus snorted in derision. "What would you know of it?"

Braden's gaze hardened and sent a chill of foreboding up Maggie's spine. "I know enough to take a stick to your arse if you don't heed my words. Now get yourself home before I yield to that temptation."

Fergus's nostrils flared. He glared heatedly into Braden's cold, deadly gaze.

For a moment Maggie feared he would push

Braden into the fight, but he must have come to his senses, for he looked from Braden to the other three men.

Fergus's shoulders slumped and he sighed. "Very well, I'll return home, but she'd best be getting herself there afore much longer."

Fergus took a step away.

"Aren't you forgetting something?" Braden asked.

Fergus turned around with a frown. "Forgetting what?"

"You owe your wife an apology," the Englishman said before Braden could.

His jaw tense, Fergus glared at the men. As his gaze swept over Ewan, Braden, Lochlan and the Englishman, he realized he'd have to fight them all unless he complied. Straightening his shirt with a tug, he looked to Bridget.

Maggie saw the indecision in his eyes until Bridget looked up at him, her pale face marred by an ugly red handprint.

The anger fled Fergus's face as he knelt by Bridget's side. "I am sorry, bride. I dinna mean to harm you. But you shouldn't have pressed me so."

Braden bellowed in rage. "Leave her, Fergus. Now!"

Maggie swallowed in fear of the tone. She sensed Braden was only one finger away from seriously hurting Fergus. Not that she would have minded if he had. Men like Fergus deserved to be beaten. She had always hated such bullies.

In fact, all four of Braden's group looked as if they were an inch away from harming him. But it was Ewan who stepped forward and quickly removed Fergus from the yard.

Maggie waited until the gate was firmly shut behind Fergus and Ewan was headed back toward them before she turned to face Braden.

"Thank you," she said, her voice carrying the full depth of her gratitude.

Braden nodded, then went with Lochlan to check on Bridget. Braden knelt by Bridget's side and gently touched her swollen red cheek. His eyes hardening, he looked up at Maggie. "How many such attacks have there been since you started this?"

"Five," Lochlan answered for her.

Maggie's throat tightened at the memory of how many women had been hurt. "Aye. The beatings are what prompted us to seek shelter with Father Bede. We had hoped by being on holy ground that the men would think twice before assaulting any of us again."

The Englishman scoffed at her words. "As if that ever stood in the way of animals."

Braden ignored the Englishman's words as he raked a cold glare over Maggie. "Did you ever stop to consider the foolishness of your actions?" Braden asked, his voice filled with rage. "How many more women are going to suffer because of your stubbornness?"

Maggie's own anger ignited at his accusatory words. She wasn't some child in need of a reprimand. She knew the consequences of her actions. They all did.

Every single woman who was now gathered around them understood.

They were mere women, subject to the whims of men, but even so they had all agreed that this was a necessary measure to ensure the well-being of all.

Maggie stiffened her spine as she confronted the four men. "Not nearly as many as the men who will die if the feud continues. Better we be beaten than our sons, brothers, husbands, and fathers *die*."

"Aye," the women around her concurred.

Agnes stepped forward from the crowd to confront Braden and Lochlan. "My bruises healed in only four days," she said, brushing her hand down her smooth cheek. "But my heart still aches for my youngest boy who died three years back under a MacDouglas sword. There will always be a hole there, aching for him."

Lochlan eyed them all. "You're not changing anything," he said firmly.

"Aren't we?" Maggie asked. "You men can't be killing and raiding the MacDouglas while you're coming here to negotiate with us. Nor can you wage war on empty stomachs."

Again the women agreed with her.

Braden opened his mouth to speak, but before he could, Maggie heard another loud shout, only this one was a cry of joy.

"Braden, my wee bairn! You're home."

The group parted as Braden's mother, Aisleen, rushed toward them.

Maggie noticed the look of hatred on the Englishman's face as he saw the tiny brunette for the first time.

Never in her life had she seen so much malice directed at a single person. Frowning, she watched as the Englishman drifted back into the crowd to where Aisleen couldn't see him.

Braden drew his mother into a tight hug. "Ah, Mother, but it's good to see you."

"And you," she breathed, cupping his face in her hands and squeezing it tight an instant before she wrapped her arms around his neck and kissed his cheek. "You've no idea how much I've worried over you. I was just this minute in the chapel saying prayers for your well-being."

"I'm sure he needs all the prayers he can get," Maggie muttered uncharitably beneath her breath.

"Now, don't be that way, Maggie," Aisleen chastised her. "This be my boy you're talking about and a fine, bonny man he is."

Bonny, Maggie couldn't argue, but fine . . .

Well, she couldn't really argue that either. He could, of course, be a little more steadfast and a

lot less of a womanizer. Anyone would agree
with that.

"Well," Maggie relented, "it was nice of him to
help poor Bridget. But as you can see, he's no
longer needed, so—"

"Mother," Braden said, interrupting her, "I was
thinking that what you women need is a
guardian."

Maggie's jaw dropped. Surely he wasn't sug-
gesting what she thought he was.

"A guardian?" his mother asked in wide-eyed
innocence.

"Aye," he said, glancing meaningfully to Maggie. "Lochlan told me that Bridget makes the
sixth woman who has been attacked. I was thinking that perhaps I should stay here and help ensure no other woman is harmed until a settlement
is reached."

Oh, he did, did he? Maggie couldn't believe
what a fool he took her for!

"I just bet you do," Maggie snapped. "Tell me,
am I the only one present who thinks this sounds
a little too much like hiring a wolf to guard the
flock?"

"Nay," Aisleen disagreed. "It sounds like a fine
idea. We be needing a man on our side, and if
Ewan will also agree to help . . . well, how can
Lochlan argue with that?"

They all turned to look at Lochlan.

"I could definitely argue with it," he said, "but
by the looks of all of you I'd be wasting my

breath. If Braden wants to be a traitor, so be it. At least I won't have to listen to him whine over my cooking and the lack of feminine company."

"Nay," Maggie spoke up. "We can't allow them to stay here. What would Father Bede say?"

"I think it's a noble idea," the priest said as he joined them. "I can't protect any of you, but with Braden here, perhaps the others will think twice before harming anyone else. I think the Lord has sent Braden to us."

'Twas more like the devil sent him to make mischief, but Maggie didn't dare contradict the priest.

"See?" Braden said to her. "I have divine sanction."

"I seriously doubt that," Maggie said before she could stop herself. "But since I seem to be the only one here who can see through you, I have no choice save to yield."

Maggie took a step toward him and lowered her voice. "Know this, Braden MacAllister, I recognize you for what you are, and if you do anything to break the oath we swore to each other about not serving a man's needs until peace reigns, I swear I'll—"

"You'll what?" Braden taunted with those gleaming dimples. "Boil me in oil?"

Oh, but he was truly a demon, to be sure. A bright-eyed handsome one who had been sent to make her life miserable. "I'm not as helpless as you think."

"That I am quite sure of."

Maggie rolled her eyes in exasperation. She looked past Braden to where his mother stood. "For all our sakes, Aisleen, watch your son while I tend Bridget. And remember, he gets no food prepared by our hands. Let him scrounge like the others as best he can."

"As you say, Maggie, but is it truly fair to make him suffer when he's only here to help us?"

Maggie didn't miss the sheepish look on Braden's face. That removed any doubt she had as to his motivations. His mother might be blind to the man, but she was not.

"Fair or not, he's to get no food from us." Maggie looked about at the women who were still ogling Braden. "Nor anything else," she said pointedly.

The women beat a hasty retreat.

Braden arched his brow as Maggie walked away. She was truly something else. What she was, he couldn't say in polite company, but never before had he met a woman quite like her.

She wasn't the raving beauty men spent their lives fawning over. Her looks were more earthly fey. Her deep russet hair had defied her efforts to secure it into a braid and little wisps of it curled becomingly all around her face. A thousand freckles covered her pale skin like nutmeg sprinkled over cream, and her eyes . . .

The deep amber color burned with her fiery spirit. Indeed, he could still see her launching her tiny frame at the lumbering Fergus. Little did she know that a blow from him could have damn near broken her fragile neck.

And for some reason that didn't bear thinking on, Braden didn't like the thought of her being hurt.

"I'll go get you some food," his mother whispered to him, before she vanished with the other women.

Once the women had all gone, Lochlan mouthed the words *"Two days,"* before leaving as well.

Sin rejoined him, then leaned over and whispered in his ear. "Your quarter hour is up and instead of the women coming out, you seem to be staying in."

Braden grinned. "She was a little more challenging than I thought."

"A little?" Sin snorted. "Face it, Braden, that little piece of baggage has you pegged."

Braden laughed at the truth of it. Aye, she did. She had known when he was playing her and she had called him on it. Never before had a woman done that. Even when they knew he was playing with them, they played back.

But not Maggie.

Not that he minded. He loved a merry chase. It made victory even sweeter.

Ultimately, he would reign victorious. Of that he had no doubt.

"By the way," Ewan said as he fell in by

Braden's side, "what were you saying earlier about charming the wench? I don't think yelling at her in front of the others was particularly charming."

"I dinna yell at her."

"Aye, you did," Sin interjected. "You damn near took her head with your words."

Realizing there was no use in fighting both of them, Braden sighed. "Very well, I shall endeavor to treat her more kindly when next we meet."

"Yea," Sin said with a pointed look. "You do that."

At the moment, Braden felt like a man trapped in a bramble bush with thorns prickling him all about. "I shall," he said between gritted teeth.

Aye, he'd treat her more kindly all right. And when he had her feasting from his hand, they would all owe him much.

"Did you see the way Braden was looking at you?" Pegeen asked a short time later as she and Maggie left the dormitory room where they had deposited Bridget.

"Aye," Maggie said. "Like a cat eyeing a mouse it wants to torture."

Pegeen gave an undignified snort. "Hardly. The man is enamored of you."

"The man is enamored of anything female."

Anything, that is, except me.

"Maggie," Pegeen chided, "what has gotten into you? 'Tis not like you to be so uncharitable toward anyone."

Maggie paused in the narrow corridor. Her friend was right. All her life, Maggie had been kind to anyone she met. Even her brothers had been impressed with her ability to settle squabbles and maintain a level head.

But Braden had always flustered her. Every time he came near, her heart pounded, her hands shook, and her senses reeled. He alone knocked her off keel and sent her careening out of control.

And all the while, he treated her kindly, but kept her at a respectful distance. Never once had he looked at her and actually seen her as a woman.

All these years she had yearned for some acknowledgment from him. Some sign that she wasn't invisible.

But no sign had ever come. Ever.

Sighing, Maggie spoke. "Pegeen, have you ever wanted something so badly that you ached to the core of your very soul for it?"

Pegeen furrowed her brow in thought. "I'm not sure I know what you mean."

Maggie leaned against the wall, her thoughts churning. Long ago, she had given her heart to a man who didn't know she existed. She had watched him grow from a callow youth into a rogue to be reckoned with. Every time she had heard tales of Braden's exploits, her heart had broken a bit more. For with every conquest he made, she knew it took him further away from her.

After a time, she'd come to realize that nothing she did would draw Braden's attention. Not the tarts or pastries she had made especially for him on the days she knew he would be coming to her home. Not even the rich perfume Anghus had brought her years ago from his only journey to Ireland. Sweet, wonderful perfume she had worn for Braden's notice.

Well, he had noticed *that*, all right. He'd sneezed until his eyes watered.

But in the end, she'd been forced to admit her love was completely and utterly unrequited.

To her, Braden was everything. He was the moon, the sun, the very air she breathed. And now he was back, spouting kind words and touching her with those wondrous hands of his. Kissing her hand in a way no unmarried woman of virtue should allow, and yet she'd been powerless to stop him.

For her, it was a dream come true.

But for him, it was a means to an end.

No matter how much she might want to pretend otherwise, she knew the truth of it. To him, she was merely another conquest to be added to the others. Or worse, an obstacle for him to remove so that his brother could continue the feud.

He only saw her today because his brother had

made him see her. She held no delusions of that basic fact.

However, Maggie was not a trifle to be forgotten. She was an intelligent, capable woman who refused to be used by any man. She would not let him past her defenses, and she would not fail her mission.

Looking at Pegeen, she promised herself that she would never, ever fall victim to her treacherous body. Her feelings could be controlled. They must be!

"I have known Braden since I was but two winters old," she said quietly, "and never once in all this time has he ever given me so much as a glance. Don't you find it odd that all of a sudden he's interested?"

"Nay," Pegeen answered. "You are very pretty."

Maggie scoffed. "Is that why men fail to court me?"

"Men fail to court you because you have six brothers. Have you not seen the looks they cast at any man who comes near you?"

Maggie thought about it. Her brothers were a bit overbearing. She was the youngest of seven, and her brothers had always watched over her like tyrants over treasure.

Still, it didn't change anything.

"Braden is only after one thing," Maggie insisted.

Pegeen crossed her arms over her chest. "And that is?"

"To get us back into our homes."

"Is that not what we want as well?" Pegeen asked.

"Aye, to be sure. But we want to go back *after* they have settled this feud. If Braden has his way, we'll go back and the bloodshed will continue."

Pegeen shook her head. "Surely he wouldn't be so cruel."

"You honestly think not?"

"But his mother . . . ?"

"She sees him through the loving eyes of a doting mother. She is blind to his motives."

"Then what are we to do?"

That was one question Maggie wasn't sure she could answer. But one thing she did know: The earth would cease to exist before she ever succumbed to Braden's honeyed words and hot glances.

Her heart might be partial to him, but her head was not. So long as she possessed her reasoning abilities, she would not let him sway her.

Maggie was the one woman on this earth who would never be moved by his charming good looks. And if there was one thing she'd learned while living with six boys, it was how to handle a man.

Aye, Braden had no idea what he was in for.

"What are we going to do?" Maggie repeated

Pegeen's question. "I'll tell you. We are finally going to see to it that the devil gets his due. If Braden wants to stay here, fine. But I promise you this: He won't enjoy a single moment of it."

Chapter 4

Braden immensely enjoyed the sight of Maggie leaving the women's dormitory and walking toward the small alcove where he was standing, concealed by shadows.

After Maggie had left to see to Bridget, Lochlan had headed back to the castle while Ewan and Sin had gone to help Father Bede repair a leak in the nave.

Left alone, Braden had decided to wait for his prey.

And such a sweet bit she was too, all fiery and passionate. He actually felt the urge to lick his lips in anticipation of her surrender.

Aye, she would be sweet to savor. Such a spirited treat, just ripe for the taking. He couldn't wait for a taste.

A gentle breeze blew across the yard, caressing

the unruly tendrils of her thick russet hair. His palms itched to unbraid those riotous curls and he ached to fist his hands in the midst of them, to spread them out across her bare white shoulders and see them flow down the length of her naked back to caress her pale hips.

Even worse, he could almost smell the sunshine in that hair, feel the warmth of it cascading around him as he held her naked and writhing above him while he dipped his hand down to play in the small russet curls covering another part of her he longed to explore at greater length.

His groin drew tight at the thought. No doubt she'd give as good as he gave her. He had an instinct for such things, and that instinct told him that she would be truly spectacular.

Aye, she'd ride him hard and fast, and please him to no uncertain end.

He smiled in expectation as she drew nearer.

Her brown kirtle was plain and threadbare, and she wore a red and black plaid over it. Still, there was such pride in her walk, such self-assurance, that a man would have to be a fool not to take notice of her.

And his days of foolishness were over.

"Maggie," he said as she walked past.

"Good Lord!" she gasped, placing a hand over her breast. "Are you trying to frighten me into an early grave?"

"Nay, I thought you saw me."

Suspicion clouded her amber eyes as she

looked askance at him. "Saw you skulking there in the shadows like some evil beastie hunting decent souls? Ha! No doubt you were lying in wait for me, Braden MacAllister, and don't you be pretending otherwise."

Braden laughed at her perceptiveness. How did she do it? How was she able to see straight through his ploys?

He smiled the dimpled smile that no woman had ever been able to resist. "Since you seem to know me so well, then tell me what I was thinking."

She narrowed her eyes ever so slightly and pegged him again with her astuteness. "I've no idea, but I'm sure it involved a woman lying in a supine position."

Her candor stunned him. But only for a second. He found it refreshing to find a woman who spoke her mind so plainly.

"Not supine," he said, dropping his voice an octave, and leaning close enough to her that he could finally smell the rich scent of wildflowers in her hair.

He reached out and tenderly touched her chin between his thumb and forefinger in a gentle caress designed to send chills the length of her body. And judging by the shuttered look of her amber eyes, he would say it succeeded admirably, even though she tried her best not to let him know it. "I prefer my women to be more active with me than that."

Her eyes darkened as her lips opened ever so slightly in invitation.

Aye, a good kiss was what she needed. His kisses had made women faint in his arms, and had even caused them to climax. One good kiss and all this would end. The women could return to their homes, and Maggie . . .

Well, he had plans for his little vexation. Plans that included paying her back for that bite she'd given him years ago. Only now he relished the thought of those white teeth of hers sinking into his skin.

He leaned closer, opening his mouth for a taste of her breath.

Just when he was sure she'd accept his kiss, she stepped back, opened her eyes wide, and pinned him with a frigid stare.

"And how many women is that?" she asked out of the blue.

Braden blinked, not quite understanding her question as his senses buzzed from her quick reversal. "I beg your pardon?"

"How many women do you prefer to be active with at one time?" she asked. "From what Meg tells me, you had her and her sister simultaneously the last time you were home."

She shook her head at him like a doddering old maid chastising a child. "Have you no shame at all?"

There was no mistaking the hurt in her gaze. Braden frowned at what he saw, unable to place the source of her emotion. "Now, why would she be telling you that?"

"For the same reason you'd be telling it to your brothers, I'm thinking. For some unholy reason, she's proud of the fact. So proud, she was bragging of the event just yesterday."

Maggie gathered her skirts, then started past him. "Now, if you'll excuse me, I have duties to be about that don't include being tupped by the likes of you."

Braden's jaw dropped in shock of her words, and he uttered the same phrase he had been uttering at her for as long as he could remember. "Great saints, woman, where have you been that you picked up such language? What does Anghus have to say about that mouth of yours?"

She stopped, her hands clenched tightly in the folds of her skirt, and turned to face him again. A terrible sadness darkened her eyes. He saw the tears an instant before she blinked them back and swallowed hard.

When Maggie spoke, her voice was hoarse. "He hasn't much to say about anything since a MacDouglas sword silenced him eternally two months ago."

The unexpected news sliced through his heart and settled painfully in his stomach. For a moment, he could scarce breathe from the sensation.

"Anghus is dead?" he asked.

She nodded, her eyes bright.

"Nay," Braden breathed, his tone betraying his

grief. "How could it be? How could a warrior and man so fine be gone?"

A single tear fell down her right cheek. Licking her lips, she quickly wiped it away. "The same way the others perished. Over a senseless feud that should never have been started!"

His heart heavy, Braden tried to come to terms with her news.

After the death of their father when Anghus was but ten-and-six, he had been the sole support for Maggie and her brothers. All the members of the clan had helped the family as best they could, but the ever-prideful Anghus had turned aside the offers: *'Tis my family, and I'll be the one taking care of them. It's my responsibility and my pleasure to watch over them.*

His old friend had been one of the finest warriors he'd ever known. They'd trained together more times than he could count. Had drank and wenched even more.

From as far back as Braden could remember, Anghus MacBlar had been like another brother to him.

"How?" Braden asked.

She spoke, her voice unsteady. "He fell guarding Ian's back."

Braden took a deep breath to stave off the agony he felt. Ian was Maggie's twin brother. The two of them had been complete terrors as small children.

He remembered Anghus tossing Ian over his

shoulder as the scamp ran after Maggie intending
to torment her.

*Lad, if you don't learn to respect your wee sister, I'll
be tearing the hide from your bones.* How many
times had he heard Anghus threaten his baby
brother? And how many more times had he seen
Anghus wrap his arms around both Maggie and
Ian and give them the love they needed?

*I'll always be here for you, little Mag-pie. I'll not let
anyone e'er harm you. So long as there's breath in my
body, I'll keep you safe.* Those were the only other
words he'd heard Anghus utter more times than
the threat.

"What of Kate?" Braden asked, thinking of
Anghus's wife and two small children.

"She's surviving. Barely. Her mother took her
in to live with them for a while. And now she al-
ternates between cursing Anghus and begging
God to let all this be a bad dream."

Braden shook his head at the agony he heard in
her voice. Dear Lord, the pain Maggie must be
feeling now. Anghus had been her one true protector, the one person Maggie had always relied
on.

What would become of her now?

Most women would have collapsed from the
weight of such grief. For that matter, most men
would have as well. And he wondered how she
was making do. How she had found the strength
to devise such a plan to end the feud that had cost
her brother his life?

He saw her in a new light, and a profound respect for her welled up inside him. "And Ian?"

"He survived, just barely." The sadness left her eyes and in its place her rage burned bright. "Now the fool wants to head out to avenge our brother."

Braden could well understand that. Nothing would give him greater pleasure than killing whichever MacDouglas follower had claimed his friend's life.

And in that instant he understood why Maggie had done what she had. "So, that's the reason for all this. You're here to protect Ian."

"I'm here to protect *all* the men who are still living. If you men had your way, we'd end up like the MacNachtans, with nothing left save small boys and old men."

He reached out for her. "Maggie—"

"Don't you be touching me," she said, stepping away from his hand. "I'm not about to let you have your way with me so your brother can lead another party out to its death. I'm sick of all this killing. I have four brothers left alive, and by the saints above, I'll keep them safe or die in that effort."

Now, that got his dander up. She acted as if it were Lochlan's fault.

"If you recall," he said, "we didn't start this feud. The MacDouglas did when he led a raid into Ken Hollow. Do you not remember the women and children who were slain?"

"Aye, of course I do. If *you* remember, my brother Aidan was one of the ones who fell that night. Do you think I could ever forget such a thing?"

"Nay, of course you couldn't."

Braden cupped her face in his hands to offer her comfort. He half expected her to pull away or stiffen. Instead, she just stared up at him, her amber eyes large.

In that instant, he saw the vulnerability inside her. The uncertainty. And he ached to soothe her in some way. Not just with physical closeness. Nay, he wanted to make her feel better from the inside out.

"I am sorry about Anghus and Aidan, Maggie, truly I am."

She placed her hand over his and looked up at him with tears brimming in her eyes. "Then stand with us, Braden, and do what is right. You know the feud canna go on. Help us to end it."

Her courage amazed him. The cunning and determination it had taken her to achieve this standoff. The woman was truly brilliant.

"Tell me, how did you do this?" he asked. "How did you get the MacDouglas lairdess to agree with your plans?"

The right corner of her lips turned up into a beguiling half smile. "I snuck myself over to their lands. Since I was just a woman alone, no man thought to stop me. When I reached the MacDouglas castle, I pretended to be a servant and went to the Lady MacDouglas's solar to wait for her. Once she heard me out, she agreed to help stop this."

He paused in thought, but what played across his mind was not to his liking. Maggie's tale had all the ingredients of a planned betrayal. "And how do you know she's not lying to you? Even now they could be planning a raid on us while Lochlan is occupied with worries over you."

"Nay," she said. "I believe her. She's a good lady and all she wants is her husband to see reason. She wants peace as much as I do."

How Braden wished it were that simple. But he knew it would take more than a few days without sex or food to make Robby MacDouglas back down. The man was out for blood. And not just any blood.

In truth, nothing short of the impossible would cow the man. "Unfortunately, little blossom, it'll never happen."

Maggie frowned at him. "How do you mean?"

Braden dropped his hand from her cheek. It was time he explained the facts of the feud to the lass. Still, he didn't want to see her discouraged. He so enjoyed her spirit that he almost hated to see her give up. But he had no choice.

And a looming deadline.

"Do you know what started this feud?" he asked.

"You said it yourself, the MacDouglas raided Ken Hollow."

Braden nodded. "And do you ken why he did that?"

She shook her head.

"Do you remember the MacRae's daughter, Isobail?"

Her frown deepened as she searched her mind. "The lass your bothers fought over?"

Braden winced at her reminder. If ever the devil wore the face of an angel, it was in the guise of Isobail ingen Kaid. Beautiful beyond description, the woman had ruined the life of every man she had touched.

"Aye," he said past the tightness in his throat, past the haunting memories that burned him through and through. "She was originally promised to Robby MacDouglas, but she couldn't stand the man and threatened to kill herself if her father forced her to marry him. My brother Kieran brought her here to escape her father's wrath."

Braden's stomach knotted as he recalled that day. Isobail had stepped into the hall, taken one look at Ewan, and in that instant decided he would make a better protector than Kieran.

"Didn't Isobail run away with Ewan?" Maggie asked.

"Aye, she did," he said, his voice thick.

The day after Ewan and Isobail had left, Kieran had killed himself.

It was less than six months later Ewan had returned home with the news that Isobail had left him in the middle of the night to be with a rich Sassenach.

The news of what had happened to Kieran had destroyed Ewan.

To this day, Braden would like nothing better than to cross paths with Isobail and send her unmerciful soul back to hell where it belonged.

But now was not the time to dwell on what Isobail had done. Now he had to rectify the lasting damage her actions had wrought.

He steeled himself for Maggie's reaction as he explained the matter to her. "And that is the reason the MacDouglas continues to attack us. He wants Lochlan to hand Ewan over to him for punishment. The MacDouglas will not see reason until he has Ewan's blood for taking Isobail from him, even though the bastard ought to be grateful Ewan spared him the lifetime of misery I'm sure she would have given him."

Instead of being deflated by his words, Maggie seemed to take comfort. She nodded grimly. "Then it's a good thing I took these matters into my hands, isn't it? Otherwise this would never end."

Braden stared at her in disbelief and fought a sudden urge to place his finger in his ear to clean it out. Surely he hadn't heard her correctly.

"It won't end, Maggie. Eventually one clan or the other will attack its women and drag them back into their homes. Do you not understand that your plan can never work?"

She lifted her chin stubbornly. Her resolve shone brightly in her eyes. "It has to succeed. Sooner or later one of the lairds is bound to listen to reason."

"Sooner or later one of the lairds is bound to attack."

"They wouldn't dare attack their mothers, wives and daughters."

"What of Bridget?"

" 'Tis different."

Braden took a deep, calming breath before he said something he would regret. How could such an intelligent woman be so foolish?

This was going to be a long two days if she persisted in her nonsense. It would serve her right if he left her to fend for herself. In truth, he'd love to see her and Fergus square off and battle each other.

But he couldn't do that. Any more than he could let her face Lochlan's wrath alone.

"Then it is a good thing I'm here to protect you," he said at last, "since you're bound to be hanged for your unreasonableness."

She looked at him suspiciously. "Don't pretend to be here as a protector. I know what you came here for. You're here to seduce one of us so that the women will no longer listen to me and will return home."

Braden smiled to cover the prick of his conscience. "Now, what would make you think that?"

"Because I know you for the randy scoundrel you are."

"You've always suspected the worst of me, little blossom, haven't you?"

An odd look came into her eyes as she regarded him. If Braden didn't know better, he'd swear it was a look of disappointment.

"There was a time, once, when I expected only the very best of you." The haunting quality of her voice tugged at Braden's heart. And when Maggie finished her sentence, it felt as though she had thrust a dagger through his gut. "Unfortunately, you grew into manhood."

"What do you mean?"

She shook her head. "Never mind. Tell me how long you intend to continue this farce of being our protector."

Braden decided to be honest with her. She had a right to know exactly what would happen should she persist. "Lochlan has given me two days. If I can't compel you from your sanctuary by then, he's going to tear down the walls and let the men have at the lot of you."

"He wouldn't dare!"

Braden nodded solemnly. "Aye, he would. You have to understand the position you've put him in. Right now the men are starting to doubt his ability to lead. If he can't bring you women under heel soon, then he will be forced to drastic measures."

Maggie felt her heart sink with his words. What would she do if they forced her hand? She had counted on the men's reluctance to harm them, but with each attack, her resolve had wavered.

Maybe she should just throw open the gates and go home.

This was just too much for a girl of two-and-twenty to deal with. 'Twas too much for a woman of eighty to deal with, for that matter.

Rubbing her hands over her eyes, she tried to think of some alternative. Some way to end this.

Whatever was she to do?

You're a good lass, little Mag-pie, with a kind heart, she heard Anghus's voice in her head. *I know I can trust you to always do what's right.*

If only she had the strength to see it through. Weary from the struggle, from the constant complaints of the women, and from the uncertainty of her own mind, she looked up at Braden.

The sunlight cast dark reddish highlights in his sable hair, and his eyes glowed with that same compelling warmth that had once soothed her when she was just a wee bairn and he a boy. Even now she remembered the inner feeling of peace his youthful hugs had once given her.

How she wished she could trust him. She needed to trust someone. Even if it was a scandalous rogue with wenching on his mind.

"Tell me," she said, "why are you here, and not helping Lochlan to plan his attack against us?"

A deep emotion burned in his eyes, something she couldn't name. "I'm here to make sure no one kills you in retaliation for your actions."

Her breath caught at his words, at words she had waited a lifetime to hear. Could it be that after all this time, he might actually have feelings for her?

Dare she even hope for it?

"And why would you do that?" she asked.

"You were always Anghus's pride. I couldn't live with myself if I let something happen to you. 'Tis the least I owe him."

His words stung her heart even more deeply than she had thought possible.

What were you expecting, an avowal of love? You know better than that, Maggie. You're far too plain and simple to turn his head.

Her heart broken once again by him, she nodded.

Two days. She had two days left to think of something.

And she would.

Somehow.

Or you'll pay a dear price.

"Thank you," she whispered, patting him lightly on the arm. "I'm sure in two days I'll be needing a guardian."

"So, you're going to carry this all the way to Lochlan's deadline?"

She nodded, wishing she could think of an alternative. But there wasn't one. No matter how hard it was, she must see it through.

"I have no choice. If I open the doors and let everyone leave, I will be a laughingstock for the rest of my life. Look, there goes that crazy Maggie ingen Blar who thought she was some great chieftain to lead the women. She led them, all right. Right back into their homes where they could be slaughtered and raped in the middle of the night by the MacDouglas and his men."

He reached for her. "Maggie—"

"Nay, Braden," she said, stepping away from him. "Both of us have the same goal—to save the life of our brothers."

She looked up at him, allowing him to see the turmoil in her heart. "But tell me this. If I give in to you and Lochlan and lead the women home, who's to say that in the next battle it isn't you or Ewan who dies? Will Lochlan still feel victorious then? Or you, if it is he or Ewan who is cut down? Where will your precious manhood be when you're standing over the grave of your brothers?"

Before he could stop her, she left him standing in the middle of the yard, mulling over her words.

Braden watched her as she entered the refectory.

Damn the wench if she wasn't right. He already knew the pain of losing a brother, and the last thing he wanted was to bury another.

There had to be some other solution to this madness. Something that would allow both Lochlan and Maggie to save face.

Clenching his teeth, Braden crossed the yard to slip through the back door of the kirk and return to the castle. He would go talk to Lochlan. Surely his brother would be more reasonable than Maggie.

If nothing else, he could try and bully Lochlan into a surrender.

After all, he was Braden MacAllister, the unparalleled, sanctified peacekeeper of the family. He'd dealt with his pigheaded brothers all his life. If he could maintain peace between the lot of *them*, then surely he could settle this petty squabble.

I mean, how hard could it be to bring peace between people who want it?

What of Kieran?

His gut tightened at the memory. Neither Kieran nor Ewan had wanted the fight that Isobail had caused. They had even tried to work it out peacefully between them before she delivered her ultimatum.

Closing his eyes, Braden tried to blot out the lonely image of the green and black plaid, impaled by Kieran's family sword, lying on the cliff above the rocks where his brother had jumped into the sea.

He had tried so hard to keep his brothers from fighting. Tried to tell Kieran that there would be another lady he would love as much.

You know nothing of it, Braden. Hearts don't just stop loving, and when a man finds the woman he needs, he'll do anything to keep her. Anything!

Aye, that was a truth he'd seen firsthand on more than one occasion. Love made a man weak. It made him do unforgivable things, and in the case of Kieran, it had cost the man his very soul.

It was for that reason Braden would never allow himself to love a woman. He would never be such a fool.

Never.

His life belonged to him and he would make certain that no woman ever held control over him.

Besides, he enjoyed his carefree life and had no wish for it to change.

At present, the only thing he wanted to change was this stalemate between two obstinate fools.

Somehow, he would get the women back to their families by the morrow. Then Lochlan would have his men under control, and Maggie . . .

Well, he had a different plan for her. One he couldn't wait to get started on.

Chapter 5

Weary and frustrated, Lochlan pushed open the door to his keep expecting an empty hall where he could sit quietly and brood over the events of the day.

What he found when the heavy door scraped open was about two score hostile men glaring at him as if he were the sole reason for their misery.

"This canna be good," he mumbled under his breath.

Lochlan paused with a frown. Never in his life had he seen a more sour-looking group. They reminded him of a gaggle of geese ready to confront the axe-bearing farmer. The only problem with the image was that Lochlan had no axe.

Nor much of anything else with which to protect himself.

And the geese were restless. They swarmed

around him, their voices loud and ringing off the stone walls as they all shouted at once.

Lochlan held his hands up to quiet them. Instead, they grew louder.

Fergus stepped forward and yelled for the others to quiet down. To Lochlan's amazement, they complied, and it was then he knew the leader of the irate geese.

"What the devil is the meaning of this?" Lochlan asked. "What are all of you doing here?"

"We've come for answers," Fergus said over the murmuring voices. "I saw the way you and your brothers cozied up to the women, and now I'm thinking you and them fancy brothers of yours are wanting to be keeping our women for yourselves."

Lochlan gaped in disbelief. "You canna be serious."

"What else are we to think?" Davis snarled.

At a score and ten years, with a thick mop of tawny hair and a slight build, Davis was normally one of the more reliable men of the clan. But by the furious look on his face, Lochlan could tell Fergus had stirred up quite a bit of mischief while Lochlan had been gone.

"All of us here know that Braden MacAllister never sleeps alone," Davis continued, "and now you've left him locked up in the kirk with our women. He's probably in a darkened corner even as we speak with one of our women wrapped about him. And God help you both if it's my wife he's with."

Davis raked Lochlan with a repugnant glare. "Where was your head when you decided to leave him in there? I'm thinking it's time we be finding ourselves a new laird! One with some common sense."

"Aye!" the others shouted in unison.

Lochlan could feel his blood starting to boil. Granted, Braden was a bit rambunctious when it came to women, but even his scandalous brother knew when to draw the line of propriety.

Most of the time, anyway.

It wasn't Fergus's or Davis's place to reprimand Braden. That was for Lochlan to do.

"I left Braden in there to get the women out," Lochlan explained.

About half the men snorted in disgust.

Dermot came forward. Only half an inch shorter than Lochlan, the older man's light gray eyes burned in anger. "I've spent the better part of a decade guarding my daughters from that randy brother of yours, and now you expect me to believe he's not in there, right now, lining the women up to choose one or even more to warm his bed? Whose knotty-pated decision was it to send him in there in the first place?"

The word "mine" faltered on Lochlan's tongue. No need to make the matter any worse than it already was. None of his men were ready to listen to reason.

Silently, Lochlan cursed his brother's raging hormones and good looks. Better he should have had a brother who looked like a warted troll than one who was forever being pursued by the fairer sex.

The men began shouting at him again.

Lochlan held his hands up to silence them.

Seeking to allay their fears, he explained Braden's plan as best he could and prayed for them to listen.

"Braden went inside the kirk to bring Maggie out. She's the only woman he's after; the rest are safe."

Bitter, cruel laughter broke out.

"What kind of fools do you take us for?" Davis asked. "None of *us* would have Maggie on her best day. Now, why would your brother be after her when he could have the best-looking among them?"

The coldhearted statement brought a sudden echoing silence to the hall.

All eyes turned slowly to Maggie's four brothers who had come inside with the others. Stephen, Ian, Duncan and Jamie looked as if they were ready to kill each man standing in the room.

"And just what do you be meaning by that, Davis MacDowd?" Jamie asked in a low, lethal tone.

Davis stammered as he regarded the four angry brothers united in defense of their baby sister. "I didn't mean much. It's just . . . you know yourself that no man here has ever courted her."

The words only served to make the brothers' faces even redder, their bodies more tense as they regarded the men around them.

"And what's wrong with my little sister?" Duncan took up the challenge.

"First, she's not much to look at," Fergus said. "And second, she's off in the head. Look what she's gone and done with the women! Not to mention, she attacked me in the kirk when I went to see my wife."

The words set off total chaos in the hall as the four brothers growled in rage, then attacked their clansmen.

Lochlan joined the fray, trying to bring peace to his men. Curses and shouts rang through the hall, along with the sounds of fists striking flesh, and breaking furniture.

Lochlan had never in his life seen such a melee.

The urge to cross the room and remove his sword from the mantel was strong, but he didn't truly want to hurt any of them. He did, however, want them to exercise a little restraint.

As Lochlan struggled to pull the brothers from the fray, five men set upon him at once. Before Lochlan could extract himself from their beefy hands, they seized him and set him down hard in a chair before the hearth.

"What are you doing?" Lochlan demanded as

three of the men held him in place while two others grabbed ropes.

The answer was plain.

After a few more minutes, Maggie's four brothers were seated next to him, the five of them trussed up like birds for the slaughter.

Cursing them all, Lochlan struggled against the ropes which bound him to the chair. If he ever got out of this, they would pay dearly for their actions.

Fergus and the others looked down upon them with evil smiles. "Now it's time we find us a laird who can actually handle the—"

"What in the name of Satan's hairy toes is this?"

Fergus's face paled at the sound of the deep bellow.

Settling down, Lochlan breathed a sigh of relief at Braden's appearance.

But his relief was short-lived.

The mob turned on Braden with a vengeance. Their angry voices again reached a deafening tone.

Until a loud whistle sounded.

The men settled down, and they drifted back, making a path from Braden to Lochlan and Maggie's brothers.

His face a mask of fury, Braden stepped forward and eyed the crowd. "Would someone care to explain to me why my brother, your laird, is tied to a chair?"

A wave of sheepishness washed through the men. Except for Fergus. He moved forward to confront Braden. "We want this matter with the women settled."

"And you think tying Lochlan to a chair is the best way to accomplish this?"

Lochlan smiled. With Braden here, he allowed himself to see the ridiculousness of the situation.

Fergus looked shamed.

Shaking his head, Braden started for Lochlan's chair. But a big, burly Enos stepped out of the crowd to block him. "Your brother isn't going anywhere until my wife is back inside my home, tending our children, warming my bed and cooking me some food worth eating."

"Aye," Fergus shouted. "I say we kill the laird and take our women back!"

The men quickly took up Fergus's shout of "Kill the laird, kill the laird."

Lochlan held his breath, afraid of what the obsessed mob might do. Damn, but he should have grabbed his sword while he had the chance.

"Whoa!" Braden shouted over them, until he shushed them once more. "Have you lost all your wits? That's your laird you're speaking of. The man all of you have sworn to follow and protect with your lives."

"He stands between us and our women!"

Braden took a deep breath as he regarded the sea of angry men. This was quickly getting out of hand. And if he didn't stop it soon, there was no telling what they might do.

Sweet Mother Mary, what had Maggie started?

"Now let's be reasonable for just a moment, men," Braden tried again. "Killing Lochlan won't get your women back. They've sworn an oath to each other and that oath has nothing to do with his life."

"Fine, then," Fergus said. "We'll kill him, send Ewan to the MacDouglas, and have our women home by week's end."

"Aye!"

"Aye, hell!" Braden roared. "You kill my brothers and you'll have me to deal with."

Fergus snorted as he raked a cold look over Braden's body. "Is that a threat? You're but one man against all of us."

Braden returned the cold glare with one of his own. "Aye. I'm one man with a full garrison of troops sitting rather nicely entrenched on my English lands. Trained knights and soldiers ready to march at my command. You touch one hair on Lochlan's head and I can promise you, I'll see every one of you in your grave."

That gave them pause. At last, Braden had found the one thing to reach through their stubbornness.

"You know, Fergus," Davis said, "he does have those lands that tie MacAllister loyalty to England, and the English king might not take it kindly if we attack him, especially now that the MacAllister is on peaceful terms with King Henry."

"Then what do you want?" Fergus asked him and the others. "We let the laird go and then just wait? I'm sick of waiting. Me bairns are screaming for their mother."

"He's right about that," Enos said. "I've heard his brood crying myself."

"Look," Braden interjected. "I was trying to work out a truce with Maggie."

Enos spat on the ground. "I say burn that witch."

"Aye," the men shouted in unison. "Burn the witch. Burn the witch."

"Burn the witch and her ugly shoes too!" Enos shouted.

Braden frowned at him.

"Well, they are ugly," Enos said defensively.

"Would you stop!" Braden shouted. "First you want to kill my brother, and now you're after Maggie. And her shoes. Is there anything short of bloodshed that would bring this matter to a conclusion?"

The imbeciles actually paused to think. And from their faces Braden could see just how much effort they were having to give it.

"I swear by the eternal saints," Braden muttered under his breath. "If it's the last thing I do, I'm going to get Maggie for doing this to all of us."

Now what was he to do? He'd come here to bicker a settlement with Lochlan, not the entire clan.

"Well," Fergus said to him at last. "What do you think we should do?"

Braden had absolutely no idea, but since one of the men still held a sword a little too close to Lochlan's throat, he didn't think this was the time to say that aloud.

"I'll go back and talk to Maggie." Which would be like arguing with a wall.

Or these men.

And of course he had no idea what to say to her, since he already knew just where she stood on the matter.

Braden ground his teeth in frustration. How on earth would he ever get this settled?

And at this point, he was tired of walking back and forth to the castle and the kirk. Enough was enough.

Sighing disgustedly, he started back through the men.

"You better not tup our sister!" Duncan snarled at him. "Or you'll be having us to deal with, Braden MacAllister!"

Braden paused midstride, turned back around, and looked at Maggie's brothers drolly. "Could I please just deal with one threat of death at a time?"

Duncan pursed his lips as he strained against

the ropes holding him down. But luckily, the boy held his tongue.

Braden paused as he regarded the five of them by the hearth. He couldn't walk off and leave them tied up like that.

He turned to face Fergus. "Let them go and I'll—"

"We'll be doing no such thing," Fergus responded, interrupting him. "How do we know you're really going to talk to that she-witch and bring them out?"

"You have my word on it."

Fergus snorted. "If it didn't involve a woman, I might accept that. But as it is, we'll be keeping your brother tied where he is until you return with the women behind you."

Now, why didn't that thought comfort him in the least?

"And if Maggie refuses?" Braden asked.

Fergus folded his arms over his chest. "We'll give you four days to convince her. If in that time the women aren't back in our homes..." His voice trailed off.

Fergus swept a look around the men watching him. "Well, you'll have to be reaching that English army, I'm thinking. If we kill you here, then they can't come and be commanded by no spirit."

That was one small flaw to his logic Braden hadn't considered. And it was one hell of a time for Fergus to find his brains and finally use them.

"Four days?" Braden repeated.

"Aye. Four days."

Well, it was a step up from Lochlan's deadline. Briefly, he wondered what he could do to get another two days. If his luck held he might actually gain enough time to think of some way out of this mess.

"All right," Braden said. "I'll have the women out in four days."

Sure you will. Why not just promise them you can walk on water while you're at it? Or turn the fishes into loaves of bread?

Hush, self, I've got enough to worry over without your intrusion.

And worried, he was. Because at the moment, Lochlan, Ewan and Maggie's lives were all depending on him. And for the first time in his life, he was beginning to doubt his ability to handle a situation.

"That's it!" Pegeen snapped, rising from the dining table and heading for the door. "I've had enough of this. I'm going home and no one's to stop me this time."

Maggie grabbed Pegeen's arm as she started past her and held the woman by her side. "Now, what's this about?"

Pegeen gestured back to the table where she'd sat eating, and to the old woman who had been sitting by her side. "I'm sick of Old Edna. She's been doing nothing but clicking her teeth while she eats. I'm sick of it. It's disgusting."

"And I'm sick of not seeing my babes," Merry chimed in from her seat in the left corner. "I haven't seen my sons in so long, I'm afraid they'll forget all about me. For all I know, Davis isn't washing their clothes or their faces. And I bet my home is dirtier than a sty."

The wails and complaints were taken up by the rest of the women. Their loud whines bounced off the walls and rang in Maggie's ears.

Suddenly the large refectory seemed to be closing in on her, the brightly colored walls, much smaller than they had appeared when she had first sat down.

Maggie felt a sudden urge to place her hands over her ears and scream.

Why, even Aisleen started complaining. And up until now, Aisleen had been Maggie's most steadfast supporter.

"Poor Lochlan is probably at his wits' end on how to cope in the castle," Aisleen said. "He's never had to worry over cooking and such. He's our laird and shouldn't be put out so."

"Silence!" Maggie shouted.

To her amazement, they quieted and looked at her as if she'd lost her wits. And at the moment, Maggie wondered it as well. Surely she must have been mad ever to think this scheme would work.

"Now, Aisleen," she said to Lochlan's mother. "I'm sure our laird is just fine. He's a grown man in charge of all our lives. I would think he, of all men, could figure out how to make a simple bowl of porridge."

Aisleen looked less than convinced, but she tucked her chin to her chest and sat back down.

Maggie took a deep breath and surveyed the other women. "As for the rest of you, you ought to be ashamed. How many times a day must we go through this? I thought we had all agreed."

"We agreed," Merry said petulantly as she picked at her roasted chicken. "But you told us the men wouldn't go more than a week without us. Well, it's been much longer than a week and there's no end in sight."

"Aye! Our men need us," they cried in unison.

"I need my man!"

Laughter broke out from the group.

Maggie cocked her brow at the last comment, unable to distinguish the voice.

Grateful for the break in the seriousness of the moment, she sighed. "I know you're all tired. As am I."

"Then let us go home," Pegeen begged.

Maggie rose to her feet. "Do you truly wish to go back home and hand the swords to your husbands and sons as they head off to battle to die?"

The women grew silent.

Maggie nodded. " 'Tis what I thought."

"But Maggie," Edna said. "What if they refuse

to end this? How much longer are we to wait? I have a garden to tend and berries to preserve for winter. Soon we'll have waited an entire month here while our work and families go neglected. At what point do we surrender?"

"Aye!" Merry chimed in again. "All of us know how obstinate men are. They'd sooner set fire to the kirk than admit they're wrong."

"What if they do come after us?" another woman asked. "How long will they wait before they punish us for this?"

Maggie closed her eyes in frustration as the women voiced her own concerns and questions. Questions to which she had absolutely no answers.

When she'd started all this, she had never anticipated the daily fights necessary to keep the women on her side.

How could they not see what she herself saw?

"It will end before much longer," Maggie assured them. Her stomach drew tight as she remembered Braden's deadline. God help her then, for she was sure the other women would go home relatively unscathed, but there was no telling what the men would do to her over this.

"When?" Edna asked.

"Soon. I'm just asking all of you to trust me for a few more days."

Edna pierced her with a glare. "My trust is wearing thin, lass."

Maggie could appreciate that, since her own

patience had been stretched so thin it was close to breaking. "Give me a few more days to see what I can do."

"All right," Pegeen said, moving back to her seat by Edna. "But don't you be asking for much more than that. I have a home to see to."

Maggie nodded, her heart heavy. Saints help her, she had no idea how to conclude this.

What she needed was help.

She searched through her mind, but only one possibility came to her.

As much as she hated to admit it, she needed Braden. He was the only one she knew of who could find a possible solution. If ever there had been a man born to negotiate, Braden was he.

But it stuck in her craw that she would have to go begging an answer from the devil's own. Even now she could see that cocky walk of his. The arrogance.

He thought himself infallible and now she would have to play into his ego.

Still, she had no choice. Her brothers' lives and those of the other clansmen depended on her.

Stiffening her resolve, she went to find the scoundrel rogue.

Chapter 6

Braden walked the well-worn path back to the kirk as he thought over what had happened and what he had left to do. The evening sun was just starting to set and if he weren't so aggravated, it would be a peaceful, cool evening. The kind of evening best suited for finding a willing maid and passing the quiet hours of the night.

But tonight there would be no willing maid in his arms breathing sweet, blissful sighs in his ear.

Tonight he would have to deal with Maggie. And worse, Maggie's obstinacy, for he held little doubt what her response would be when he asked her, yet again, if she would surrender her women to Fergus and his bunch.

It would be as futile as asking the sun not to rise. Or the walls around him to breathe.

Clenching his teeth, Braden wanted to start

knocking heads together. Was there no end to the frustration?

Why couldn't someone, other than he, be reasonable?

What had Fergus been thinking when he had decided to go after Lochlan anyway?

When Braden entered the small chapel to find his other two brothers, he swore he could feel his blood starting to boil. His every nerve tense, he needed all his strength not to slam the chapel door and rattle its hinges.

The setting sun filtered into the room through the two large stained-glass windows that showed the birth and death of Christ. A myriad of colors dappled the old stone floor as he made his way toward the back of the kirk.

There was an iron stand for candles to the left of the nave, where his brothers were working. Sin held a ladder while Ewan stood on the next to the last rung repairing the ceiling. Braden headed for them, then quickly told them the latest bit of *wonderful* news.

"Are you serious?" Sin asked as soon as Braden finished his tale.

Ewan descended the ladder. "What do you mean, they've taken Lochlan captive?"

"You heard me," Braden said. "As soon as Fergus left here, he went 'round to the homes, gathering up men and inciting them. When Lochlan returned to the castle, they seized him."

"Those bastards!" Ewan roared. "Give me a sword and I'll—"

"What?" Sin asked, interrupting him. "Bleed all over them? I realize you're quite a bit larger than the average man, but we're still just three against how many?"

"Two score in the hall even as we speak."

Sin shook his head. " 'Tis too many to fight."

"*Sassenach!*" Ewan spat.

Before Braden could blink, Sin grabbed Ewan's collar and jerked his head until their gazes were locked. The black, evil look on Sin's face would have made any other man wet himself.

"Don't you *ever* insult me again, *brother*," Sin said, his quiet voice carrying the wrath of hell. "You forget which of us was cast out of Scotland into the hands of our enemies. I was fighting for my life while your lily arse was being coddled by a doting father and loving mother. If you've a desire to learn firsthand what I was taught, then grab your precious sword and meet me outside."

For the first time in his life, Braden saw uncertainty creep into Ewan's eyes.

And Braden had had enough. Growling at Sin, Braden separated them by prying Sin's grip from Ewan's shirt and stepping between them.

"Jesus, Mary and Joseph, is there not a single soul in the whole town who can go more than a second without letting their emotions get the better of them? Leave him be, Sin, or I swear, in the mood I'm in, I'll tear your head off your shoulders and use it for a footstool."

Sin's face was a mask of utter disbelief as he looked skeptically at Braden.

Few, if any, men had ever stood up to Sin for fear of the knight's honed skills and short temper. And if Braden hadn't been so angry, he would have laughed at the expression on Sin's face.

However, at this moment, Braden couldn't find much humor in anything.

Recovering his stoicism, Sin said sharply, "Believe me, there is nothing more I would love than to stain my sword red with Scottish blood, but should we storm the castle, the first casualty would be Lochlan."

Braden nodded. "They said as much before I left."

A tick started in Sin's jaw while he thought the matter over.

When Sin spoke again, his tone was ominous. "Let us not forget that we are dealing with men here. Men who are horny and hungry. In their state, they are capable of most anything."

"So, what are we to do?" Braden asked.

Sin stroked his chin in thought. "How much time did they give you?"

"Four days. If the women aren't out by then, they'll kill Lochlan and storm the kirk."

"Four days," Ewan repeated. "Well, it gives us time to poison the lot of them."

Sin gave a short half laugh. "Remind me to

take you along on my next siege, little brother. I like the way your mind works. However, if we poison the men, then we'll have the women out to kill us for the deed."

"He's right about that," Braden concurred. "After all, they're hiding in here to protect their men."

Silence settled between them as each tried to think of something to end the stalemate.

"I'm afraid we have no recourse," Sin said at last. He met Braden's gaze. "You'll just have to complete what you started. Seduce Maggie."

How simple that sounded. If it were anyone other than she, Braden had no doubt of his success. But at the moment, her seduction was nearly out of the question. "It's not quite so simple a matter anymore."

"How so?"

Braden sighed. "You realize that if I continue pursuing her after she told me she's doing this to protect her brothers, she will think I'm a total monkey's arse for it."

Sin arched a brow at him. "Are you telling me you've never seduced a woman who thought you were a monkey's arse?"

"Nay," Braden said, aghast at the very idea of what Sin intimated. "Women love me."

"Lucky you," Sin said dryly. "Most of us have to work for our bedmates."

Braden gave him a droll look. "I'm not most men and you're not amusing."

"Actually, I am, but that's another conversation. Right now, we must stay focused. You work on seducing Maggie, and I shall see if there's a way to get Lochlan out alive."

"Let me help," Ewan said.

Sin shook his head. "You're too large to skulk about. They'd see you in an instant."

Braden nodded his agreement. "He's right about that. You'd end up bumping your head or if you had to hide, you'd never get all your body parts into a single nook or cranny."

"I'm barely an inch taller than Sin."

"Aye," Sin said, "but I've had a lot more practice at being deceptive than you have."

"Fine, then," Ewan said resignedly. He looked at Sin. "You go skulk, I'll repair the roof, and Braden gets to have all the fun."

"Doesn't this remind you of childhood?" Sin asked sardonically.

Braden snorted. "All except for Lochlan being tied up."

Sin arched both his brows.

"On second thought," Braden said, finally smiling, "we did do that to him a time or two, didn't we?"

"Just a time or two." Sin started away from them.

When Sin reached the door of the kirk, he paused in the doorway and gave Braden a meaningful stare. "Braden, don't disappoint me."

* * *

"Braden, I am *so* disappointed in you!" Maggie snapped as she glared at him.

Braden's lewd proposition rang in her ears. Surely the man had gone daft.

But worse than his casual invitation to spend the night in his bed was the fact that in her heart she really wanted to accept that which was unacceptable.

How could her heart want something her head knew was wrong and impossible?

Confused and disappointed with herself for her conflicted feelings, she lashed out at the source of it all: Braden.

Why on earth had she thought, for even an instant, that he might be the one to help her?

He'd help her, all right. But only if the helping involved a little tupping. To the devil with that. She didn't care if he *was* the most handsome man in the world, or even that she was, if she dared admit it, attracted to him. Physically, at least.

The man was the devil!

Anger and pain mixed inside her. And to think she had actually started liking him again.

He'd been such a dear boy. Her hero. How many times had he come to her rescue back then?

More times than she could count.

In those days, he would scoop her up in his arms and fight or scare off whichever brother was after her. She had looked to him as her champion.

Why did that dear, precious boy have to grow into such a man? A man who had no soul.

"How can you come back here and try this with me after I told you the reason we're here?" she asked. "Have you no shame, man?"

Braden sighed inwardly as he wished he were the one tied to the chair, and Lochlan left to woo Maggie.

I am a monkey's arse.

This is what I get for listening to Sin. I should have known better. The only advice Sin can give that's worth a damn is when it involves war, not women.

The entire day was starting to wear on his nerves. Would it ever end?

Taking a deep breath, he tried again. "Maggie, my love, don't you understand that Lochlan can't just give in to you? If he does that, it'll make him look weak before his men, and what man is going to follow a laird who got led about by a mere lass?"

Maggie glared at him. How could he be as dense as the others?

"Damn you men for your pride," she said between clenched teeth. " 'Twas that pride that led two of my brothers into their graves. Can any of you ever admit when you're wrong?"

His smile charming, Braden reached out and touched her cheek in a gentle gesture that sent chills the length of her body. "We are complicated beasties, to be sure, but no more so than you women."

Even worse than the touch, the light teasing in those greenish brown eyes reached inside her and made her yearn for a time when they weren't on opposite sides.

It would be so easy to give in to him.

But she couldn't. Not when she had so important a goal. And not when giving in to him would ultimately break her heart.

"This is nothing to jest about, Braden," she said more harshly than she meant. In truth, she wasn't as angry at Braden as she was at herself for letting him affect her this way. "Lives are at stake here."

"Aye, they are. More even than you know."

She frowned at the note in his voice. A shadow passed over his face and it was then she knew he was hiding something. "What do you mean?"

Dropping his hand, he hesitated a few minutes before he spoke again. "The clan is ready to shed blood to get you women back home."

Maggie clenched her teeth in exasperation. Men! How insufferable they all were. It seemed to be the eternal plight of women that they were forever drawn to the unreasonable oafs.

"Does everything with you men have to come down to bloodshed? Canna one of you just sit down and have a conversation?"

He tilted his head in a beguiling, attractive manner that showed off those deep dimples. "If we did that, then we'd be women and you wouldn't love us as much as you do."

"Aye, but we might *like* you better."

He arched a questioning brow.

Rolling her eyes, Maggie didn't understand how he could be so nonchalant about the matter.

"How can you make light of this?" she asked. "Are you not worried about dying in battle?"

"Nay, love," he said gently. "None of us are. We're Highlanders. Born to fight and to wench. Personally, I prefer the wenching part, but as you well know, I've never shirked from a fight."

Irritated by his words, Maggie tried to think her way through this. How could she get Lochlan to end the feud? "Then what am I to do?"

"Surrender," he said simply.

"And nothing changes."

"It will change. Lochlan can negotiate peace with the MacDouglas."

"But *will* he?"

She saw the uncertainty in his eyes. And the debate. She could almost see the workings of his mind and she wondered what lie he would devise to feed her.

Finally he spoke, "Nay, even I am not such a beast that I'd lie to you about this. Not when it's so important to you. Lochlan canna stop the feud so long as the MacDouglas is after Ewan's life."

Which was exactly what she suspected.

Still, she respected Braden for being honest. The man might be a scoundrel and a rogue, but he did draw the line at lying. It was nice to know at least one moral was still intact in his wicked body.

However, that didn't help her for the moment.

How could she end this if . . .

Maggie paused as an idea occurred to her. It was ludicrous, really, but no more so than the idea of getting the women to withhold themselves from their men. Surely, if she could get the Lady MacDouglas to follow her, she could get Robby MacDouglas to listen to her?

After all, the entire feud had started because of a woman, and now that he was married to another, why would he continue the feud over Isobail?

Perhaps he was even looking for a way to back out without losing face himself.

Aye, 'twas a possibility.

Maggie let the idea loose in her mind. The more she thought it over, the more reasonable it seemed.

It really *was* a possibility. And if it was the truth, then maybe if she got to the MacDouglas, she would be able to make him see the futility of continuing the feud.

Right?

The very least she could do was try.

Making up her mind, she met Braden's gaze levelly. "If I can't get Lochlan to end this, then I'll have to get to the MacDouglas and talk sense into him."

Braden laughed aloud at her words. "Are you insane?"

"Nay, I am serious. If I explain it to him, he'll—"

"Laugh in your face, then cleave your head from your shoulders and hang it from his walls."

"I will make him see reason."

Braden stared at her in numbed disbelief. Never in his life had he met her ilk.

She was something to behold, no doubt about it. Unfortunately, that something wasn't sane.

And by the tilt of her chin, he'd say her mind was as fixed as Fergus's had been. There wasn't going to be any way to talk her out of this.

Still, he felt the need to try. "Is there anything I can say that would sway you from this madness?"

"Nothing at all."

"Not even the fact that the MacDouglas will more than likely rip out your heart and toss it to his dogs?"

"It changes nothing. I have to try."

"I thought you'd say that." Braden sighed. "Can I add another thorn to your bramble bush, then?"

Maggie froze at his words, terrified of what he might say. Every time he got that look on his face, he tossed another formidable obstacle at her. And right now, she was tired of hurdling them. "What?"

"If you women don't give up by the week's end, the men will kill Lochlan and storm the kirk."

Her jaw dropped at his words. Surely he was jesting, but the sincere light in his eyes told her he spoke the truth. "What?"

"It's true. Lochlan is at the castle even as we speak, tied to a chair."

If the situation weren't so dire, she'd laugh at the image in her head. But this wasn't funny. Not in the least.

"Och, you men!" she snapped, angered over the thought of what they had done.

"Hate us if you must, but I canna let my brother die any more than you can."

"Nay, and I couldn't live with myself if they killed him," she said quietly.

Leaning her head back, Maggie closed her eyes and shook her head. She was weary and tired and frustrated.

When had things gotten so complicated?

Well, it didn't change anything. It just gave her less time to work a miracle. And by God's will, she would have her miracle. Or die in that effort.

At least four days gave her time to reach the MacDouglas.

She hoped.

"Here, take this." She pulled from her little finger the ring that her father had given her on her tenth birthday. It was a thin gold band that had the impression of tiny wildflowers on it. All the women of the clan knew it to be hers, and in her absence, they would know it spoke for her.

"At week's end, give my ring to Pegeen and tell her to take the women home."

Braden held the gold band in his hand. Her warmth still clung to the metal. It was such a tiny piece of jewelry, so frail and delicate, and yet at the same time strong and unbending. It reminded him much of its owner.

He remembered a time, long ago, when he and Maggie had been friends. When she had actually saved him from being ambushed by a group of the clanswomen who had been lying in wait to mob him on his way to her house.

He couldn't honestly remember a time in his life when he hadn't known her and her stubbornness.

He'd never before thought about just how much of his past she was. Not until he thought of her marching off to the MacDouglas and getting herself killed.

For some reason, the thought of her death stung him far more deeply than it should.

Braden handed the ring back to her. "Do you honestly think I'm going to stay behind and let you brave the MacDouglas on your own?"

"Of course. They would be suspicious of a man they didn't know, but a woman—"

"Would stand out mightily, since all of their women are in hiding. Is that not right?"

Maggie opened her mouth to speak, then snapped her jaw shut. She'd forgotten all about that. Her journey to MacDouglas lands wouldn't be so easy this time. They would be suspicious of any stranger, and as a lone woman in their midst while their own women were shunning them . . .

It didn't bear thinking on.

"And might I point out," Braden continued, "that if they ever figure out *who* you are, your life will be worthless. No doubt they all know your name by now and curse it with every breath they take."

"Very good points," she said, her mind whirling as she sought to think of an alternative.

There wasn't one.

She would merely have to alter her original plan of reaching the MacDouglas. "I shall have to dress as a lad, then."

"A lad would never be traveling alone," he said. "You'll need someone to go with you."

How she wished she could have an escort, but if anyone found out Braden's identity . . . Well, she didn't want to think what the MacDouglas clan would do to the brother of their enemy.

She had started this alone and she would finish it that way. "Braden—"

"Nay," he said firmly. "I doubt the MacDouglas will listen, and when he demands your head for it, you'll be needing someone to get you out of there."

"You can't fight all of them."

"You'd be amazed what I can do when my life is at stake."

Actually, she wouldn't. She had seen him train enough to know quite a bit about his abilities to protect himself and others.

Still, the fact that he was willing to risk his life for hers meant quite a bit to her. Braden might be an arrogant man, but he usually wasn't a foolish one.

"Why would you risk your life for me?" she asked.

"I have no idea. But come, we need to find you some clothing and give Ewan your ring and instructions."

"Are you mad?" Ewan asked after they had found him outside the kirk, putting the ladder away in a small shed.

"Is who mad?" Sin asked as he joined them.

Ewan turned to Sin with a disgusted look. "Braden is going to take Maggie to see the Mac-Douglas so that she can talk the MacDouglas into stopping the feud."

Sin whirled to face Braden. "Are you mad?" he asked in disbelief. "He'll have you impaled before you get halfway to his castle."

"Nay, he won't," Maggie said, then she laid out the plan for them.

When she had finished, Sin shook his head. "It'll never work."

"Forgive me," Maggie said softly. "I don't mean to be rude, sir, but I don't even know who you are, and I have no idea how this matter concerns you."

"He's my brother Sin," Braden said softly in her ear.

Maggie's eyes widened and she formed a small O with her mouth. Everyone in the clan knew the terrible tale of how Sin had been taken forcibly from the castle.

And even worse, the story of how, as the king's men were struggling to force the youth on a horse, his father had turned his back to them, then coldly closed the door and left his son to his enemies.

The instant the door had shut, Sin had stopped struggling, stiffened his spine, and ridden off with the promise that he would never return.

Anghus had been there when it had happened, and the tale had always haunted her. How could any father just turn his back on his blood and let him go?

Now she regretted her harsh words to him. No doubt, Sin had heard worse, but she didn't want to add any more to a man who had suffered so much.

"Forgive me," she said to Sin, "but it's been quite some time since last we met."

Sin gave an almost imperceptible nod, but said nothing.

And now that she knew who he was, she asked, "How do you know my plan won't work?"

A wicked, almost evil smile curved Sin's lips. "Because when it comes to planning attacks, I have no equal. If I say it won't work, you can wager your life on the fact that it won't. I've never been wrong."

A chill went down her spine. There was something hidden in those words. Something that scared her.

"Speaking of plans," Braden interjected, "how did the reconnaissance go with Lochlan?"

Sin shook his head. "It's hopeless. They have him and four others tied in the center of the hall where they can all keep an eye on them. Even if we came in through the gallery, they'd see us in plenty of time to kill the five of them, or us."

"What four others?" Maggie asked.

Braden went cold at her question. Oops. In his concern for Lochlan, he had let that other little tidbit slip his mind.

He turned sheepishly to Maggie. "Did I forget to mention the small fact that Fergus has all four of your brothers tied up with Lochlan?"

She narrowed her eyes on him. "What?" she roared. "What do you mean—"

"It's all right, Maggie," Braden assured her. "Nothing will happen to them."

"Why didn't you tell me?"

"I didn't think it would change anything."

"Well, it certainly does! I'm not going anywhere until they're safe."

Maggie faltered as soon as the words were out of her mouth. Once again, she was caught. "I have no way to get them out, do I?"

Braden shook his head. "Not unless you throw open the door to the kirk and lead the women home."

She sighed. "Then we'd best follow my original plan."

"Then I go with you," Ewan said.

"Oh, aye, that'll work well," Sin said sarcastically. "If there's one person the MacDouglas would rather lay hands to than Maggie, it's you. Good plan, that."

"Could you please refrain from sarcasm?" Ewan snapped.

"Could you please refrain from fighting?" Maggie inserted. " 'Tis a wonder any of you survived childhood." She glared first at Sin, then at Ewan.

"I knew I should have stayed in England," Sin said under his breath. "But no, I just had to come back with Braden and had to stick my bloody nose in where it doesn't belong. If I had any sense, I'd go back home right now and leave all of you to your idiocy."

Braden ignored him. "Ewan, you keep Maggie's ring, and at week's end, hand it over and save Lochlan. That should keep the men from doing anything against the MacDouglas or his men until we can reach the MacDouglas. When you free Lochlan, tell him what we're doing and make certain he doesn't lead any kind of attack against the MacDouglas unless he's sure we're dead."

His eyes full of reluctance, Ewan nodded slowly.

Braden clapped him on the back. "Maggie and I will leave just after dark."

"What should I do if the women miss her over the next four days?" Ewan asked.

"Tell Mother what we've done in the morning. She'll help you keep the women from getting suspicious."

"Just remember," Maggie warned, "you have to give us the whole four days to reach the MacDouglas. If you let the women out sooner, one of the men might attack the MacDouglas, and it could get us killed before we even reach the castle."

Ewan's face belied his fear for them, but finally he agreed.

Sin growled in his throat. "I suppose this is where I toss my gauntlet in to join this suicide escapade."

Braden arched a puzzled brow. "Meaning?"

"I can't very well let you go alone, little brother. In the highly likely event the MacDouglas decides to kill the two of you where you stand, you'll need another sword."

"Oh, here's where I get to be sarcastic," Ewan said. "Can I point out how much you'll stand out wearing English clothes as you prance across MacDouglas territory?"

Braden nodded. "He's right, Sin."

The glower on Sin's face would have quelled Goliath. "I'd sooner wear a kirtle than put a plaid on this body."

"Well, then, you'll have to stay here," Braden said.

"I'll be fine in my own clothes."

"Nay," Braden said firmly. "I'll not chance it. I couldn't save Kieran when he died any more than I could keep our father from sending you to the English. But this I can stop, and I will. I'll not lose another brother. Not so long as I live."

Sin's glare intensified as he tapped his thumb against his thigh in agitation. "You know, there's this voice in my head that keeps telling me to return to England. No doubt I'm going to wish I'd heeded it."

His lips curled, Sin turned to Ewan. "Find me a damn plaid and I'll wear it."

Braden stifled his laughter at the look of repugnance on Sin's face.

"Now that we have that settled," Braden said, "the next question is, how do we find our way across enemy lands and into the very heart of the MacDouglas's territory?"

Maggie smiled. "I'm so glad you asked."

Chapter 7

Hours later, as the sun set over the lush, rolling hills of the Highlands and darkness stretched across the land, Maggie stood in the small courtyard behind the kirk. The entire area was enclosed by shrubs and roses that Father Bede spent most of his days lovingly tending. And those roses smelled wonderful in the early twilight.

A solitary bench rested against the far wall and if she listened closely, she could hear the voices of the women in the nearby dormitory. Faint laughter rode the wind and brought a smile to her lips.

It was beautiful out here, and she loved her blessed Highlands. Even though the sun had descended over the farthest hill, a dapple of pink, purple and magenta played across the dark blue clouds as the first stars of the night came out to twinkle. A pleasant chill settled on the earth and the night animals began their soft, gentle serenade.

Maggie had seen the evening descend thousands of times in her life, but never before had it struck her quite the way it did tonight. It was then she prayed that when all was said and done, she'd be back to witness another beautiful sunset from MacAllister lands.

A few weeks ago, when she had devised her plan, she'd had no idea that it would lead to this. Any more than she'd guessed Braden MacAllister would step forward to be her defender in this strange sequence of events.

He was a good man, to risk his life for her. And though he had told her he was only doing it for Anghus, she liked to think that maybe there was more to it than that.

Perhaps he would even be a little sad should something happen to her.

What a silly fool you are, thinking such thoughts. The man has better things to worry over than a plain, dowdy lass like you.

Still, Maggie dreamed. Dreamed of impossible things with a man who had stolen her heart.

But most of all, she recalled a time long ago when she had been a wee lass of seven and had first given her heart over to her hero. . . .

"Help, save me!" she had screamed as she ran through the great hall of the laird's donjon as fast as her wee legs could carry her. The clip-clopping

of her shoes echoed loudly and was silenced only by her fearful shouts.

She had to get away. She had to escape before the great, angry beastie on her heels overtook her.

"He's going to kill me for sure," she shouted as she looked about for someone to deliver her from Satan's dreadful spawn. "Please, please don't let me die. I'm just a tiny bairn, too young to die yet."

"No one's going to save you from me," the demon snarled. "So you might as well stop running, so I can kill you right proper."

Maggie gulped in fear and ran even faster. Where were all the grown-ups?

Where was her da?

Terrified, she glanced over her shoulder to see her twin brother Ian closing in on her.

"Help m—"

Maggie didn't get a chance to finish the word. Out of nowhere two arms appeared to wrap around her. She thought her father had finally come to her rescue until she realized her rescuer was only slightly taller than she, and her unexpected weight had knocked him off balance.

Falling to the right, she and her savior ended up careening toward one of the castle's wall hangings, becoming entangled in it, then landing with a solid thump on the floor. A loud rending of fabric filled her ears as the tapestry was torn from its rod and came fluttering down around them.

The rich, red fustian cloth covered her completely. Maggie tried to pry the fabric loose, but she was hopelessly trapped in it. Worse, her movements unsettled the dust and she began sneezing repeatedly.

This was no good, no good at all! She could hear Ian's breathing just a hair away from her. And if he laid hands on her, she was certain her young life would be over.

"Get out of there, you fishwife," Ian snarled as he pulled at the fabric, trying to get to her.

"I'm not a fish's wife," she shouted back. "I'm too young to be married, and I don't like fish."

From the depth of the fabric, a musical laugh filled her ears. "I doubt if either of you even knows what a fishwife is," the voice said.

In an instant, she recognized her savior. Her heart stopping, Maggie widened her eyes at the voice of the laird's youngest son.

Good heavens, she was sitting on top of Braden MacAllister!

Again.

Scrambling to get up, she accidentally elbowed him in the stomach and kneed him in the side. He groaned, then captured her arm in his hand.

"Easy, now, lass," he said softly. "Let me get us out of here afore you damage me any further."

"Forgive me, my lord," she said hurriedly. "I didn't mean to kill you."

"I'm not dead yet," he said, laughing again. "Though I'm beginning to suspect being around you might be hazardous to a lad's health."

Maggie bit her lip as she remembered the last time they had met, just a sennight ago. She'd been up a tree gathering apples when Braden and her brother Jamie had come along. She'd overreached her balance and had toppled out of the tree directly onto poor Braden's head.

Jamie had called her rotten fruit ever since and had warned her to keep a fair distance from the laird's son afore she killed him.

She'd tried to do as Jamie had asked, for she liked Braden a great deal. He often brought her small trinkets when he came to visit her brothers Jamie and Anghus, and unlike her brothers, he never tried to truss her up or make her eat worms or other despicable things.

With a few tugs, Braden managed to uncover the two of them.

The first thing Maggie saw was Ian's enraged face as he lunged for her.

Shrieking, she started to run, but Braden caught her to his side with one hand, while he held Ian back with the other.

"Here, now," he said to them. "What is all this about?"

Ian held up his toy horse, which had only three legs. "She broke my horse and I'm going to break her head for it."

"I didn't mean to do it," Maggie quickly defended herself. "I told you it was an accident. I fell with it because you were trying to hit me."

"I wouldn't have been trying to hit you had

you not been playing with it, you reeky, mouse-eaten cotquean!"

Braden threw his head back and laughed mightily. "Cotquean?" he asked Ian. "Lad, do you even ken the word?"

Ian poked his lip out. "Aye, me da uses it all the time."

"And it means?"

"Faint-livered."

Braden shook his head. "How old are you now, Ian?"

"Seven, same as *her*." He sneered the word as if Maggie were the lowest of the low.

"Well, then, for future insults, you should know cotquean is a man who does women's work, and so is hardly fit for insulting your wee sister."

"Oh," Ian said sullenly. "She's still mouse-eaten, though."

"I'm not mouse-eaten," Maggie said. "You toad's pizzle."

Braden choked on her insult. "Where on God's precious soil have the two of you been, to pick up such language?"

"Me older brothers, mostly," Maggie said.

"Someone should have a talk with Jamie and Anghus," Braden said as he handed the horse back to Ian. "I tell you what, Ian MacBlar, I have a painted horse in my bower. If I give it to you, do you promise to leave your sister alone?"

"Only if she promises not to touch it." His glare intensified as he stared at her. "Ever."

Maggie pursed her lips and felt tears prick at her eyes at his words. She wasn't a bad girl, and she never meant to hurt his toy. "It's not my fault. I only wanted to hold it."

She looked up at Braden. "They never let me play with their toys. And since our mother died last winter I haven't had anything new to play with at all."

"It's because you're a girl," Ian spat the word. "Girls don't play with horses. Girls don't deserve them."

Maggie reached to strike him, but Braden caught her again.

"You know, Ian," he said to her brother, "you should take more care with Maggie. Sisters are special treasures."

"How would you know? You've only got brothers."

"That's how I know. If I had such a special little blossom for a sister, I would take care of her. Watch after her."

Ian sneered. "Then you can have her. Just give me the horse and she's yours."

Maggie looked up at Braden as a tear fell down her cheek. "I don't want to be a pest," she said to him. "I just want to play with them, but they think I'm no fun. They say I can't play anything because I'm a girl." More tears fell. "I hate being a girl. I hate it, I hate it, I hate it."

Braden drew her into a tight hug. "There, now, little blossom. There's nothing wrong with being a lass. The good Lord made you what you are, and one day your brothers will come to realize just what a special gift they've been given."

For the first time in her seven years of living, she believed that. If Braden liked her, she couldn't be all bad, could she?

Her brothers were just mean.

"What are the two of you doing in here?" Her father's angry tone split the air.

Maggie pulled away from Braden to see her father's irate face.

Her father stalked toward them and took her hand, then reached for Ian. "I thought I told the two of you to stay in the wagon until I finished my business with the laird."

Maggie swallowed. There would be a beating for this, to be sure. And all because she'd wanted to play for a few seconds instead of sitting in the stinky old wagon.

Life was just so terribly unfair!

Her father apologized to Braden, then quickly returned them to the yard where their wagon waited.

Maggie scurried up the back of the empty wagon and took a seat on the remnants of hay while Ian settled up front. Her da left them with a dire warning should either of them move again.

Her heart heavy, she tucked her feet beneath her dirty saffron kirtle and watched her father disappear into the stable.

Oh, what a wretched, awful day. Why couldn't

she ever listen to what her da told her? Perhaps Anghus was right after all. She did have a demon in her.

Sighing, she kept her head sedately bowed and studied her folded hands, and prayed that her da wouldn't be overly harsh with his beating.

A few minutes later, a painted horse appeared just before her teary eyes.

Gasping, she looked up to see Braden's wonderful, ten-year-old face smiling at her.

"I named him Connor," he told her, "but he said he'd like to play with a wee lass for a bit. He thinks a lass would be more fun than playing with a mean old boy."

"Thank you, my lord," she breathed, cradling the horse to her chest. It was painted a deep rich brown with great big black eyes. Never had she seen anything more incredibly beautiful. "I'll take good care of him for you."

Braden nodded, then handed Ian a white one. "Remember your promise, Ian. You can't kill your sister."

"Can I hit her, then?"

"If you do, I'm taking the horse back."

"Oh, all right," Ian said huffily.

Maggie watched as Braden left them and in that instant she realized she loved the young lord.

He was her hero.

Clutching the horse tightly in her hands, she vowed that one day she wouldn't be a fish's wife. One day she would be . . .

One day, she would be Braden MacAllister's wife.

Maggie smiled at the memory.

Fifteen years had passed since that day, and yet in some ways it seemed like yesterday.

So much had happened to her and Braden since then. So many things had come between them, and her promise to marry him.

Of course, most of those *things* were other women. Women like the tall, beautiful Nera, who had caught Braden's eye when he turned ten-and-five.

But how she missed those days of childhood when she would go fishing or swimming with Braden and her brothers.

How she wished she could go back for just a moment to when her life was simple.

"Are you ready, then?"

Maggie jumped at Braden's voice behind her. She'd been so lost in thought that she hadn't even heard his approach.

She pushed her reminiscing to the back of her mind as she turned to face him. "I was but waiting on you."

Standing beside the dark kirk with a pack thrown over his shoulder, he was incredibly handsome. The fading light played across his face, which made the angles of his cheeks even more pronounced than normal. Even so, it in no way detracted from the perfection of his tanned face.

At that moment, she wished she were his feminine equal. That she was as perfectly formed as he, with long ebony tresses and creamy skin unblemished by freckles.

If she were, then perhaps . . .

Maggie pushed the thought aside. She was what she was and there was no help for it.

Banishing her wishful thinking, she picked her own pack up from the ground at her feet and went to stand beside him.

Braden assessed her as she drew near. Never before, in deference to his friendship with Anghus, had he paid her much notice. But tonight, he saw her in a way he'd never seen her before. As a woman.

With her breasts flattened down to make her look more mannish, she reminded him of some fey creature caught between childhood and womanhood. She'd even added girth to her waist.

Even so, he vividly recalled the luscious curves of her body.

Her breasts were just the perfect size to fit into a man's hand, and though her waist wasn't fashionably narrow, it was thin enough to be pleasing, and shapely enough to be all woman.

A tiny smile hovered at the edges of his lips as he dipped his gaze down the red and black plaid she wore draped over her. Like his, it stopped just above her knees and showed her legs off quite nicely.

And what attractive legs she had. Strong and

curvy. He could just imagine running his hand down over the smooth skin, tasting the strength of those legs with his tongue as he trailed it along the curve of her calf, to the back of her thighs, and then higher, to her . . .

He paused at the thought.

With a curse, Braden realized no one could ever mistake *those* legs for a man's.

"What is it?" she asked.

Braden gestured toward her. "Your legs."

Her eyes narrowed in warning an instant before she matched his curse with one of her own. "I am not a chicken!" she snapped with such rancor that it took him aback.

"I beg your pardon?"

She dropped her pack to the ground, bent over to where she could look at her knees, then she started pulling the hem of her plaid lower.

"You know, I had six brothers, which means I don't need the likes of you telling me everything that is wrong with my body. And in spite of what Ian, Jamie and Duncan always said while we were growing up, I do not have the legs of a scrawny, half-dead chicken."

Braden tried not to laugh, but for his life he couldn't help himself. The image of her plucking at the plaid and gesturing in sharp, stiff movements reminded him quite a bit of poultry. Even the manner of her speech in short, angry bursts reminded him of a chicken clucking.

However, the heated glare she shot him when she straightened up succeeded in checking his humor.

At least until he made the fatal mistake of looking at her boots. Enos's words rang in his ears as he tried not to notice that the frayed brown boots really were ugly.

Burn the witch and her ugly shoes too.

Braden held his breath, but still the laughter bubbled up until he had no choice but to laugh or choke. Throwing his head back, he gave rein to his humor.

Maggie balled her fists at her side as she glared at him. "You better be glad I'm a woman, Braden MacAllister, or I'd be taking a sword to you right now."

And she probably could best him too, especially in those ugly shoes.

The thought made him laugh even harder.

"You beast!" she said, an instant before something wet slapped him upside his head.

"What the . . . ?" Braden pulled it away from his head to see a damp cloth in his hand.

"You'd best be glad I didn't have anything harder in my pack or else I'd have used it on you instead."

"Just so long as it's not your shoes," he said, choking back another wave of laughter. "I could survive anything but that."

"My shoes?" she asked, her anger wilting beneath her confusion.

Braden cleared his throat as he fought with himself. "I wasn't laughing at your legs, little blossom. But rather at something Enos said earlier."

Suspicion hovered in her eyes. "You swear it?"

"On my completely unrepentant soul, and if it wasn't for the fact that I'm sure you'd find something harder to slap me with than that cloth, I'd be willing to show you just how unlike a chicken I think those legs of yours really are."

Her cheeks pinkened at his compliment as she looked about bashfully. "Then what were you going to say about my legs?"

"That they're by far too feminine to be exposed. We need to lower your plaid and pad your . . ." In spite of himself, he laughed again, "Boots."

"Oh," Maggie said quietly. "I'm sorry about the wet cloth, then. I hope it didn't hurt." She came forward to take the cloth from his hand.

"It didn't hurt," he said, releasing the cloth to her.

Her hand gently scraped his, and for a moment he couldn't focus on anything except the gentle softness of her skin fairy-light on his own. Unbidden, his gaze dipped back to the exposed flesh of her legs, and his mind played through several interesting scenarios he'd love to experience with her.

Aye, as passionate as she was, he could already hear her deep throaty moans as he taught her the true meaning of pleasure.

He lifted his gaze to her flat chest and the laces that drew her saffron shirt closed. In his mind, he could see himself reaching out and unlacing them, exposing the binding on her chest and then freeing her breasts to his touch.

His body drew hot and hard as his mouth watered for a taste of her skin.

"You know, Maggie . . ." Braden stopped himself before he propositioned her again. Any other woman would be his in an instant, but to get this woman, he would have to play the game more slowly. Skillfully.

She wasn't the type of woman just to fall into his arms and demand his kiss.

"What?" she asked, folding the cloth and returning it to an animal skin bag in her pack.

Change the subject, his mind warned. *Now!*

"Why are you carrying that?" he asked in a deliberate effort to refocus his thoughts.

"In case it's needed. I always pack a damp cloth for washing and such."

Braden didn't understand that, but then there were many things about women in general he didn't understand. And a lot of things about Maggie in particular that defied even his best cognitive abilities.

Letting the matter go, he dared a glance at those ugly boots. "We'll have to find something to pad your boots with. Do you have—" He broke off as he finally looked up at her head and noticed her hair.

The moonlight caught in the strands he had assumed she'd braided or twisted about her head. And it was only standing this close to her that he could finally see what the dark auburn locks really looked like.

"Good Lord, woman, what have you done?" he asked in disbelief as he fingered her sheered locks. Her soft hair curled about his fingers as Braden carefully brushed his hand over her head.

"I didn't want my hair to betray us."

Braden felt as though he'd been slapped in the face with something a lot harder than her rag. Her hair barely reached her thin shoulders. And it was then he noted the tears in her lashes. He cupped her cheek in his hand and ached to pull her close to comfort her. "Maggie."

"It's just hair," she whispered. "It'll grow back."

"But it was beautiful hair. Hair a man dreams of holding in his hands and burying his face in."

Her eyes sparkled in the moonlight as she looked up at him. "Did you ever dream of that?"

Placing his hands on her cheeks, Braden answered her question with a kiss.

Maggie moaned at the fierce tenderness of his embrace. Never in her life had anyone kissed her, and the thought that it really was Braden who had finally done so thrilled her more than anything else had in her entire life.

Mo chreach, but it was wondrous. This feeling of those strong, beautiful lips on hers as his arms wrapped about her, pulling her closer to his rock-hard chest. It was better than even her sweetest dreams. And her entire body thrummed with the rush of excitement.

He smelled of sweet, decadent elderberries and tasted of ale and honey. Of raw, earthly desires, and in that instant she understood why the women had complained so mightily at being deprived of their husbands.

Who would want to give this up for even an instant? She wished she could die right now. Right in this moment of pure heavenly bliss. If she lived to be a thousand years old, she'd never forget the taste of his mouth, the feeling of his arms holding her tight as her senses whirled from the earthy scent of his body.

For this one tiny moment, he was hers. And she reveled in it.

Braden's head swam at the sensation of her lips beneath his. Her breath mingled with his as her tongue gently explored his mouth. He could tell by her hesitation that he was the first ever to lay claim to her lips, and that knowledge only added to his pleasure.

Aye, she was a spirited and bold lass, one who beguiled him in ways he'd never known.

"Maggie," Braden whispered against her lips, savoring the feel of those two syllables against his tongue while he longed to savor even more intimate parts of her body. Slowly. Leisurely.

Aye, he wanted to lay her down and make love to her for the rest of the night.

And right now he could kill the MacDouglas for the absence of her hair. How he wished he had known in time to stop her. Never had a woman done such for him, and all because she didn't want to betray him.

It was much more of a sacrifice than a scoundrel like him deserved.

Braden trailed his lips from her mouth to her jaw, then down to her neck. He inhaled the sweet fragrance of her skin and drank the moonlight and warmth from her flesh.

She ran her hands over his back, wrenching a groan from him as he lifted the hem of her plaid from behind and found out just what she wore beneath it.

Nothing.

The thought drove him close to madness.

Aye, he would have her.

Now. This instant.

He fisted his hand in the plaid as he licked the gentle hollow of her throat. He both felt and heard her moan as she tilted her head back and gasped for more.

"Am I intruding?" Sin's voice sliced through Braden's pleasure, almost instantaneously stifling it.

Damn the man's presence!

Reluctantly, Braden lifted his head to see Sin

standing in the shadows. Braden narrowed his gaze on his brother, wishing the man had learned a little better timing in his years of warfare.

Unperturbed, Sin met his gaze with just a hint of a smile. "If you want, I could take a quick walk about the church and come right back. That should be enough time to finish the deed, should it not?"

Releasing the plaid to fall back around her hips, Braden gave Sin a droll stare at the insult to his stamina. "For you, perhaps. I, on the other hand, prefer to satisfy my women."

Braden felt Maggie stiffen in his arms an instant before she pulled away. "It's dark now. We'd best be going."

Braden clenched his teeth, but as Sin stepped out of the shadows and into the bright circle of moonlight, he forgot his anger in another wave of laughter.

Maggie looked at him with a frown.

Braden couldn't speak; all he could do was motion to Sin's legs, which were almost gleaming white beneath his plaid.

"Do you want to die?" Sin asked nonchalantly.

"Nay," Braden choked. "But have you seen your legs, man?"

Sin growled low in his throat as he shifted the pack over his shoulder. "Aye, and I know they're whiter than a dove's tail. With any luck the sun should blister them up fairly well on the morrow and by the time we reach anyone who might care, they should be a half-normal color."

Sin inclined his head to Maggie. "Given how hers look, I doubt anyone will ever notice mine anyway."

The thought sobered Braden instantly. "Aye, I thought of that myself. We'll have to be finding her a larger pair of boots, I'm thinking, and some padding for them."

Sin tossed a brown pair of boots to him along with two worn plaids. "I always plan ahead."

"Good lad," Braden said as he handed the boots and cloth over to Maggie. "You must come in handy on all those sieges the English love so well."

"I hold my own." Sin looked about the small courtyard. "So, where are our horses?"

"We'll be walking," Maggie told him as she sat down on the ground and exchanged the new boots for her old worn pair. "We'll draw less notice that way."

The stunned, horrified look on Sin's face was comical.

"Walking?" Sin choked. "Och, now, lass, are ya tryin' tae kill me?"

Braden laughed at Sin's brogue. "Do yourself a favor, brother, if we come across anyone we don't know, don't open your mouth. Your brogue is more likely to give you away than your legs."

Sin glowered at Braden. "I don't want to hear

another word from you about my legs. I'm sure by the end of tomorrow they'll be acceptable even to you."

"Let us hope so. For as it stands now, it'll be a race to see which of you gets us hanged first."

Sin cast an interested stare at Maggie's legs. "Aye, but between the two, I must say I prefer hers."

Braden smiled lecherously as he ran his gaze over them as well and wondered how long he'd have to wait before he got a full taste of them. "As do I."

Rising to her feet, Maggie flushed. "Would you two stop? Is there ever a minute in the day when a man doesn't have wenching on his mind?"

"Aye," Braden said with a smile. "But it usually involves the minute and a half that we're eating."

She shook her head. "And Lochlan wondered why I chose the method of reaching his warriors that I did."

Before Braden could retort, a door opened from the dormitory across the yard.

Maggie gasped as she dodged into the shadows. The men quickly followed suit.

Pegeen paid them no heed as she crossed the yard to the chapel, then vanished inside.

"That was close," Maggie whispered. "We'd best be leaving before someone sees us."

Braden nodded solemnly before leading the way out the small postern gate that Fergus had used earlier that day.

They moved quickly through the heather-covered moor behind the kirk and into the thick woods that separated the MacAllister and the MacDouglas lands. None of them spoke as they put as much distance as they could between themselves and anyone who might want to stop them.

It was nearly two hours later, and long after the dense, dark trees shielded them, that Maggie dared to speak. "Do you think we stand a chance of changing Robby MacDouglas's mind about the feud?" she asked the men.

"Not a bit," they said almost in unison.

A deep frown drew her brows together. "Then why are the two of you willing to do this?"

Braden gave her a grim look. He'd been dreading this question, and though he knew he should probably lie, he couldn't bring himself to be dishonest with her. Maggie was probably the only woman he had never lied to, and for some reason he wanted to keep it that way.

"Because," he said, "if you fail, then I know a certain way to end this feud once and for all."

"And that is?"

"I plan to kill Robby MacDouglas."

She stumbled at his words, then stopped dead in her tracks, her mouth open. "Nay, you canna be serious."

"Of course I am," Braden said. "You want this feud to end and this is the only guarantee I know."

Maggie felt tears prick her eyes. How could he? And all this time she had assumed he was going with her strictly to protect her.

Foolish woman, her mind snapped. *You should have known he didn't do this for you. Do you honestly think he'd care whether or not you live or die?*

But she couldn't say that out loud. Instead, she whispered, "I thought you were being chivalrous. You said you couldn't let me go alone."

"Listen to me, Maggie. The only reason I'm allowing you to come along at all is that I know you well enough to know you'd trail along after us on your own, anyway. At least this way I can keep my eye on you. Believe me, I did learn a thing or two about you while you were growing up."

"And I learned a lot of things about you as well, Braden MacAllister, most of which left me in tears. But of all the heartbreaking lessons I learned, I never thought I'd see the day when you'd just go off to murder someone."

Her words stung his conscience. Braden had no intention of murdering the MacDouglas. It would be a fair fight. But when he left MacDouglas lands, the feud would be over.

One way or another.

"If you're too squeamish to do what must be done, woman, then I suggest you hie yourself home where 'tis safe."

Frustrated, she turned to Sin. "Could you please talk sense into him?"

"Why?" Sin asked. "For once, I completely

agree with him. I would think the life of the Mac-Douglas would be paltry when compared to those of your family."

Maggie was aghast. "You would honestly walk up to him and just cut his throat?"

Sin's dark gaze became empty, dull. "I've done worse things in my life."

Braden flinched at the tone, for he knew only too well just what sort of things his brother had done. He patted Sin on the back.

"Maggie," Braden said quietly, "I am willing to do what I know is foolish. I'll give you time to talk to Robby MacDouglas. If you succeed, then there will be no more bloodshed. But if you fail . . ."

Anger darkened her eyes. "Thank you for adding that." Her sarcasm made a mockery of Sin's usual tone. "Let's see if I have all this correctly. Right now I have hanging on my shoulders the lives of our laird, your brother Ewan, and my four surviving brothers, as well as the hopes of all the women of both our clan and the MacDouglas's, and now the very life of Robby MacDouglas rests with me too. Have I forgotten anything?"

"There are a few things more," Sin added dryly. "If you fail, you'll probably get yourself killed, along with Braden and myself. If the Mac-Douglas kills Braden, I'm rather sure Lochlan will spend the rest of his life trying to eradicate all the MacDouglases from this earth. Should I die, King Henry would be rather put out himself, and since he's not overly fond of the Scottish and completely fond of me, there's no telling what he might do to retaliate. Knowing the king as I do, I'm sure it won't be pleasant."

Braden cleared his throat. "This would probably be the place where I might mention that Sin is one of the king's chief advisors and a close personal friend."

Maggie rolled her eyes toward heaven. "Sweet Mother Mary," she breathed. "Now you've got me responsible for two countries going to war?"

"Aye, but that's only *if* you fail."

Maggie squared her shoulders as she started trudging through the forest. "Very well, then. I shall not fail."

And then under her breath she added, "I hope."

Chapter 8

By the time they finally stopped for the night, the full moon hung high above their heads. A thick, eerie mist clung to the forest floor as the cool white light dappled all around them, streaming through the trees and shrubs at strange angles. Braden took a deep breath and savored the smell of clean air that held a hint of heather and pine.

It was the kind of night for fairies and other fey creatures to frolic, and for more earthly creatures to take advantage of in quiet, undisturbed embraces.

It was also the kind of night Braden had once used to frighten a young Maggie into a screaming fit years ago.

Braden smiled at the memory.

No older than ten, Maggie had trotted along after Anghus and him one night when the two boys had snuck out of her small cottage in search of dragon's treasure. What they found was a red-haired imp who wanted to tattle on them unless they let her join them.

Being the clever ones, they had told her she could come along only if she could keep up.

Anghus had led her forward slowly while Braden had run ahead under the pretense of scouting for trolls and pixies. Once he was out of sight, he had doubled back to come up behind an unsuspecting Maggie.

Just as they were reaching the cave that was their destination, Braden had goosed her and shouted.

Terrified, she had screeched like a banshee, cocked him with one swift kick to the groin, then ran home shrieking the whole way with her arms flapping above her head.

To this day, he swore he could still feel the pain of that kick. But how funny she'd looked running through the forest, screaming that a dragon was after her.

He wondered if she recalled the event. If she did, she showed no signs of it tonight as they stopped. She just looked weary-eyed and exhausted.

Silently, they took shelter beside a narrow stream, in a small clearing of grass and heather. Braden handed Maggie her pack as Sin headed off to gather wood for a fire.

Maggie unpacked the dried meat, cheese and skins of ale and made them each a small meal.

Once Sin found enough wood, Braden started the fire while Sin used a stick to clean mud and wet leaves off the soles of his black leather boots.

"How far do you think we've come?" Maggie asked before placing a piece of cheese in her mouth.

Sin snorted. "Since we're on foot, my wager is less than half a league."

Braden tossed a handful of dried leaves at his brother. "Could you be any more pessimistic?"

"Aye, but for the lady's sake, I'm trying to behave."

The worst part was, Braden knew Sin's words for honesty. And God save them if Sin gave full rein to his biting sarcasm. The man could make Job leap from a cliff.

Choosing to ignore his brother, Braden answered Maggie's question. "I'm sure we've covered a few leagues. How long did it take you to reach the Lady MacDouglas last time?"

She hesitated as if she were silently debating something. "Four days," she said at last.

"Four days?" Sin cursed. "Why didn't one of you say that to me before we left? Haven't any of you people ever heard of horses?"

Braden shook his head at Sin's typical anger. He placed another piece of wood onto the fire before rising to his feet and moving to sit by Maggie. "He's teasing you."

"The devil I am. If God had meant man to walk about, he'd have made smaller horses."

Befuddled by the logic, Braden frowned at Sin. "That doesn't make a bit of sense."

"Well, if I weren't so tired from *walking*, I'd be able to think up something more intelligent to say," Sin retorted.

"Excuse me," Maggie interrupted them. "Do the two of you always carry on in this manner?"

"Mostly," Sin said, before Braden could respond.

"Well, then, I beg you to cease. I canna take any more of it tonight."

And so they withheld their conversation while they ate a light repast.

Maggie was grateful for the silence, not that they were really all that annoying with their bantering.

In truth, it was funny at times.

But what she feared was that one of them might become enraged by the teasing and lash out as her brothers so often did. She couldn't begin to count the number of suppers that had started out with just a good-natured jab or two and had ended in all-out warfare as one of her brothers lost his temper and attacked the other.

Both Sin and Braden were large and dangerous enough to inflict serious damage on the poor hapless soul who angered them. She doubted if a quick dousing of water would calm them as it did her brothers.

Most likely, if she tried, they would turn on her. And that would be truly terrifying.

After they finished their modest supper of bread and cheese, Braden banked the fire while Sin took up watch on the edge of camp. Maggie dug her large woolen green and yellow plaid out of her pack and settled down just before the fire.

To her instant chagrin, Braden laid down behind her.

Close behind her.

"What are you doing?" she asked, rolling over to look at him.

"Combining our warmth," he said nonchalantly as he snuggled up to her spine.

"I'm quite warm enough," she said quickly. Indeed, with him this close, her body felt as though it were on fire.

"What?" Braden asked with a teasing note in his voice. "Are you afraid of me?"

"Nay," she answered honestly. It was herself that scared her. As well as the strange emotions his presence evoked.

"I won't hurt you, little blossom," he said, smoothing back a lock of her shorn hair.

Mo chreach, his hand felt good in her hair. His strong fingers did the most wicked things to her scalp.

He gently rolled her back to her right side, facing the fire, and positioned his body right behind hers, not quite touching, yet so close she could feel the warmth radiating from him to her.

"Just close your eyes and go to sleep," he said, his breath stirring her hair.

As if she could really do such a thing while so much thrumming heat pounded through her body. She'd never felt so alive or alert.

Every tiny part of her body could *feel* Braden. The skin over her neck where his breath fell in a soft, rhythmic pattern. Her back where his body heat warmed her through and through.

But worst of all, she felt him in her heart. For it was there where he made her feel secure. There where she ached for a dream that could never come true.

Her throat tightened at the thought.

And it was through her pain that she wanted to enjoy this night. To pretend that for one moment he was hers and they were lying here as lovers.

With the dream foremost on her mind, she tried to relax. But that was as impossible as sleeping.

Aggravated at herself and her foolish dreams, she propped her head on her arm and forcibly closed her eyes.

A few minutes later, her arm fell asleep. The rest of her remained painfully conscious. Unwilling to let Braden know how much his presence disturbed her, she tried to wad her plaid up into a small pillow.

Her shoulder began to ache.

Over and over, Maggie shifted her head and arms trying to get comfortable.

It was useless.

Just as she resigned herself to a sleepless night, Braden reached out and touched her arm.

"Here," he whispered, pulling her back against his front. "Lean on me."

She wanted to argue. Nay, she needed to argue, but she couldn't. Not when he felt so good.

Reluctantly, she allowed him to cradle her against his chest.

Now, *this* was comfortable!

She lay with her head on top of his biceps, where she could feel the strong muscle as it shielded her from the hard ground. Though his body felt as strong as steel, it made a most wondrous pillow.

Closing her eyes, Maggie savored the wicked feel of Braden wrapped around her and the rich masculine smell of him. He encased her with his presence and it seeped into her very soul.

And still she couldn't sleep.

Worse, she knew Braden was all too aware of the fact that she was lying there, stiffly, in his embrace. In fact, she could feel his stare on her even though she kept her eyes stubbornly closed.

A braver lass would never lie so passively while the man of her dreams held her so intimately. But she didn't know what else to do.

What would it take for her to make him see her as a woman? Or, more to the point, make him see her as the only woman for him? She didn't want to be just another female in a long line of females, she wanted to be his only one.

Aye, she wanted to tame the wild wind. To touch his heart where no other woman had ever reached.

But that was impossible.

Even if she dared be bold with him, she was terrified he would deny her. How would she face him if he pushed her away, or worse, laughed at her feeble attempts?

Oh, what's the use, Maggie? You know what happened the last time you tried to impress him.

Her mind drifted back to the day she had turned ten-and-four. She had taken extra care to dress for mass that morning, for it was on that day that for the very first time in her life she had felt she really was a woman.

And she knew Braden would be at the kirk.

Over and over as she struggled to dress, she had told herself it was going to be *the day* Braden noticed her. He'd take one look at her in her finery and he'd realize that she was finally grown and that she was the only woman he would ever want. The only woman he would ever love.

In her mind, she had even pictured him going down on his knee before the entire clan and vowing his eternal, undying love for her while all the girls who had been mean to her would look on in envy. Then the two of them would ride off together and live happily ever after.

Certain of her success, Maggie had meticulously coiled her hair about her head, and worn her mother's best kirtle and plaid. True, the yellow kirtle had been a bit large and mature on her, but to her it had been beautiful, and it had made her *feel* beautiful. She had even worn a special pair of high-heeled slippers for which she had paid the cobbler two dozen eggs.

When she had joined her brothers for the wagon ride to the kirk, they had frowned at her clothes, but none said a word about her attire.

They didn't have to. The other boys of the clan had said plenty.

"Look," Davis had said the moment she arrived at the kirk and descended from the wagon. "It's a scrawny, speckled chicken with a skinny chicken neck, wearing a grain sack three sizes too big." The others had taken up the cry of "*Bock, bock,*" and to this day their scorn resonated through her soul.

They had chased her back to the wagon, where her brothers had stepped in and sent them running, but the damage had already been done. Her beautiful hair had fallen down around her shoulders, and she had broken one of the heels from her shoes. Her mother's dress was stained and her plaid torn.

At that moment, she had hated herself. Hated the way she looked and hated the fact that her mother hadn't been there to help her be more attractive. More ladylike.

The only saving grace of the day had been Braden's absence. At least he hadn't witnessed her humiliation.

Nay, Braden would never be interested in her. Especially since the only attractive part of her, her hair, was gone. Sighing in regret, she fought the tears that wanted release.

Braden watched Maggie. Something was troubling her, and his heart wrenched for all she had suffered in her young life.

Maggie had always been strong. Even now he could remember the way she had looked when her father had been buried. It had been the coldest day of winter and she had stood there with tears brimming in her eyes as the icy wind cut through all of the mourners, but not one tear had fallen. Anghus had been so shaken, he could barely walk. It had been Maggie who helped her brothers home. Maggie who took care of them.

Braden had gone to offer his condolences, and as he rounded their small cottage, he had found her doubled over in grief. But the moment she had seen him, she had straightened, dried her eyes and pulled herself together with a strength of will that amazed him to this day.

Lord, what a hard life she had lived. Her brothers, and most of the boys in the clan, had been unmerciful in their teasing of her. Her father had censored everything she had ever done to please him.

And still she was the most giving, kindhearted woman he had ever known.

Without conscious thought, he reached out to

gently stroke her hair. The silken, russet strands caressed his fingers and stirred his hunger for her.

Is it her you want, or is it just a woman?

For the first time in his life, Braden paused.

Never before had he considered such a thing, but then, he'd never had to. Women had always come to him. Sought him out and offered their bodies to him without reservation.

But Maggie was different. She had never pursued him. Instead, she had always withheld herself, almost as if she feared him.

Tonight, that bothered him.

Leaning forward, he inhaled the floral scent of her hair, allowing it to wash over him and captivate his senses. She was luscious and soothing, like a warm summer breeze.

Losing himself to his impulses, he trailed his hand from her head, down her arm, and snuggled even closer to her warmth.

Maggie's eyes flew open.

Was he . . . ?

Aye, he was! Braden was actually running his hand down her hip as he smelled her hair.

Is he supposed to do that?

Nay, woman, you know better than that. You're supposed to be married to a man before you let him sniff your hair and run his hands over you.

Aye, but his hand felt good. Wonderful, in fact.

Maggie!

Torn between wanting to let him have his way

and knowing it would be wrong to do so, Maggie cleared her throat. "Braden, would you behave?"

"I am behaving," he purred against her ear.

See? her mind argued. *He said he was behaving.*

But she didn't believe either one of them. Not for a minute.

"Nay," she said, noting the odd sound of her voice. "You're groping."

"Only a little groping."

Oh, the man was shameless! A little groping, indeed!

If she didn't stop him now, there was no telling what it might lead to. . . .

Actually, she knew exactly where it would lead, and even though her heart might want this with him, her head knew the dire consequences of such an act. She would not be another of his conquests. No matter how she felt about him, she wasn't going to let herself be used.

Her only thought to save herself, she grabbed his hand tightly in hers and moved it to her stomach, just below her breasts, to keep it still.

"So," Braden whispered in her ear, his voice husky and deep. "You want me here, do you?"

He reached his hand up ever so slightly and cupped her bound breast in his hand.

Maggie struggled to breathe as a fierce wave of desire tore through her. A strange ache started at the core of her body and it was all she could do not to moan.

"Braden!" she choked. "You're not supposed to do that."

"Nay?" he asked, nuzzling his face against her hair.

She closed her eyes as his breath tickled the back of her neck. He felt so good, and right then she wanted a kiss from him so badly that it took all her will not to roll over and claim his lips.

"Braden," she tried again. "If you don't let me go, I swear I'm going to sleep with Sin."

He froze at her words. Then he laughed.

"What's so funny about that?" she asked with a frown.

"My brother would sooner geld himself than lie down with a Scotswoman."

"Oh, you," she scolded as she rolled onto her back to glare up at him and that handsome, dimpled smile of his. "That's not what I meant and well you know it. You're terrible. Wicked. Incorrigible!"

His smile deepened and she didn't miss the dark hunger in his eyes. "Actually, I've been told I'm rather good. Especially when it comes to—"

Maggie placed her hand over his lips to stifle the rest of that sentence. "I've heard enough from you. And I'm not about to let you have your way with me out here in the woods like some harlot. I'm a good, respectable lass, and I intend to stay that way."

And then a terrible thing happened. She realized how soft his lips were beneath her fingertips. Then she remembered what those soft lips had felt like as they kissed her own.

Heaven. His kiss had been total heaven.

Startled by the thought and the fact that her will had begun to falter, she removed her hand and clenched her fingers into a fist.

A tic started in his jaw as he regarded her. He dipped his gaze down her lips and she watched the debate play across his face.

Finally he sighed and pulled back.

Maggie took a deep breath in relief as he settled himself a few inches away from her.

"Tell me," he said quietly. "How did you make this trip the first time, all by yourself?"

What an odd question. Why would he . . .

She paused at the thought as she noticed a part of him that was quite a bit larger than it had been before. Her face flamed. He was trying to distract himself, and unless she wanted to make it worse, she'd best help him do just that.

"I was riding a horse," she said under her breath to keep Sin from overhearing her words.

Braden laughed softly.

"I rode during the day and stayed at my cousin's the first night. Then once I reached Mac-Douglas lands, I kept to the roads and paid for lodging."

"And it took four days?" he asked.

Maggie blushed again as she recalled her earlier words to him regarding how long the trip had taken. "Nay, I was gone only two days. I'm guessing it'll take us four on foot."

Maggie cast a fearful glance to Sin. "I didn't want to tell Sin how I had traveled lest it make him even angrier that we are on foot."

"You're wise beyond your years."

Braden leaned forward ever so slightly and trailed his fingers through her hair again. "Do you know, your hair is as soft as silk?"

Not again. If he kept this up, she was going to be hopelessly lost.

Maggie bit her lip as she enjoyed hearing him compliment her. "Nay," she whispered. "I've never felt silk."

His eyes darkened again as he moved his head a little closer to hers. "I would love to wrap you in it," he confided in her ear, sending a thousand chills over her entire body. "Aye, a deep green sheet, one that would set off the creaminess of your skin and the highlights in your hair. Believe me, there's nothing more sensuous than silk skimming over your naked body."

"Braden!"

His smile was completely unrepentant.

Maggie shook her head at him. "You can't help it, can you?"

"Help what?"

"Flirting with every woman you meet."

"Who says I'm flirting?"

"I do, because I know if Nera or Adena were here this moment, you'd be off with one of them and giving no thought whatsoever to me."

He recoiled his head as if she'd slapped him. "Och, now, Maggie, I don't know which of us you just insulted most with that statement. Do you honestly think I would . . ."

Braden paused as he truly thought about her words. And in that moment, he learned something about himself he didn't like.

She was right. He couldn't even guess how often he'd been with one woman when another, more attractive woman had come along and "distracted" him.

"You were saying?" she asked.

"Nothing," he said, glancing off into the dark forest. For the first time in his life, he felt guilty over some of what he'd done in the past.

Maggie settled back down on the hard ground and he watched her struggle for comfort.

In spite of himself, Braden pondered what he would do if a more attractive woman were here. Would he flit after her the first chance he had and pay no more heed to Maggie?

Could he truly be that shallow a person?

The most painful part of all was that he didn't know for sure whether he would or not.

He *was* an ass and a scoundrel. And for the first time in his life, he wished he were different.

Why couldn't he be more like Lochlan? Steadfast and loyal, or like Ewan.

Nay, he thought quickly. Not like Ewan. Ewan was too monkish for his tastes. But he could be like Sin. Sin was respectful and discreet, and women threw themselves at him as much as they did Braden.

Unbidden, his gaze went back to Maggie lying stiffly on the ground. She deserved so much better than a scoundrel like him. She deserved a man who could love her, and her alone. In truth, she needed such a man.

And in his heart, Braden knew he could never be that man. He wasn't capable of giving himself over to just one single woman. Ever. He loved his freedom too much. He loved his women too much.

For that reason, he would have to keep himself from her. Because in the end, he could offer her nothing more than a broken heart, and he didn't want to add any more unhappiness to her life.

Still, thoughts of Maggie drifted through his mind. Thoughts of her earlier kiss. The softness of her pale skin beneath his hand. The sound of her breath whispering in his ear.

But even worse was the imagined sight he had of her lying naked beneath him, her amber eyes dark with hunger as she cradled him with her entire body and urged his hips with her hands as he lost himself deep inside her.

His hunger for her was enough to drive him mad. Never had he felt such a strong, alluring need to find out exactly what a woman's passion was like. But with Maggie, he wanted to know. Nay, 'twas almost a need to find out if she was as hot and passionate without her clothes as she was in them.

Leaning forward ever so slightly, Braden closed his eyes and inhaled the sweet, feminine scent of Maggie's hair and he ached to trace his fingers over the creamy skin of her cheek.

Too well, he remembered her passion. The taste of her breath mingling with his as he plundered her mouth and laid claim to her virginal lips.

At that moment, he wanted nothing more than to claim the rest of her for his very own.

His body stirred violently at the thought.

Aye, she was a lass to savor. A vibrant treasure that he wanted to spend weeks exploring.

His gaze drifted over the length of her wrapped beneath the plaid. Only a few pieces of cloth separated their bodies. Separated him from the part of her he longed for most.

It would be so easy to lift the hem of her plaid and bury himself deep inside her. To listen to her moans of pleasure as he taught her the oldest, most intimate dance a man and woman could ever share.

In all these years, why had he never noticed her before? What had kept him so blinded?

There were no words to describe her spirit or her conviction. Never had he met such a woman, and yet there had never been a moment in his memory when he hadn't known *her*.

"You know, little blossom, you could be safe in your bed this night."

"Aye," she whispered, staring into the fire before her. "I could. But it wouldn't do anything to stop the dying. I would give anything for this feud to end."

"Except let me kill Robby MacDouglas."

She grew quiet as she mulled over his words.

"Perhaps I judged you harshly," she whispered. "Perhaps I should hate him for the deaths of my brothers. If not for him and his bloodlust, they would be alive now. But somewhere deep inside him, there must be a part that wants an end to this as much as we do. Surely, after five years of fighting, he must be weary of it. Aren't you?"

He didn't respond.

"Braden?"

"I'm thinking on it."

She turned to look at him, her face incredulous. "You still want to fight?"

"There is something to be said for it."

Her eyes burned bright in frustration and she growled low in her throat, then she pushed at his shoulder.

Braden laughed as he pretended to tussle with her.

"Do I need to go for a stroll?" Sin's voice cut into their play.

"Nay," Maggie said quickly, moving away from him. "I am merely trying to kill your brother."

"Ever the charmer, eh, Braden?"

"Hold your tongue, Sin."

"I would, but with my luck, one of your giant Scottish bugs would land on it. Besides, it makes my hand wet and pruney when I do that."

Braden rolled his eyes, wishing he had something close enough to toss at Sin.

Maggie laughed softly.

"Good night, Braden," she said, returning to her original position.

"Good night, little blossom," he whispered. But inside, he knew a night without her kiss could never be called good.

A few hours later, Maggie awoke with a start to find Braden's arms wrapped protectively around her. At some point in the night, they had drifted even closer together and she lay perfectly entwined with him before the fire.

An odd, foreign need beat at the center of her body as she enjoyed the strange sensation of his masculine thigh pressing high between her own. Oh, but it was a wicked, wicked feeling. One she was certain a young woman shouldn't be experiencing with a man not her husband.

At first she wasn't sure what had awakened her until she realized Sin was just behind them.

He stooped and gently nudged Braden awake.

Maggie quickly closed her eyes and feigned sleep.

"Your watch, little brother," Sin whispered softly.

She felt Braden stiffen as he came awake and wondered if their position shocked him as much as it had her.

Carefully, he extracted himself from her, and to her amazement, he placed a folded plaid beneath her head to cushion it from the ground. The tenderness of the gesture touched her deeply.

The two men stood over her and she felt the stares of both. Uncomfortable with their attention, she started to say something, but for some reason she couldn't bring herself to betray the fact that she was no longer sleeping.

"I canna believe she cut her hair off," Braden whispered.

"She is definitely unusual."

"Aye. I've never met another woman like her."

"Many would call her mannish."

Braden snorted. "And I'd call them fools. There's nothing mannish about her."

Sin didn't respond, but Maggie could hear him making a pallet on the other side of the fire.

After a few minutes, someone placed another plaid over her. Maggie slit her eyes open to see Braden rising to stand in front of her pallet. He leaned over and brushed his hand gently through her hair, then pulled the plaid up to her chin.

His kindness touched her so deeply that for a moment she could barely breathe.

"Are you going to take the post or continue to coddle her, Braden?"

Braden turned to look at his brother. "She could use a little coddling, I think."

And with that Braden left her.

Once they were alone and Braden was positioned away from them, Sin spoke to her. "I know you're awake."

Maggie fluttered her eyes open to meet his black gaze over the fire. "I suppose Braden knew as well."

"Nay, he'd never have spoken so freely of you had he known."

She frowned. "Then how did you know?"

"Intuition, observation," Sin said quietly. "Things I had to cultivate to survive. Braden isn't nearly as suspicious as I am."

His words confused her. What had made him say such?

"And are you suspicious of me?"

His hard look froze her all the way to her toes. "Woman, I'm suspicious of anyone who acts altruistically. I've only known a handful of people in my entire life who were actually kind. The vast majority of people only help others when they know it'll benefit them in some manner."

Even more confused than before, she lifted her head to stare at him. "You think I want something from Braden?"

"I know you do."

"And that is?"

"You want him."

Shocked by his words, Maggie opened her mouth to argue.

"Don't deny it," he said, cutting her words off before she could even begin. "I can see it in your eyes every time you look at him."

Maggie glanced to where Braden sat on the edge of the forest and wondered if her feelings were as clear to him. Inside, she hoped Braden wasn't so astute. For if he knew how she felt, that meant he had been deliberately ignoring her feelings all these years, and that cut her all the way to her soul.

"I admit I fancy him," she said reluctantly, "but that doesn't mean I want him. A person may fancy a snake is beautiful, but only a fool would try and claim one."

Sin arched a brow at her. "So, that's it, then."

Her head began to ache from trying to figure out Sin's mind and cryptic comments. "What?"

"You're afraid of Braden."

"Aye," she admitted. "I'm not a fool. Braden isn't the type of man who would stay by a woman's side. He'd take me, then be off frolicking with the first lass who turned his head. I've no desire to be my mother, to cry alone in my bed while the man I love is out for the night with another."

Sin propped his head against his arm. "You ask for a lot in this day and age, milady. Most women accept the fact that men will forever prowl."

"I am not most women."

He smiled at her and nodded. "That you are not. Now you'd best be getting back to sleep."

Maggie closed her eyes. But what she saw in the darkness of her eyelids disturbed her greatly. She had two clear memories of her mother. One of her mother holding her tight to her chest and singing to her. The other was of a quiet summer's night after her mother had taken ill.

Maggie had been trying to sleep that night too, but her mother's crying had awakened her. Scared of the noise, she had crept from her bed to where a hanging cloth separated her bed from her parents'. Her mother had been weeping in the arms of Maggie's aunt.

"How could he be with her while I lay dying?" her mother had cried, her voice filled with such agony that it haunted Maggie to this day. "The least he could do is wait until I'm in the ground."

"I know," her aunt had soothed. "Men will be men. You know that."

Her mother had died just a few hours later. Alone in her bed, waiting for her husband to come home to her.

And worse, her father had never married the woman he had gone to see that night.

"But Blar, you know I love you. I'd be taking care of your bairns for you if you'd let me," Sila had begged her father outside their cottage one night three months after her mother's passing.

"Sila, you're a good lass, but I canna marry you now. Not after what has happened. Every time I look at you, all I can think of is the night she died. I should have been here with her, not out with you. The guilt of it is more than I can stand."

"Aye," Sila had wept. "You had no business with me. I never should have listened to you when you told me I meant something to you."

With that, Sila had run off into the darkness, and her father had come inside their small cottage.

He had glanced at Maggie standing in the shadows, and by his face she knew her father realized she had heard everything. He'd said nothing as he walked past her and went to his bed.

Like Braden, her father had been a good man, but a man nonetheless. And Maggie would rather die an old maid than be put in the position of either her mother or Sila.

Nay, she had dreamed of Braden the whole of her life, but it was time to let such foolish dreams go. Braden belonged to the world, and she . . .

She belonged to herself.

Maggie looked wistfully to where Braden sat several yards away.

"Good night, my love," she whispered. "And good-bye."

That night, Maggie was tortured by dreams of Braden. Dreams of his sweet kisses. Of his arms holding her close.

I'll never leave you, little blossom. His sincere voice made her heart soar.

She dreamed of having a home with him, of having his wee ones running about.

And then her dreams turned more wicked. Turned to things Maggie had overheard her brothers discuss when they thought her asleep.

Aye, she could see Braden slipping her clothes from her, running his hand over her body as he kissed her until she lost all reason. She could feel his hands sliding over her bare skin, cupping her body as his lips toyed with the sensitive flesh of her neck.

"Braden," she whispered, her body on fire with a need she could barely understand.

She wanted him.

And then, from a distance, she heard the cruel laughter of the men in her village as they taunted the only boy who had ever noticed her.

I would have thought she was below even your standards, they had said to David.

Maggie jerked awake as that haunting laughter rang in her head.

Disoriented, she glanced about to find Braden and Sin talking in low whispers a few feet away. The smell of fresh-roasted hare greeted her.

Her hands trembling, Maggie tried to banish the memory of her dreams. The sound of the boys laughing at her the day David had helped her run an errand for Anghus.

Barely seven-and-ten, she had been so touched by David's kindness as he carried her heavy basket to Father Bede, but the other boys had mocked him for it.

You know, Davey, if nags are to your taste, I have one to sell ya.

Maggie covered her ears with her hands to blot the memory. At times like this, she wondered why she even cared whether or not her male tormentors perished under a MacDouglas sword. Most of the men around her age had earned that fate, given the misery they had heaped upon her over the years.

But as soon as the thought occurred to her, she felt shamed for it. They didn't deserve to die for their meanness, but in all honesty, she wouldn't mind seeing them taken out and thrashed for it.

And in that moment, she realized why she had always loved Braden so much. Out of all the men in the clan, he was the only one near her age who had never laughed at or mocked her.

Not once.

"Are you all right?" Braden asked as he looked past Sin to see her sitting up.

Maggie nodded as she let her hands fall away from her ears.

"Why did you let me sleep so late?" she asked, noting it was already midmorning.

"We decided you needed your rest," Braden said as he handed her a skin of watered-down ale.

"But we need to reach the MacDouglas as soon as possible."

"And so we shall," Braden assured her with a gentle, dimpled smile. "A couple of hours will make little difference."

For a minute, she thought of Lochlan and his predicament, until she remembered that Braden's mother would take care of it.

Still, once the women were free, they had little time to persuade the MacDouglas to peace.

In that moment, she wished she had brought horses. But then, three unknown "men" riding across MacDouglas land would have invited the kind of attention and confrontation she would rather avoid. Especially since two of them were Braden and Sin.

There was no telling what either might do when confronted, and Maggie certainly didn't want to find out.

Braden handed her part of the hare. "Eat and wash, then we'll get started. We still have plenty of the day left to travel by."

Maggie nodded. She ate quickly, then took a few private minutes in the denseness of the forest to attend her needs before rejoining the men.

They had already put out the fire and had everything neatly stored in the packs. Maggie reached for hers, but Braden draped it over his shoulder.

She smiled. "I appreciate the thought, Braden, but should we come across others, I'm rather sure they would think it odd you carry my pack."

"She's right," Sin agreed. "It defeats the whole purpose of having her dressed as a boy."

"Very well," Braden said, but before he would let her have it back, he put half the contents into his own pack. "There's no need in you getting tired unnecessarily."

Maggie's heart pounded at his thoughtfulness. Aye, Braden was an easy man to love. Kind, considerate. If only loyalty to women were one of his numerous virtues.

"Are you all right?" Braden asked as he handed her the pack. "You seem troubled."

Aye, troubled by a handsome man who haunts my dreams and my heart.

"I'm fine," she said, offering him a smile. "Just thinking of the task ahead." As well as the fact that when this was all over, she would return to her little cottage alone and he would be off . . .

She didn't finish the thought. She couldn't.

Sin gave her a knowing, sympathetic look, then led them through the forest toward MacDouglas lands.

They walked through the rest of the morning and well into the afternoon. Instead of stopping for a meal, they ate pieces of bread while they walked, and spoke very little as they kept mostly to the ancient forest.

It was midafternoon when a strange tingling sensation started on the back of Maggie's neck and ran over her scalp. An eerie shiver went through her.

It felt as though someone were watching them.

She turned her head to scan the dark trees and shrubs, but saw nothing. She heard nothing.

And yet . . .

At first the men appeared to notice nothing strange. Until she noted the tenseness of both their spines. The way they both walked with one hand on their sword hilts.

Aye, they felt it too.

"Braden—"

"Stephen?" he asked, quickly cutting her off, and that more than anything else verified her suspicions. They were being watched, and both he and Sin knew it.

"Never mind," she said, dropping her voice an octave.

Still, she saw and heard nothing.

It stretched on for so long that she had just begun to think her imagination was running amok. Until they topped a small rise in the forest. Just as they neared a giant yew tree, a figure casually stepped out from behind it.

He was a large, burly man, but not quite as tall as her escorts. His dank, dark hair hung limply about his beefy shoulders and his dirty beard obscured most of his face. He arched a bushy black brow as he narrowed one eye on them and leveled a sword toward Sin.

"Well, well," the burly man said evilly. "What have we here?"

"Looks like we got some little pigeons just right for a plucking," a man said from behind them.

Terrified, Maggie looked around as a total of ten men surrounded them. They were thieves, by the looks of them, and would be bent on God only knew what once they learned that the three of them carried little money.

Sin and Braden exchanged looks with each other that were a terrifying mixture of wry amusement and anticipation. And that made her tremble from the inside out.

This was not good. Not good at all.

Chapter 9

"**W**ell, well," Sin said to Braden, mocking the leader's words and tone. "What have we here?"

"Looks like a pack of fools wanting to die," Braden said, a cold, deadly smile on his lips.

Maggie quickly crossed herself as she realized the situation was about to escalate into something she really didn't want to witness.

She just hoped they all survived it.

Tension sizzled so thick around them that she could nearly smell the raw, pungent odor of it. All the men were stiff and wary, their eyes darting over each other as they evaluated the mettle of their opponents.

Her stomach drew tight in fear.

The outlaw leader returned Braden's cold

smile with one of his own. "Now, *friend*, there's no need for us to spill your blood or your guts. Give us your money and we'll leave you to peacefully go about your way."

"There's just one wee problem with that," Braden said, his voice ominously calm and patient, his greenish brown eyes menacing. "You're not my friend and I'm quite a bit fonder of my gold than I am of you. Now, given that, why would I want to turn my gold over to your clumsy hands?"

Maggie's panic rose.

The leader's face turned dour. "In that case . . ."

The others attacked so quickly, Maggie barely had time to duck the one beefy thief who came after her and hurl herself into the shrubs for protection.

Braden and Sin unsheathed their swords in unison and used them to drive back their attackers.

The big thief she had dodged moved to grab her, but didn't make it before Braden caught him by the scruff of his shirt and shoved him in the opposite direction into a rather large oak tree, where he rebounded with a resounding thud, then went sprawling atop the peat-covered ground.

Maggie sighed in relief, hoping no one else noticed her.

But an instant after that thought, she saw another thief inching toward Braden's unguarded back, the thief's sword raised to strike.

Panic swelled inside her. Braden was so occupied with the man before him, he didn't even notice the one at his back.

Her only thought to save Braden, Maggie scrambled from the bushes. She grabbed a large, leafy limb from the ground and used it to whack the thief against the back.

The leaves smacked his spine, neck and head, but didn't do anything other than make the big man angry. He whirled on her with a vicious curse.

Too late, she realized her attack hadn't been very well planned or executed.

Awkwardly, she held the limb before her as she struggled to protect herself. The thief laughed cruelly as he whacked the leaves and wood almost playfully with his sword.

"Mother of saints preserve me!" she whispered, then bashed him in the head with the limb.

He staggered for only an instant, then his face darkened in rage. "You'll die for that."

"The devil you say," Braden growled as he grabbed the thief and spun him about to face him.

Braden sent him spiraling to the ground with one backhanded blow. She barely had time to thank him before another man attacked.

Maggie watched in awe as the brothers made short work of the men without actually killing any of them. But there were wounds aplenty and many a swollen noggin as the thieves fell like rotten apples on the ground, then lay moaning and holding their bruised limbs and aching heads.

Maggie still clutched her tree limb, too afraid to let it go until the thieves were gone.

Braden cornered the leader against a yew tree and held his sword just below the man's chin. His hand steady, Braden's fierce look would have quelled the devil himself and it sent a raw shiver over Maggie.

"Now, then, *friend*," Braden said, "do I have to kill you, or will you go on about your business and leave us in peace?"

Sin clucked his tongue as he glanced longingly at the men on the ground around him. "Oh, come now, can't I please kill one of them? How about the large one with only three teeth, or maybe the short one here with bad breath?"

Braden gave a mocking half laugh at Sin's pleading tone, but his eyes never left the thief before him. "Should I let him have his fun?"

The leader shook his head. "Nay, we'll be going, if it's all the same to you."

Braden took a step back and lowered his sword.

With a speed that amazed her, the highwaymen gathered themselves and vanished into the trees.

Maggie could barely stand, she was shaking

so badly. That had been just a little too close for her liking. Never had she experienced such an event.

Mo chreach, what would she have done had Braden and Sin not been with her?

Truly, it didn't bear thinking on.

Even worse was the thought of what might have happened to her had the thieves come upon her the first time she'd made this journey alone, dressed as a woman.

Her stomach shrank, and a wave of panic whipped through her. If she lived to be a hundred, she would never forget this terrible feeling inside her, or the uncaring look on the leader's face when he had first stopped them.

They would have killed them all without a moment's concern!

Maggie took a minute to thank the Lord and His saints for their mercy and to pray that she never again experienced such a thing.

"Are you all right?" Braden asked as he pried the tree limb loose from her hands, then tossed it aside.

"Thank you," she breathed weakly. "Thank you."

"My pleasure," he said as he held her shaking hand in his own.

Heavens, the man was handsome. And in his hazel eyes, she saw the concern and care, and in her heart, it soothed and warmed her greatly.

Yet in those eyes she also saw a deep compelling light that looked strangely close to humor.

Surely Braden couldn't find anything about their attack funny.

Nay, she was misreading him.

Braden cupped her cheek in his hand and lightly stroked her cheekbone with his thumb. It was all she could do not to close her eyes and sigh in pleasure. His soothing, quiet touch was pure bliss and it sent wave after wave of desire coursing through her as it melted away her fear and concerns.

Braden had protected her. Again. And she wondered if he even realized just how many times in her life he had been her champion.

"Thanks for protecting my back," Braden said softly.

Maggie frowned. There was something hidden in his tone. And in an instant she knew what had him amused.

"You knew the man I hit was behind you the whole time, didn't you?"

"I did," he said with a short laugh. "But I'm glad you thought enough of me that you distracted him. And even more so that you risked your life to do so."

Another shiver went over her, but this one had nothing to do with her panic and everything to do with the fierce warrior before her.

Glory, but the man was incredible when he smiled.

How in the world could any woman deny him anything when he looked at her like that, dimples flashing, his gaze warm, his touch hot?

He paused his tender stroking on her cheek and stared intently into her eyes. " 'Twas a very brave thing you did for a scoundrel like me."

"And you *are* a scoundrel," she said, knowing it in her heart and for some reason not caring about the fact at the moment.

"Aye," he said with a devilish grin, dipping his head toward hers. "The absolute worst."

Without conscious thought, she opened her mouth for him, aching for another kiss.

Braden closed his eyes and started to accept her invitation until Sin cleared his throat.

"Do I have to separate the two of you again?" Sin asked. "I swear, but this is getting tedious."

Maggie jumped in Braden's embrace.

Braden pulled back instantly and sighed. "Remind me to thank you more properly later," he whispered to her.

Maggie was too stunned to respond. Her senses reeling, she could do nothing more than nod.

Good heavens! What had she almost done?

You almost kissed him.

Again.

Oh, lass, where's your head, to be letting such a man have his way with you?

Biting her lip, she looked to where he and Sin were standing together.

Why, Braden, why do you have to flit from one

woman to the next? And worse, why couldn't she hate him for it?

Because it would be like hating the wind for blowing or hating the sun for shining. It was his nature. To change it would more than likely change the man, and with the exception of that one bad habit, she liked Braden a great deal.

Nay, she didn't want him to change. It was his carefree spirit that enticed her. She would just have to guard herself more closely around him and not let herself suffer any more hurt by him.

"Do you think they'll return?" Maggie asked as she rejoined Braden and Sin.

"Aye," Sin said at the same time Braden said, "Nay."

Sin looked drolly at his brother as he sheathed his sword. "You honestly think they'll just be off without retaliating in some way?"

"Aye, we got the better of them. Why should they return?"

Sin's eyes flared with such intense emotion that Maggie took an involuntary step back from it.

"Vengeance is a strong motivator, little brother," he said flatly.

It was then she knew Sin harbored a deep hatred. Against whom she could only guess. But she pitied the poor soul who had evoked such an enemy as Sin, and in the back of her mind she couldn't help but wonder what terrible fate Sin had heaped upon that person's head.

She didn't think for a minute that the person still lived. From what she had seen of Sin, he no doubt had taken the person's life swiftly. And with relish.

Braden met his brother's gaze with an almost imperceptible nod and some deep understanding passed between them. "You would know that better than I."

Sin looked away. He rested his hand on his sword hilt and walked past her.

"I want my horse," he muttered as he passed by, then headed off into the dense forest.

Braden sighed as he watched his brother stalk off. He picked his pack up from the ground and started after Sin.

Maggie followed quietly as she looked back and forth between the brothers.

Braden could be as dangerous as Sin, but there was an aura of irrepressible humor and fun about Braden that drew her into his charisma. He took nothing from anyone, and yet he gave so much to those who knew him. Everyone in the clan, when they weren't ready to kill him over a dalliance, liked the warrior.

In truth, she'd never heard a word against him unless it involved his lust.

If only she could understand what it was about men, and Braden in particular, that drove them from bed to bed. Was it ever possible for a single woman to satisfy a man? Even Anghus, as much as he had loved his wife, had slept with another woman while he was away in Ireland.

Over and over, she tried to think of one man who had never cheated on his woman. And to her dismay, she couldn't think of any.

Surely there must be one, somewhere?

As she pondered possible men, they walked on in silence. After a time, Sin started mumbling beneath his breath.

"What was that?" Braden asked.

"What?" Sin asked, turning his head to look back at his brother.

"What did you just say?"

"I was again cursing your ill-bred Scotsmen and wishing myself home."

Braden shook his head. "I swear, you grumble more than an old woman. Tell me, do you complain so around Henry?"

"Nay, I don't have to. No one in England is stupid enough to try my patience."

Braden laughed softly, then spoke to Maggie. "I wonder how many Englishmen are lying in their graves because they dared to look askance at him."

Maggie agreed. "Your brother is a strange man."

Braden laughed louder.

"What?" she asked, wondering what he found so amusing.

"I was just thinking how each of us has our

own role in life. Lochlan is the sensible one. Ewan the serious one. Kieren was the passionate one. Sin the dangerous one, and I . . . I am the wicked one."

His summation was perfect. "And you relish your role, don't you?"

Those greenish brown eyes sparkled. "No doubt I will one day burn for it, but aye. Life is too short to spend it moping about. Look at Sin."

She did. With his handsome brow furrowed and his eyes narrowed, Sin looked as if he were ready to kill the next person who annoyed him.

Braden continued talking. "Sin is one of the wealthiest men in all of England, with holdings stretching from Canterbury to Scotland to the Holy Land. He is one of the few men alive who can call Henry by name to the king's face, and yet he is brooding at best, angry at worst. He spends his entire life completely alone and isolated from everyone."

Braden shook his head. "I couldn't stand to live that way. Any more than I could follow Ewan into the mountains and live like a hermit."

Maggie understood why Ewan was withdrawn after what had happened with Isobail. But then, he had always been a shy man who preferred isolation to company.

Sin, she didn't remember all that well. She had scarcely been more than a babe when he had been taken by the English. The only real memory she had of him was when he had chased Davis off for calling her names.

"Tell me," she said softly. "Given how Sin was taken away against his will, why is it he now prefers to dress and act English?"

Braden took a deep breath. He turned his head to look at her and she saw the trouble in his eyes. And the pain.

"When Sin turned four-and-ten, Henry was crowned king of England, and as part of the king's coronation celebration, Henry allowed the Scottish hostages Stephen had taken to return to their families."

Maggie frowned. She had never heard that. Nor did it make sense. If Sin could return, why hadn't he? "Why would Sin choose not to come home?"

A tic started in Braden's jaw. "He wanted to, but my father refused. He sent word to King Henry that he could keep Sin, as he had no use for a Sassenach son."

Maggie's breath caught in her throat. She couldn't imagine such cruelty. Dear saints, the pain Sin must have felt when he had learned of his father's response.

Suddenly her own father's criticism of her didn't seem so terrible.

"Why would your father do such a thing?" she asked. "What did your mother have to say over it?"

Braden looked away and she saw the torment in his eyes. And a strange guilt she couldn't fathom.

"My mother was the reason Sin didn't return," he said, his voice strained. "My mother refused to have him in the same house with her."

"Why?" Maggie asked.

What could make Aisleen not want her son to return to her?

Braden sighed. "Sin's mother was an English lady my father trysted with the one time he'd gone to London. Sin was conceived just a few short months before Lochlan."

Maggie flinched at his words. So that was it.

Clenching her teeth, she shook her head in disbelief. Men and their unfaithfulness. How could Braden continue to carry on with women like he did after seeing the consequences of infidelity so close at hand?

Poor Sin, to be cast out because Aisleen didn't want to see the evidence of her husband's actions.

Her heart heavy, she felt for both of them.

"What of Sin's mother?" she asked.

Braden curled his lip in disgust. "She had no use for him. That was why she sent him to live with my father in the first place. She'd decided years ago that Sin was an embarrassment to her."

"So, he was discarded by both his parents?"

"Aye. He is a bitter man, but 'tis well understandable."

Maggie agreed. Now she understood the hostile look Sin had directed at Aisleen when she had appeared in the kirk yard.

He must hate her passionately.

She couldn't imagine the way he must have felt when both his parents turned him out. It was more than any soul should have to bear.

Looking at Braden, and the pain in his eyes, she wondered what he truly thought of his parents. And in her heart, she knew it must sting him too.

Braden walked in silence as he remembered when Sin had been forced from his home.

To this day, he couldn't quite forgive his mother for her deplorable actions. How any woman could turn a child, even one not her own, over to a mortal enemy was beyond him.

It had been on that very day that he had decided never to marry.

Should any child ever show up claiming to be his, Braden would welcome it with open arms. He would have no wife to hate it. No woman to badger him into an unforgivable act.

Worse was the unrelenting guilt in his soul that Sin had been the one his father gave up that day. For in his heart he knew that, as the youngest son, he should have been the one to leave, and Sin, as the eldest, should have been the one to stay in Scotland.

But Braden's mother had saved him from the English.

Over the years, Braden had often wondered if

all women would have done as his mother, or if it had merely been a flaw in her character alone.

"Tell me," Braden said to Maggie before he thought better of it. "Had you been my mother, what would you have done?"

Indecision played across her face as she thought it over. "I don't know."

"So, you would have sent him away as well?"

She looked up at him, her amber eyes pensive. "I honestly don't know. On the one hand, I would hate to say that I could ever turn a child out, but it would be hard to have proof of my husband's infidelity so close at hand. I can't imagine what your poor mother must have felt every time Sin came near her. Still, children are innocent of such things, as none of us ever ask for the gift of life." She sighed. "I suppose 'tis not for me to judge her actions or to say for certain what I would have done unless I'm faced with a similar choice."

Braden felt his jaw tic at her words. If he lived an eternity, he would never understand how his mother had done what she had. And though he loved his mother, he found her actions that day selfish and cruel.

Maggie adjusted the pack on her shoulder. "You and Sin are terribly close, aren't you?"

Braden nodded. "In spite of the years we lived apart, we are. Over the last eight years, I've traveled to England several times to see him."

"Is that how you got your English lands?"

Braden grinned. "In part. Henry also wanted a

way to assure himself of Highland loyalty should he have need of it. Having me swear fealty for English lands seemed like a good way to make an ally of a powerful clan."

She smiled gently. The sunlight caught against her freckled face and the softness in her eyes was truly something to behold. "You're a good man, Braden MacAllister."

"Am I?" he asked, amazed she would say such. For some reason, he had the impression she had spent far more time condemning him than praising him.

She looked at him askance. "Now, don't be thinking anything of *that*."

He laughed at the outraged tone of her voice. It was plain she thought he would use her praise to seduce her and that she wouldn't welcome such a thing. "You don't think very much of me, do you?"

She furrowed her brow in thought. "I do, and I don't."

"What does that mean?"

She stopped walking and turned to look at him. "I know there's goodness in you, but there's an equal part of the devil too. If you weren't so very fickle, you'd make some woman a fine husband."

Her choice of words amused him. People had called his activities any number of choice things over the years, but no one had ever used the term "fickle" before. "Fickle?"

"Aye, fickle. Do you not think I know how

many women you've been with? Why, I doubt there's more than three women in all of Kilgarigon between the ages of ten and five and two score years you haven't had."

"Och, now, Maggie, you wound me." And she did too. He hadn't been with *that* many women. He wasn't some randy rooster just out to tup every woman who crossed his path. In fact, he had turned down more offers than he had ever accepted.

"The truth is often painful," she said, her voice and eyes sincere.

His humor died as she passed a sharp, judgmental look over him. One that ruffled him more than just a wee bit.

Now, this was getting out of hand. He wasn't the only one to blame here. True, he'd been with a lot of women, but he had never forced any of them. In fact, he usually wasn't even the one doing the pursuing.

"Tell me, Maggie, have you ever asked yourself why it is I might be such?"

She didn't hesitate. "Because you're a man."

He snorted at her response. She made it sound as if his being a man explained all the questions of the universe. "In part, but have you failed to notice how many women come after me?"

Her jaw dropped and she raked him with a scathing, repugnant look. "And that's your excuse? They come after you and so it frees your conscience up to just take what it is they offer? Consequences be damned? You're disgusting."

"Nay, I'm not disgusting," he said quickly. "You say I am inconstant. Well, what of your fine feminine friends? I can hardly be inconstant alone."

"So, what are you saying?"

"I'm saying that I'm not the only one to blame here. As you said yourself, I'm a man and it's hard to resist a woman when she's crawling naked into your bed begging for your favor, or pressing her body up against yours while she whispers in your ear all the things she wants to do to you."

She looked aghast. "Are you trying to tell me that all the women are seducing *you*? That you are just a humble little lord walking about, minding your own business, when some evil woman sneaks up upon you and forces you to take her?"

"You don't believe me?"

"Of course I don't believe you. It wasn't me doing the seducing last night, Braden MacAllister. It was you breathing in *my* ear and making free with *your* hands on *my* body."

"That was different."

"How so?"

He didn't honestly want to think about it. But in his heart, he knew it was different.

Seeking to change the subject before she made him say something they would both regret, he said, "Did it never occur to you that if I could ever find a woman who was completely loyal to me, then I would certainly be loyal back? I would love to find one woman on this earth who would be concerned for me, and never ask me to do unconscionable things to please her. To have a woman who wouldn't stray from my bed to the next man who turned her head."

She scoffed. "Now, there's a bit of irony." She gave him an incredulous look as if she couldn't believe what he had said. "Would you really be able to confine yourself to one single woman?"

"Aye. Do you not think I wouldn't love to have a home with children? I'd give most anything for it, but I'll not be made a fool of by a bonny lass. My brother Kieran killed himself over a fickle woman who wasn't content with him but had to have Ewan as well. And the woman they loved, after tearing our family apart and causing Kieran's death, abandoned Ewan the first chance she got to go off with a richer man. Women, in case you've been asleep during Sunday mass, are the root of all evil."

He could tell by the look on her face that she would love to strangle him, but to her credit she merely glared at him. "Women would never be evil if it weren't for men such as yourself leading them down the fiery path to hell."

Now, that made him see red. How dare she

blame it all on his gender. "You can't be blaming men alone for it."

"Can't I?" she asked, her voice high-pitched and angry. "As you said yourself, it takes two to form a tryst. More often than not, 'tis the man doing the leading."

Braden couldn't believe that came out of *her* mouth when she, of all women, ought to know better.

"That so?" he asked. "Do you not remember the time when I was but ten-and-six and your friends laid an ambush for me? Why, I barely escaped with my life."

It truly had been unnerving. He had come down a path near a copse of trees when ten girls had launched themselves at him. They had tackled him to the ground and started screaming in his ears how much they loved him and how they wanted him to marry them. They had ripped his plaid and tugged his hair until he was bloody from it.

Somehow, he'd managed to find his way out of their groping hands, and Maggie had hidden him inside the hollow of an oak tree, then sent the girls off in the wrong direction.

It was the last time he had ventured to her house without an escort.

He saw the recollection on Maggie's face as her eyes turned a bit sheepish.

"And," Braden continued, "what about that

time at your house when you pretended to fall down, and when I tried to help you up, you latched on to me so tight that you almost strangled me?"

Her face turned bright red and he knew in that instant that she had been as guilty of laying a trap for him as the other lasses.

"That was different," she said defensively.

"How so?"

"It just was."

Braden narrowed his eyes on her, certain now of his victory. "You may not like the truth, Maggie, but the truth is that most women are up to no good."

Her face was a mirror of disbelief. "You arrogant, apish, underhonest lewdster!"

Braden laughed at her insults. He had to give her credit, she could rival his brothers for creativity.

Her body rigid with rage, she whirled around and stomped ahead of him.

Braden hurried his step until he stood directly behind her and Sin.

Sin cast a curious glance at him over his shoulder before looking at Maggie.

Her eyes snapped amber fire. "Your brother is a beslubbering, churlish, hell-governed princox, and I hope one day he gets the beating he deserves for it."

Sin threw his head back and laughed.

"You find that funny?" she asked incredulously.

"Indeed," Sin said, smiling. "You're the only woman I have ever known who insulted him. And you do it so well."

Braden joined Sin's laughter.

Now she was furious at them both. If only she weren't so beautiful when she was angry, Braden mused ruefully. Aye, bright red looked good in her cheeks.

"Men," she fumed as she stomped on ahead of them. "Who needs them?"

Chapter 10

"**B**raden," Maggie called. "I need you. Help!"

Braden paused at the plea, amazed by it.

It had been nearly an hour since they had lost sight of Maggie in the dark forest. Yet they had known the entire time she wasn't too far ahead of them because her angry, often derogatory tirade against men in general, and Braden in particular, had kept them highly amused.

"Braden, please!"

It must have cost her dearly to utter those words after the large amount of condemnation she had heaped upon him, his hide, his soul and every human being who had ever met him.

Normally such a plea from a woman would have him rushing to her side. However, Maggie's tone was too rational for her to be in any real danger. It sounded more as if she were merely annoyed.

Resuming his walk over the peat-covered path, Braden looked at Sin. "Did we not hear her say, several hundred times in the last hour, 'Men, who needs them?' "

"That we did."

"Think we should ignore her cry, then?" Braden asked.

The baffled frown on Sin's face was priceless.

Braden chucked Sin on the arm. "I'm jesting. You know I would never leave a woman in distress."

" 'Tis what I thought, but you looked a little too sincere just now."

And for a fraction of an instant, Braden *had* considered ignoring her. Especially given the severity of some of her curses. God help him if any of them ever came true. Why, he'd be a two-headed, three-toed, monkey-nosed, blind son of a cesspit-licking lackey if she had her way.

But, in spite of her uncharitable remarks, he couldn't leave her in whatever condition she was currently in.

All in all, as much as he hated to admit it, he actually liked the hellion.

"Braden!"

"I'm coming," he assured her, stepping around a large shrub to see her. . . .

Braden froze. Not even in his wildest imaginings had he thought to see her like *that*!

Her posterior wiggling and thrusting about rather provocatively, she lay bent over. And heaven help him, but it looked as if she were battling the very forest, or at least the hapless shrub in front of her.

Sin burst out laughing.

Braden probably would have laughed too, had a breeze not ruffled up the hem of her plaid, gifting him with a bountiful sight of her creamy buttocks. As well as a glimpse of other things that stirred a man's interest and loins.

Desire flooded through him, sending a painful throb straight to his groin.

The lass truly had a beguiling bottom. One of tempting proportions that would contour just perfectly to his body. And in that instant, he swore he could feel the softness of her thighs in his palm, hear her moaning as he buried himself deep inside her over and over again until they both cried out in blissful release.

Braden ground his teeth as his need for her flamed so hot that for a moment it rendered him immobile.

"It's not funny!" Maggie snapped, trying to pull herself out of the tangle of brush and limbs. All she succeeded in doing was baring more of her backside to him.

At this rate, the plaid would be gathered up at

her waist in another move or two and her entire bottom would be bared for his hungry view.

His eyes feasting on her, Braden held his breath in expectation. And for the first time in his life, he realized he was actually salivating over the sight before him.

"Braden!" she shouted again. "Please, help. I can't move. Every time I try to pull out, it just gets worse."

Nay, love, he thought wolfishly, *it only gets better.* Much better, point of fact.

"Braden?"

Braden briefly closed his eyes as an image of her writhing in his arms flitted through his mind. Too easily, he could picture her surrender, imagine the sound of his name on her passion-drunk lips.

And when he opened his eyes, he was again greeted by the plaid just barely concealing her natural charms.

It was all Braden could do to force his gaze away from her wiggling hips and move around her to where he could see her flushed face.

He would definitely like a few more leisurely minutes to explore her—

"What is taking you so long? Would you *please* help me?" she asked again.

Aye, he'd help her all right, but what he really wanted to help her do, she'd slap him into eternity for.

Focus, man, it's not like you've never seen a woman's backside before.

True enough, but he couldn't ever remember a woman's body tempting him *this* much.

Dropping his pack on the ground, Braden eyed the contraption on top of her with a frown. Maggie lay on what appeared to be a leaflike table while more branches and leaves had fallen on top of her and held her pinned face down.

"How did you get in there?"

She arched her back to where she could glare at him. "Oh, I don't know. It just looked like a good place to stop for a bit of a rest."

Sin laughed again as Braden rolled his eyes at her sarcasm.

"Well, Lady Venom Tongue, perhaps I should leave you in there."

Panic flitted across her brow, then she quickly added, "I was walking, then I tripped over something and all of a sudden this giant mass of leaves fell on top of me. Now would you please help me get up?"

Braden ran his gaze over her body. She was in quite the perfect position for—

"Braden!" she snapped, as if she could read his thoughts.

He couldn't resist teasing her. "Think you, we should leave her here?" he asked Sin.

"Well, she did say, 'Men, who needs them?' Perhaps we should, just to prove a lesson."

"You wouldn't dare leave me here like this," she said. Then she added less forcibly, "Would you?"

Braden gave her a devilish, dimpled grin. "Why don't you catch up to us after you get yourself free?"

Maggie groaned, cursed him yet again beneath her breath, then fell prone on the bed of leaves. "If you were a gentleman, you wouldn't even consider leaving me here like this."

"Well," he teased, "according to you, I'm not a gentleman, but a lust-ridden, warted sow's ear fit for naught save eating, belching and chasing after other men's wives."

Her face flushed even redder. "You heard that?"

"Aye, and I wouldn't be surprised if the king of England sitting on his throne in London heard it as well."

Maggie wanted to bury her head in shame. She hadn't meant for him to hear her words, and she didn't really mean any of them. She used those words to stiffen her resolve and try to keep herself focused on his flaws. Her only real problem with him was that she loved the scoundrel entirely too much.

Well, except for this moment. Right now, she would like nothing more than to choke his arrogant hide as he stared at her with humor dancing in his greenish brown eyes.

Sighing, she tried again. "Very well, I'm sorry for what I said. Men are good for some things. Now please help me."

Braden looked skeptically at Sin. "I just don't feel she meant that apology. What say you?"

Maggie huffed and squirmed. "Please," she said, stressing the word.

Pressing his lips into a grim line, Braden shook his head. "Still it lacks sincerity."

She froze and glared at him.

Braden bit back a laugh as he regarded her anger. If her amber gaze could kill, he would definitely be shredded by the malice she directed at him.

"If you don't get me out of this, Braden MacAllister, I swear I'll haunt you for an eternity."

"Now, *that* could be frightening," Sin said.

Or it could be a whole lot of fun.

Braden's gaze drifted back toward her bottom. A whole lot of fun, indeed.

Stifling the thought, Braden used his foot to move his pack out of his way, then leaned over to try and move the leaves from her back.

It didn't work.

Braden frowned as he looked more carefully at the limbs. "This was a trap of some sort," he said, noting the way the branch had been rigged to fall from behind Maggie.

"Probably some child wanting to trap another. You can tell it wasn't meant to hurt anyone, just pin them down for a bit," Sin said as he examined it as well. "Sort of like the ones we used on Kieran and Lochlan."

Braden laughed at the memory.

"While you two admire the handiwork, would one of you please find a way to free me?"

"I'm working on it," Braden said.

He moved to stand behind her so that he could pull the limb back in the direction from which it had swung.

It suddenly dawned on him what he'd have to do to free her. And in his gut, he knew she wasn't going to like it.

He, on the other hand . . .

Braden licked his lips in anticipation.

"Maggie, my love, I'm going to have to get really close to you to free you."

"I don't care what you have to do," she said sharply. "Just please do it and let me go."

Braden dropped his gaze down to her hips as his hunger for her grew even more, as well as another part of him that stiffened and strained, begging for her softness.

Well, if that's the way she wants it . . .

He stood directly behind her, then had to lean forward, over her back, to pull the limb off her. As he did so, his painfully aroused groin made full contact with her bottom.

She gasped, then jerked her hips to where they collided fully with his swollen shaft. The action wrung a deep moan from him.

"This is a priceless sight," Sin said from behind them. "Should I leave you two alone?"

"Shut up, Sin," they shouted in unison.

Braden struggled to breathe against the agonizing pain of his need for her. He had never wanted anything as badly as he wanted to take her right then and there.

Forcing himself to move, Braden pulled the limb away from her spine. Maggie scooted out from between him and the leaf-table lightning quick. Her face was the same color as her hair as she looked about at anything *other* than him.

"Thank you," she said.

"My pleasure," Braden said before he thought better of it.

Her eyes flashing, she met his gaze with fury smoldering in the amber depths. "Only *you* would take advantage of a woman in that position."

There, she was wrong, and if he were the demon she thought him to be, he'd have done a whole lot more to her than just free her.

"I wasn't trying to take advantage of you. I was simply trying to get you out as quickly as possible."

"Oh, I'm certain of that." Her sarcasm made a mockery of Braden's even tone as she tugged her plaid back down to her knees.

"Well," Sin interjected, "while the two of you catch up on insults, I'm going to scout us a place to sleep."

Sin quickly vanished into the trees.

Maggie glared while Braden fought down the smile he knew would only anger her more.

The air between them was rife with awkwardness. An awkwardness Braden didn't like.

As far back as he could remember, there had always been the easiness of friendship between them, and he didn't like the sudden change in her demeanor.

"Did you get hurt?" he asked.

The anger dimmed a bit as she shook her head. "I'm uncertain how I fell. I'm usually very surefooted."

"Well, even the best of us occasionally falls into the wrong trap."

She looked down as if his words triggered something in her memory; then, unexpectedly, she smiled.

He delighted in the change it made in her. Her eyes glowed warmly as her entire face lit up. The lass was beautiful when she smiled.

"What?" Braden asked, wondering what had brought about this sudden change.

"I was just remembering another trap."

"The one where I goosed you at the cave?" Braden asked.

She frowned for a second, until she recalled the event, then she gave a short laugh. "Nay, I was thinking of the trap you mentioned earlier when Nera, Mairi, and the others ambushed you on the way to my house."

Braden squirmed at the memory. "You know, I still have scars on my body from it."

To this day, he had a thin spot on his crown where one of the girls had pulled a handful of hair from his scalp. "When I first ran into you that day, I thought you were in with them."

"I know," she said, smiling. "I'll never forget the terrified look on your face when you ran me over. 'Tis the only time I've ever seen you panicked."

"And I was too. I had no idea how to get away without hurting one of them."

Then Braden recalled how he had escaped the lust-crazed lasses.

Looking at Maggie, he smiled. "And I'll never forget how you shoved me into the hollow of that oak tree, then sent them off in the opposite direction."

"I was shaking," she confessed, "terrified they would learn I'd lied to them and set upon me with a vengeance."

That wasn't the way he recalled it. Barely ten-and-three, she had appeared out of nowhere to save him. He didn't remember her looking afraid. "You looked poised and calm to me."

Braden stared in awe of her as memories played through his mind. Memories of Maggie sneaking him out of the tree, then the two of them literally crawling through the bushes to reach her house undetected by the girls.

And later, Maggie bandaging the cuts and bruises the lasses had inflicted upon him. She had even hummed a gentle tune as she smoothed the salve across his skin. Her touch had been so light and soothing. Her voice pleasant.

He couldn't remember whether or not he had thanked her that day. But right now, with the sunlight on her face and the fire in her eyes, he wanted nothing more than to kiss her until eternity came and went.

Impulsively, Braden reached out and ran his fingertip over the freckles covering her cheekbone. "I've always wondered why you saved me that day."

She didn't pull away. Instead, she looked up at him with a strange emotion in her eyes. "I was but returning the favor."

"What favor?"

She drew her brows together. "Don't you recall it?"

"I don't think so."

Maggie's frown deepened. "You truly don't recall saving my life?"

As he toyed with the delicate, soft skin, Braden searched his memory, but for his life, he couldn't remember ever saving her from anything except one of her brothers, and none of them would ever have truly hurt her. "Nay."

"I was but seven when you came to my rescue."

"I would have been ten."

"Aye. My father had gone to the castle to deliver wool. Ian and I were supposed to stay in the wagon, but I snuck his toy horse from his side and when he realized what I had done, he started after me."

Braden smiled as he finally recalled the event. The two of them had been quite a sight. "You were running through the great hall, screaming for help."

"Aye, and I thought he was going to kill me for sure."

"You ran straight into me and sent us careening into my mother's best tapestry."

They both cringed at that part of the memory.

Maggie bit her lip. "She wasn't overly angry, was she?"

His mother's wrath had been immeasurable, and she had given him quite a thrashing over it. Why, even to this day, she brought it up every time he displeased her.

Braden started to make a quip about it, but then caught the look of concern and guilt in Maggie's eyes. And for some reason he couldn't fathom, he wanted to soothe her. "Nay, she wasn't overly angry."

Relief settled across her face. "I'm still sorry I kicked you while I was trying to get up. But you know what I remember most?"

This time, he couldn't resist teasing her. "The knee to my groin you gave me when you sat up?"

She flushed and bent her head down.

Braden ran his hand through her hair, caressing the shiny locks.

"Nay," she said. "It was after my father had scolded us and returned us to the wagon. I felt so terrible, and then all of a sudden there you were with your painted horse."

"Connor," Braden added, remembering the toys his uncle had carved for him. He'd loved those horses. But the dark brown stallion he had given her had been his favorite. To this day, he didn't know what had possessed him to give it up to her.

It had been another impulsive act his mother had taken him to task over.

Still, he recalled the happiness he'd seen on her tear-streaked face as she had cradled the tiny horse to her chest. "You looked as if I had just given you a king's treasure."

"You had," she said softly. And in that instant Braden felt in his chest a very strange tenderness toward her. One he couldn't define.

Never had he felt anything like it.

And when the edges of her lips turned up ever so slightly, it was as if lightning struck him.

"I still have it."

Her confession amazed him. He would have thought she'd have tossed it out years ago. "Do you?"

She nodded.

"Why?"

She shrugged sheepishly. "It was the kindest thing anyone had ever done for me," she said. "I couldn't believe you gave me such a valuable gift."

It touched him that even at so young an age, she had known the true value of the horse. Then again, Maggie had always been wiser, more insightful than most girls her age.

"Well, I felt badly for the way your father shouted at you. It wasn't your fault."

"Nay," she said, her eyes dancing as she wrinkled her nose. " 'Twas Ian's for wanting to kill me."

Laughing, Braden stared in wonder of her as foreign emotions swept through him. She was so different from most women he'd known. So giving and kind, yet fierce and independent.

"We've known each other a long time, haven't we?" Braden asked.

"Aye, we have."

"It's strange where life takes us," he said, thinking aloud. "I remember the first time I ever saw you. You had just started walking. Your head was as bald as it could be and you had the biggest eyes I'd ever seen."

"Far from a flattering image."

"True," he said as he traced the outline of her cheek with his forefinger. "But for a baby, you were passable enough."

Too easily, he could recall the day he'd first seen her pulling herself up to stand by his side. She'd looked up at him with a big, sweet grin that had warmed his heart. She had cooed at him, then laid her head down on his knee. At first he had ahhed the gesture until she had laughed, then bitten a piece from his thigh.

He had yelped, and she had cried, and his leg had worn that bruise for days. After the experience, he had approached wee bairns with much more caution.

"Is that all you remember?" she asked him.

"Nay," he said, tucking a stray piece of hair behind her ear. "I remember the way you laughed at me. You had such a happy laugh and most every time I went to your cottage you had a smile on your face. Until your mother died."

Maggie nodded, her eyes turning sad at the memory. "My da expected me to care for the boys."

He hated to see her sad. For some reason, it made his own heart ache and so he decided to lighten the conversation. "Aye, and from that day on, you were always so serious. Especially on the days when you were trying to kill me."

Maggie dropped her jaw at his words, offended that he would think such a thing. "I never tried to kill you."

"What about the night you set my bed on fire?"

"I never . . ." Maggie's voice trailed off as she recalled the event. It had been the night she had snuck into Anghus's room to see Braden sleeping.

What she had never expected to see was him lying spread out on the bed with no shirt. The covers had been pushed all the way down to his waist, where they gathered just below the tiny hairs that ran below his navel. He'd held on to the covers with one clenched fist, while his other arm had been curved above his head.

To this day, she remembered the sight of his tawny, flawless chest gleaming in the candlelight, rising and falling with his deep even breaths.

So intent on him, she had forgotten the candle in her hand. One minute she had been admiring him, and in the next the candle had slipped from her hand and set fire to his mattress.

She had tried to stamp it out, but it had spread quickly. Braden had jerked awake an instant before she grabbed the pail of wash water from the floor and doused the fire, and him with it.

He had come up sputtering, his brow puzzled as he glared at her.

To this day, she was mortified by the event.

"It was an accident," she told him.

" 'Tis glad I am to know you weren't really trying to kill me."

Maggie diverted her gaze to her feet. Oh, the things she had done to him over the years. All in all, it was amazing he still spoke to her.

"You know, Maggie, I never noticed before just how beautiful you are."

She looked up at him doubtfully. "You're only saying that because I'm the only woman you've been around for the last two days."

"I'm saying it because I know it."

How she wished she could believe that. But she knew the rogue too well. His heart only belonged to his lady of the moment.

So, then, be his lady of the moment, her heart whispered. *'Tis better than never having him at all.*

If only it were that easy. As much as it hurt for her to see him pursue other women now, she couldn't imagine how much worse it would be to give herself to him and then watch him leave her behind.

Her heart couldn't take such a thing.

Maggie reached up and touched his face. "I wish I could believe it, but you've said it yourself many times. You were put on this earth to love women. Notice that is plural and not singular."

"Is that what it would take to win you?"

"Aye. I want a man who will never stray from my side."

"You ask a lot."

"Too much, I've been told by my brothers."

"And so you're content to grow old alone?"

Maggie watched the way the light danced in his eyes, entranced by it. "I'll hardly be alone. My brothers have enough children to keep me occupied."

He frowned at her. "Do you not want your own?"

"More than anything. But I don't need a husband for that, now, do I?"

The shocked look on his face made her laugh. "I dinna hear what I think I did."

"You misunderstood me," she added quickly. "There are children aplenty with no one to love them. Your brother was one. When I am ready, I am quite certain I'll be able to find a child who needs a mother's love."

Braden shook his head. "Do you depend on anyone for anything?"

"Do you?"

"That is different. I am a man. It would be remiss of me if I depended on others."

"And it would be remiss of me to burden another for my welfare. I have always stood on my own, and I will continue to do so."

Braden stared aghast at her. "You're a strange lass, Maggie ingen Blar."

"You forget headstrong and unreasonable."

"That had to come from Anghus."

"Actually, it comes from your brother Lochlan most recently. But also from anyone who has ever had to deal with me."

He laughed.

Before he could speak, Sin stepped out of the woods in front of them. "There's a small clearing a bit farther ahead, if you're interested. I'm going after dinner now."

"You need any help?" Braden asked.

Sin shook his head. "You'd best stay with Maggie in case one of our *friends* returns."

"Good idea."

Braden picked up their packs from the damp peat and handed Maggie hers before he started off in the direction Sin had indicated. "Let's go find our camp."

Maggie stared at his back as they walked, longing for the impossible. Too easily, she could imagine having such a kind and wonderful man to call hers. If only he could be trusted with her heart.

But she knew better. And she had cried enough tears over him. She would content herself with his friendship and try to protect her heart as best she could.

When they found the place where Sin had left his pack, Braden made a small fire.

Maggie sat down and took her pack off her arm. She groaned a bit at the ache in her shoulder from the weight of it.

"Here," Braden said, kneeling behind her. "Let me help."

Before she could protest, he placed his warm hands on her shoulders and gently massaged her aching muscles.

Och now, that felt good. Really, *really* good.

Closing her eyes, Maggie enjoyed the sensation of his hands sliding along her collarbone and upper arm, where his hands clenched and unclenched in a soothing, seductive rhythm. His touch was both light yet firm, hot and masterful. And when he pressed his thumbs beneath her shoulder blade and wiggled them about, she gave an involuntary moan.

Oh, his firm, hot touch was heaven, pure and complete heaven.

He leaned so close to her that she could smell the raw, earthy scent of him. Could smell the elderberries in his hair.

"Better?" he asked, his voice thick and deep.

"Aye," she breathed, her body melting.

Braden reached his right hand around her and gently cupped her face in his hand, angling her chin until she looked up at him. Maggie stared in awe of his handsomeness. At those beautiful greenish brown eyes darkening as he watched her expectantly.

And then he kissed her.

Maggie moaned at the contact of his lips on hers as molten heat tore through her, pooling itself at the center of her body, where it throbbed and ached in a primal need she barely understood. Braden's touch was both gentle and demanding. Fierce yet tender.

Maggie wanted him closer. Needed him closer.

She wrapped her arms about him and Braden willingly obliged her unspoken request, moving his body until nothing but clothing separated them.

He left her lips to trail slow, scorching kisses over her cheek to her neck, where he teased her flesh with his tongue. Maggie hissed at the sensation as chills spread all through her. She reeled from the feelings inside her that coalesced into something indescribable. And it was Braden, her Braden, who was making her feel this way.

Her breasts swelled and ached as the deep, painful throb became even more demanding than before.

In that instant, she wanted him. Wanted him as she always had.

How many nights had she lain awake, clutching her pillow to her, pretending it was Braden she held?

Not even her best dream could compare to this reality. She was really here and Braden was finally holding her in a true lover's embrace.

He loosened the laces of her shirt, then buried his lips against the column of her throat as he worked on the piece of linen she had binding her breasts down tightly to her chest.

Her body on fire, Maggie swallowed as she ran her hands through the black silken strands of his hair.

Braden pushed the linen down and she shook as the cool air caressed her hot skin.

"So very sweet," he breathed, moving his right hand lower, and lower until he seized her taut breast.

She cried out in pleasure as he teased the tip, then parted her tunic so that he could replace his hand with his hot, sleek mouth.

Maggie knew she should push him away, and yet she couldn't bring herself to do it. Not after all the years she had dreamed of having him, of holding him just like this.

In fact, she could say nothing at all, only feel. Feel his breath scorching her, feel his hand and lips teasing her flesh as his delectable weight pressed her down.

Braden inhaled the sweet floral scent of her as he teased her taut nipple with his tongue. His head dizzy, he could think of nothing save her. She filled him with need and wonder, with a strange peaceful feeling that defied his ability to name.

And he wanted to taste more of her.

Pushing back the saffron shirt, he licked his way toward her other breast and thought of other places he intended to taste before he was through with her.

Aye, she would be branded on all his senses before the day was through, and he would claim her as no man had ever claimed her before.

And take her in more ways than she could imagine. He wouldn't stop until she was weak from his touch, drained and spent in his arms.

Only then would he have mercy on her. And on himself.

Maggie sighed in pleasure as he ran his hand down between their bodies. It was so incredible, she thought, amazed by the sensations flooding her.

She felt consumed by fire. His hand skimmed over the curve of her hip to touch the flesh of her thigh. Instinctively, she arched her body toward his hand, as she delighted in the feel of his skin against hers.

She wanted more. Needed more.

He returned to claim her lips with his own.

Maggie buried her hands in his hair while his hand moved to her inner thigh, skimming up higher and higher until he touched the delicious ache between her legs.

She jerked in surprise as he touched her where no one had ever touched her before.

Was he supposed to do that?

And yet it felt so deliciously wonderful.

His tongue toyed with her mouth, matching the rhythm of his fingers as they slid around the center of her body, teasing her, stroking her until she was ready to scream.

And then suddenly she felt him deftly slide a finger inside her body. She moaned deep in her throat as she instinctively lifted her hips to draw his hand in deeper.

Never in her life had she felt the like. Clenching her teeth, she bucked her hips against his hand, wanting more. Craving more.

Braden wanted to roar in triumph. He had her right where he wanted her and she was his for the asking.

Deepening his kiss, he continued to toy mercilessly with the tiny nub of her, taking delight in her pleasurable moans.

She was so hot and slick and tight, just waiting for him to fill her to capacity. And he would.

Aye, he would fill her deep and hard, and have her screaming out in release, begging him for more until they were both covered with sweat and thoroughly spent.

Kissing her, he circled her once with his thumb, then plunged it deep inside her.

"Please, Braden," she moaned.

And in that miserable, awful instant, reality

came crashing down upon him as he felt her maidenhead with his finger.

She was a virgin. And until he had come along, she had been completely untouched.

Against his will, he saw himself for the first time through her eyes. A wandering rogue with no thought of anyone save himself.

He had seduced her to this. And come the morning, she would feel used by him.

She would hate him.

Or worse, she would hate herself.

His painfully aroused body begged for hers, but he couldn't take her. Not like this. Not out in the woods like some hoary beast with no regard for her or her feelings. She was a maiden and she deserved a better first time than this.

She deserved . . .

She deserved to be taken by a man who loved her.

Damn it to hell! he roared at himself.

And damn her for giving him a conscience.

Infuriated at both of them, Braden forced himself to pull away.

She looked up at him with a frown.

"I'm sorry, Maggie," he breathed. "I forgot myself."

And then he saw the shame in her gaze.

Worse, tears filled her eyes as she pushed herself to her feet. Without a word, she took off running through the woods.

Braden went after her, catching her before she ran too far ahead.

"What is it?" he asked.

"I canna believe I let you do that," she said. "I'm not a whore, to—"

He silenced her words with one finger over her lips. "Nay, you are not a whore. If you were, I wouldn't have stopped."

Her frown deepened.

"There is nothing wrong with what we did," he said quietly. "You are a woman full grown and it was wrong of me to take advantage of you. If you want to hate someone for what just happened, then hate me. But never hate yourself."

Confusion and pain mixed on her face as she studied him. "Why did you do it?"

"Because I want you," he said, his voice breaking with need and emotion. "Even now my body craves yours in a way that is most painful."

"Then why did you stop?"

He moved his hand to cup her face. And right then, it was all he could do not to kiss her. Not to finish what they had started.

"Because I didn't want you to hate me for it," he told her. "Or worse, to hate yourself."

"I don't understand."

"I know you don't. Tell me, Maggie, when you were making those plans of growing old without a man, did you never give thought to what you might be missing?"

"Of course I did."

Braden arched one brow. "Does that include what you just felt?"

Heat crept over her face. "I didn't know about that. I mean, I knew about that, but I didn't know . . ."

"What it felt like."

She nodded.

He leaned his head forward until their foreheads touched, and he buried his hands in her soft russet hair. It was all he could do not to touch her more intimately, because right then, being intimate with her was all he wanted.

Indeed, he wished he could just crawl inside her and stay there for eternity.

"What you felt, little blossom, is nothing compared to the pleasures to be had. And I wish to all that is holy that I could be the one who shows it to you."

Maggie stiffened in his embrace. "Are you asking to marry me?"

Braden pulled back to see the indecision on her face. "Would you have me if I did?"

"Nay. I know you too well. You're not the type of man to ever content himself with one woman."

It was true and he knew it in his heart and with every fiber of his body. He couldn't see himself coming home night after night to the same woman. He needed variety, spontaneity.

Worse, he could never give her his heart. That

was one part of him that he refused to share with any other person.

And Maggie needed . . . nay, he corrected himself, she *deserved* a man loyal to her. One who would never break her heart and leave her weeping.

Still, his body didn't listen. It craved her with such ferocity that he swore his groin would grow blisters from the heat.

"So, where does that leave us?" he asked.

"At a standoff, I fear."

"Nay," he said, laying his hand on her shoulder. "Not a standoff. We both know I can never have you." *Because I can never be the man you need me to be, and I would sooner die than hurt you.*

"I know," she whispered.

Braden kissed her forehead lightly, then pulled away and led her back to the camp. Both their moods were dark as they quietly tried to ignore each other. But it was hard.

On second thought, it was impossible. Her taste and smell was branded into his memory and all he could see was her smile. All he could hear was her moaning his name.

And God help him, he wanted more.

The sweet bliss they could have together . . . but Maggie wasn't the kind of woman a man made love to and left. She was the type of woman a man married.

You could . . .

Braden wouldn't even let his mind finish that thought. He could never marry. Especially not a woman with whom he could see himself falling in love.

Chapter 11

Maggie spent the entire evening trying to avoid Braden as best she could. But how did a woman manage to avoid someone who meant so much to her?

Even now, as he sat across the fire beside Sin, not even looking at her, she could feel his presence as acutely as if he sat directly next to her. The firelight played across his face, making his eyes appear a midnight black like Sin's.

His mood had been so serious since their discussion, and she missed his lighthearted teasing. And more than ever she wished she were the type of woman who could just walk over there, seduce him for the night, and be content with his leaving her come morning.

Perhaps her brothers were right. She did ask too much of a man.

But then, didn't she have a right to ask for the same commitment and devotion from a man that men demanded of women?

Oh, it just didn't seem fair to her.

Unaware of her thoughts and sidelong glances, Braden licked the grease from his lips in a way that made her body yearn.

How could any man be so scrumptious? And why, oh, why couldn't she get him out of her mind?

She averted her gaze.

But what was the use? She could still see those wonderful greenish brown eyes teasing her. Hear him calling her "little blossom," and feel his strong hands roaming over the most private parts of her body.

The man was simply too gorgeous for her own good. And in that instant, she wished she had never seen him. She could only imagine the years of peace she would have known had she not been trying to gain his attention.

Sin rose as soon as he finished eating. "I'll take first watch again."

Her own dinner forgotten, Maggie stood in a hurry as memories of the night before coursed through her. The last thing she needed was to awaken once more in Braden's arms.

She had to do something to put distance between them. "Perhaps I should take a turn at watch?"

Both men stared at her as if she'd lost her mind.

She had, but that was beside the point. Worse, Braden gave her a knowing, rakish smile.

"No offense," Sin said dryly, "but I prefer to *live* through the night."

"I was just trying to be helpful," she said.

"Then get plenty of sleep," Sin said, turning his back to her.

Maggie wished she possessed some of Sin's sarcasm to come up with an appropriately biting retort, but all she could do was sit back down and return to her food.

Braden ran his tongue wickedly over his bottom lip as he leaned to one side and stared at her over the fire. She looked down and tried not to notice how delectably long those legs of his were stretching out.

He propped his head on his hand and looked invitingly at her. "Ready for bed, my love?"

And you had missed that teasing?

Whatever had she been thinking?

Maggie fought the childish urge to stomp her foot at him. How dare he tease her like *that*, knowing how much she wanted him, as well as the fact that there could be nothing between them.

By the light in his eyes, she could see he was doing it on purpose just to nettle her.

It was then another urge possessed her. One to return the gesture to him. 'Twas time he was on the receiving end of such tactics.

"Aye," she said.

Then slowly, seductively, she smoothed her

hair to rest behind her right ear and gave him an inviting, taunting smile of her own as she leaned forward. "And you?"

He didn't speak. His eyes bulged ever so slightly as his gaze fastened on the small amount of cleavage her position afforded him.

"You have no idea what you're playing with," he said, his voice an octave lower.

"Aye, but I do." She wrinkled her nose at him as she playfully bit her lower lip, imitating his earlier gesture. "You'd never force yourself on an unwilling woman, now, would you?"

"Of course not," he said, his tone offended.

She sat back on her heels and trailed one hand slowly over the laces of her shirt. "Then look all you want, for that's the only pleasure you'll ever get from me."

To her dismay, he threw his head back and roared with laughter.

"Oh, Maggie," he said after he sobered. "If I dinna know better, I'd swear you were an experienced little minx. Now go to sleep. I already told you, I have no interest in tupping with you in the woods. But when I find a bed . . ."

She'd run as fast as her legs could carry her. After what had already happened, she knew she couldn't resist him for long once he touched her.

And his kisses . . .

It was enough to make a woman forget herself, for sure.

Realizing the virtue of retreat, she settled herself down before the fire. She had just begun to relax a bit when Braden joined her.

"What are you doing?" she asked hurriedly as she remembered the way his body had felt shielding her from the ground.

"I'm bringing you an extra plaid," he said, draping it over her.

"Thank you," she whispered, trying her best not to notice the way his scent clung to the fabric. Or worse, the way his hands felt on her body as he smoothed the material over her.

When he left her, she could feel her entire body temperature drop.

Her heart felt torn as he settled himself across from her. The rational part of her was grateful, but her heart ached at the loss of his comfort.

Sighing, she forced herself to concentrate on what she would say to the MacDouglas when she met him. That was a relatively safe topic. One that diverted her thoughts from Braden.

At least for a little bit.

That night, Maggie slept from sheer exhaustion.

She came awake just after dawn to see Braden looking straight at her, his face unreadable.

Self-conscious from his attention, she brushed her hair with her hands and wondered what he had been thinking as he watched her sleep.

"Good morning," he said in greeting.

"Good morning," she responded, pushing

back the plaid as she stood. She glanced to where Sin slept a few feet away. "Should I wake Sin?"

"Not if you're of a mind to be keeping your head on your shoulders."

She frowned at his words.

Braden moved to stand between her and his brother. Instead of reaching out to touch Sin, or speaking, he pulled his sword an inch out of the scabbard, so carefully that only a tiny, barely perceptible rasping sound disturbed the air.

But it was enough.

Lightning quick and in one fluid motion, Sin rolled to his feet. With the toe of his left foot, Sin caught his scabbard and kicked it from the ground into his hands, where he unsheathed his long sword in a quick, graceful arc and whirled to face them.

The blade came to rest a mere inch from Braden's neck as Maggie froze, too scared to breathe.

His face deadly and tight, Sin only relaxed when he realized it was she and Braden who had disturbed him.

Sin cursed. "I really hate it when you do that," he said to Braden, sheathing his sword.

Braden gave her a warning stare. "Never touch him while he sleeps. Or if you do so, duck."

"I will remember that."

As if unperturbed by the strangeness of his actions, Sin stretched casually, then yawned. "Still no sign of our bandits?"

Braden shook his head. "Not yet."

"Pity. I feel the urge to kill something." Sin left them to tend to his needs.

"Kill something?" she asked Braden when they were alone. "Is he jesting?"

"Most likely not," he said, matter-of-factly.

A chill went down her spine as she left Braden and rolled her plaid up, then placed it into her pack. Sin was a scary, scary man. But then, Braden could be so as well.

Dismissing them from her thoughts, she made herself concentrate on the task ahead.

Once Sin returned, the men gave Maggie her privacy as Braden prepared food to break the morning fast.

Braden glanced longingly into the trees where Maggie had vanished. He'd spent half the night just watching her. Watching the way her chest rose and fell with her deep, even breaths. The way her arm gracefully curled under her head to support it.

The way she had gently reached up in the middle of the night to scratch at her cheek and rub her eye like some adorable little child.

Sleep did the most incredible things to her. It softened the tautness of her face and made her appear like a fey imp. The same imp who had once filled his boots with flour. He laughed.

Where had the time gone?

One day they had been children, running

through the heather-filled moors together as they chased butterflies, and now she was grown. Grown into a strong woman who captivated him.

And this attraction he felt for her. What was it? Where did it come from?

It must be the allure of forbidden fruit, he decided. He knew he couldn't have her and so he craved her all the more. Aye, that was it. That made sense to him.

Once they were around others and he could find another woman, all would be set right. Maggie wouldn't haunt his thoughts or torment his body. He would be his old self once again, the Braden who made fathers cringe in their sleep and women giggle at his approach.

And yet some part of his mind argued. It told him that she had changed him. That somehow, some way, he wasn't the same man he'd been when they started this journey.

Braden didn't listen.

He couldn't afford to.

Maggie returned to the camp and in less than an hour they were on their way. They spoke little as they made their way through the forest, ever vigilant for the thieves.

As the day wore on, the sky above became dark and forbidding. A storm was coming, and they would need shelter for the night.

Reluctantly, Braden led them out of the forest toward a small village, brimming with activity. The wattle-and-daub huts were uninviting, and there was a large Celtic Cross in the center of them.

As they approached the unfamiliar people, Braden glanced down at Sin's legs. True to Sin's prediction, they had actually darkened and were no longer so obviously white.

Maggie's still looked a bit too womanly for his tastes, but with any luck no one would notice that, and if they did happen to glance her way, they would merely attribute it to youth.

He hoped.

As he watched her, he saw the fear and trepidation settle on her face as her gaze darted about the people and she tightened her grip on the pack. He hated to see her scared. She had nothing to fear, not so long as he was there. He would never let any harm come to her.

So he sought of a way to make her smile.

"I wonder if there's a bed to be found here," he whispered teasingly in her ear.

Her face turned bright red at his words. "I'm sure there's nothing more promising than a stable," she mumbled under her breath.

Sin opened his mouth to speak, but Braden caught him on the arm. "Not a word, brother. We're no longer on MacAllister lands, and in this area, that English accent of yours will quickly get our throats cut."

Sin shot him an arrogant look that spoke loudly, *Let them try it.*

However, Braden wasn't in the mood to fight,

and luckily Sin glared at him but kept his lips in a tight, grim line.

Braden moved ahead of them and approached a man who was loading hay into his wagon. About two score years in age, the man had hard lines around his face and a full gray beard laced with just a hint of brown. Though the man appeared clean and well kept, his brown and yellow plaid was ragged around the edges.

"Good day to you, sir," Braden said to the man.

The man paused in his loading and eyed him suspiciously. "Who are you?"

Braden answered without hesitation, "My name's Sean."

"And who do you follow?"

"Ewan of the Clan MacLucas."

The man's silvery eyes narrowed even more. "I never heard of him."

"We're from the isles," Braden said. "My brothers and I are on our way to MacDouglas lands to see our sister and her new babe. I was wondering if there might be a place we could spend the night."

The old man accepted his words with a laugh. "MacDouglas lands, you say? You'll not have a happy time there, I'll wager."

"How so?"

The old man scratched his beard. "My sister married a MacDouglas, and I heard from my brother-in-law that she and the rest of the clan's women have taken over the castle from the men.

They're standing the battlements like a group of Amazons and have threatened to tar any man dumb enough to venture near them until the MacDouglas ends the feud with the MacAllister."

Braden feigned disbelief. "You don't say?"

The man's visage turned dark. "Aye. 'Tis an evil, demonic thing that has possessed the women. I heard the MacDouglas has petitioned the bishop for an exorcism."

"To be sure," Braden said, then dared an amused glance to Maggie, whose cheeks seemed to be a shade or two redder than they'd been a few minutes ago. "Imagine a woman not wanting her man. Saints preserve us."

The man nodded gravely, then his mood seemed to lighten a degree. He returned to loading his hay. "Old Seamus rents to strangers. Damn fool, he. You'll find his place down near the stable."

"My thanks," Braden said, then turned and led Maggie and Sin toward the south end of the village where the stable lay.

"Sean?" Maggie whispered as he drew near her.

"I didn't want to chance the name Braden, lest it jog someone's memory."

"Quick thinking," she agreed.

As they drew near the stable, Braden had to force himself not to curl his lip. Old Seamus's home was about as clean as a sty.

Still, it would keep them out of the rain, and

the last thing any of them needed was to catch their death before the MacDouglas had a chance to kill them.

He found Seamus outside his house, fetching water from a well. The old man paused at their approach and eyed them with great reservation.

"I don't have beds for three strapping lads," he said after Braden had asked him for a place to stay. "But I do have the stable, if you're of a mind to use it."

Maggie cast him a smug *I told you so* look.

"It's not fancy," Seamus continued, "but it comes with a meal, and it'll keep the coming rain off your heads."

It would do. And judging from the smell of the man, the stable would be preferable anyway.

"How much?" Braden asked.

The old man stroked his chin thoughtfully as he swept them with a measuring gaze. "Free, if you lads don't mind doing some chores for me."

Braden noted the strained look on Sin's face. He could tell his brother would sooner brave the rain than do anything menial for a Highlander. Indeed, knowing Sin, it was a wonder he didn't turn berserker and start laying waste to the entire village.

He would make it up to Sin later. For now they had to be practical.

"Sounds good," Braden said. "What can we do for you?"

"There's a pile of wood in the back that needs chopping and a fence that needs repair."

Braden clapped Sin on the back and headed toward the area.

"We'll get busy, then," Braden said to Seamus as he led them off.

"Hey, lad?" Seamus asked, stopping him midstride.

Braden turned to look back.

"What are your names?"

"I'm Sean, and this"—he gestured to Maggie— "is my brother James, and"—he indicated Sin— "Durbhan."

Seamus eyed them cautiously. "They don't talk much, do they?"

"Not much to say," Braden said.

He seemed to accept that. "Fine, then, but I do warn the three of you to keep your hands off me daughters. I may be an old man, but I've got a bow and a shovel, and no one here would care what I did with the lot of you."

"Yes, sir," Braden said, trying his best not to laugh at the warning. Sin would never lay hands to one of his daughters, and Maggie . . .

He'd best not even think of *that* lest it make him laugh.

"Shall we chop wood first?" Braden asked them as he led them to the small yard behind the house.

"Chop wood, my arse," Sin sneered in a low tone. "I'd sooner—"

"It strikes me," Braden said, interrupting him, "that you're supposed to be mute." He looked at Maggie. "Have you ever met a mute who spoke more?"

Maggie didn't look one tiny bit amused. She said nothing as Braden dropped his pack, then grabbed the axe from the stump where the old farmer had embedded it.

Fury smoldered on Sin's face as he picked up another axe from the ground and glared at Braden, who half expected his brother to lob the axe at his head.

Instead, Sin turned on his heel and cleaved a large log in two with one angry whack.

Shaking his head at Sin, Braden grabbed another limb and set to work on it.

Maggie stood back as they started breaking the large pieces of tree into fire logs. Her heart ached as she remembered the farmer's warning about his daughters.

Why, oh, why couldn't the man have sons?

Maybe they're ugly.

Maggie paused at the thought. Aye, maybe they were toothless like the farmer, and large, heavyset women with warts and pockmarks who wouldn't tempt Braden at all.

Seizing that hope, she moved to lift one of the large logs, but Braden stopped her. "You can get the kindling. Let us take the larger ones."

Without a word, Maggie set the log down and picked up the smaller bits, then took them to the woodpile next to the wattle-and-daub house.

Turning back toward Braden and Sin, she paused to watch the men in awe as they hefted the heavy axes and broke the logs with ease. A fine sheen already covered their bodies and she couldn't help but stare at the way Braden's shirt drew taut over his muscles every time he brought the axe back.

Mesmerized, she clenched her hands into fists as she fought the urge to touch the bulging muscles of his arm. Or wipe his damp black hair back from his forehead.

Oh, but the man was glorious and disturbing to her well-being.

Desire coiled through her in a way she'd never before known. Now that she had a taste of Braden, she was like some possessed drunkard craving more ale. For the first time in her life, she understood obsession. Understood *true* desire for a man.

And heaven help her, but she wanted him more than she ever had.

Just when she was certain she could stand no more, she felt the hairs on the back of her neck stand up. A chill of foreboding ran down her spine.

Someone was watching them. She was sure of it.

Half expecting to find the thieves, Maggie

looked up to see an attractive girl of about a score of years, watching the three of them intently.

When the girl realized Maggie had noticed her, she smiled widely, displaying a *full* set of perfectly white teeth, and toyed with her long blond braid, giving Maggie a come-hither stare that would have made any man puff his chest out in prideful interest.

Damn her luck! The girl was more than just attractive, she was downright beautiful.

It was then the girl was joined by four more equally attractive lasses, ranging in age, Maggie guessed, from ten-and-three to just over a score of years.

Maggie went cold.

Oh, bother, they were in trouble now, she realized. She knew the look on the lasses' faces.

Man-hungry.

Maggie gulped in fear. The last thing she needed was for one of those lasses to come groping on her body and discover they had a lot more in common than any of the girls could suspect.

Worse, as Maggie looked at them, she knew without a doubt where Braden would be spending the night. And it surely wouldn't be as her pillow.

Her sight dulling at the thought, Maggie grabbed the small stack of kindling and moved to pile it with the rest.

"Beg pardon," the eldest lass said as she

brazenly approached them. Her light blond hair shined even in the murky daylight, and her proportions were the type Maggie's brothers often fantasized about. "Me sisters and I thought you might be wanting a drink."

The girls giggled as they came forward to hand each of them a cup of ale. Maggie took the cup and quickly put a few feet between herself and the lass who had handed it to her.

The girl poked her lips out in an obviously practiced pout, but Maggie couldn't care less as she turned her attention toward Braden.

He took a cup from the eldest. The buxom lass rested her hip against the stump nearest Braden as she fondled the axe handle in a suggestive manner and stared hungrily up at him.

"I was just telling me sisters how nice it is to have such strong . . ."—the blonde's gaze dipped to Braden's chest, where his saffron shirt was damp with perspiration—"men around to help with chores."

Braden's eyes darkened speculatively, and worse, he smiled. "And what be your name?"

"Tara," she said, purring her name.

Maggie had the sudden urge to wrench every strand of blond hair from the young woman's head.

"I'm making a special hotchpotch tonight," Tara continued, "just for *you*." She reached out to touch Braden's chest.

Braden cast a quick glance at Maggie, who glared at him with the full weight of her displeasure.

The smile faded from his lips, and then he removed Tara's hand from his chest. "I'm sure we'll enjoy it."

Still, Maggie's heart ached as she wondered if he'd have bothered removing Tara's hand if she weren't standing right there watching them.

Tara pulled her hand back to rub it slowly along her collarbone as she trailed her gaze over Braden's body, pausing it briefly at the area where his thighs met.

"I'm sure you'll enjoy it," she said, her voice conveying a thick double entendre.

Maggie turned her back on the two of them, unable to stand anymore.

Let him have the harlot. Maggie had more important things to do, like gather up this stupid firewood so that she and Sin could have a roof over their heads while Braden gallivanted with that strumpet.

Maggie dumped the kindling, loudly, then turned to gather more.

She caught Braden's gaze. Tension sizzled between them as they stared at one another for a long minute, motionless.

"Here, now!" Seamus shouted as he came around the side of the house and broke their unspoken exchange. "What are you girls doing out here? I told you you were to stay inside while the lads be working."

"But Da," Tara said, stepping away from Braden, "we just thought—"

"I know what you be thinking, and you'd best be getting back inside. You might be grown, but you're still me daughters and I've a good strap for your backsides if you don't listen to me."

Tara poked her bottom lip out, then reluctantly did as her father ordered.

Seamus cast a malevolent glare at them until he saw the woodpile. "That should carry me through the winter!" he said gleefully. "Now, if you'll see about that fence, I'll see about your food."

Braden didn't move until Seamus left them.

At least he had the good grace to look ashamed as he approached her. "Maggie—"

"Don't," she said, cutting him off. He didn't have to explain it to her. She knew.

Bock, bock. She heard the cruel, taunting laughs of the boys from her clan as they mocked her. Women who looked like her didn't turn the heads of men who looked like Braden.

At least, nowhere other than in her dreams.

"There's work to do," she said, stepping around him.

He sighed, then led the way to the broken fence.

Sin frowned at her as she walked past him.

"What?" she asked.

Sin started to speak, then locked his jaw and followed Braden.

Maggie felt like throwing her hands up in defeat. Sin's look had been accusatory. Though why he would accuse her of anything, she couldn't imagine. She hadn't done anything wrong.

Braden was the one who needed to be chastised. His behavior was deplorable.

Oh, bother anyway. They would soon reach the MacDouglas and then she wouldn't have to worry over it anymore. Then she could go back home, and Braden would be free to make lustful eyes at all the pretty lasses who caught his fancy.

Besides, she didn't need a man. She'd never in her life needed one. All they did was gulp down food without so much as a thank you, belch and sniff.

Why, she'd be better off with a pet pig.

And yet, deep in her heart, she didn't believe her words. For it was there she knew the truth. And not even the harshness of her thoughts could protect her from caring. Because she did care. She wanted Braden for herself and the thought that he could just dismiss her and claim another woman cut her to her soul.

Saddened, Maggie joined the men at the fence and they worked in silence.

Once the fence had been mended, Seamus brought their food.

They barely made it into the stable with their platters before the storm broke. Sin shut the door as thunder clapped and hard raindrops pattered against the wood.

Maggie paused and looked around the dim interior as Braden lit two lanterns.

Inside, the stable's worn wood was faded to a light tan, but the structure appeared sound. Two cows mooed from their stalls to her right, and an old nag chomped at its hay on her left. There were four nicer horses huddled in a large stall to the back of the stable.

Braden led them to the center of the building, where bales of hay could provide makeshift tables and chairs. He sat on the one closest to the door while Sin sat to his left. Maggie took the smallest bale, farthest from the door, and set her platter on it.

As they ate quietly, the rain pelted the roof and more thunder rumbled.

" 'Tis a good thing we stopped here," Sin said after a few minutes.

"Aye," Braden agreed. "It would have been a miserable night otherwise."

To Maggie, it already was.

When they finished eating, Braden gathered up their platters and cups. "I'll return these to Seamus."

Maggie narrowed her eyes on him and the lie he was spilling. Did he honestly think she was too stupid to know what he had planned?

"What?" Braden asked innocently as he caught her glare.

Averting her gaze, she said nothing as he shook his head at her and walked off. If he was that dense, then she truly had nothing to say to him.

Still, she fumed. Did he honestly think she didn't know what he was going to do? He wouldn't give those dishes to Seamus; it was Tara he was aiming for.

Damn him!

"Why don't you hit him and get it over with?" Sin asked as soon as they were alone.

Maggie looked up to see him reclining on his own pile of hay. "I beg your pardon?"

Sin tugged his boots off and stretched his legs out. "If looks could kill, Braden would be smeared all over yon wall."

"That's right," she said churlishly, "side with your brother. After all, 'tis the right of your gender to strut around after anything in a skirt."

In a royal tiff, Maggie ignored Sin as she pulled her sleeping plaid from her pack. She struggled to make a pallet and as she worked, her pain over Braden built until tears gathered in her eyes and fell down her cheeks.

Angrily, she wiped them away.

"Maggie," Sin said with a tenderness in his voice that she wouldn't have thought him capable of. "Why don't you tell Braden how you feel?"

"Why?" she asked, her voice breaking on a sob. "So he can laugh? Or worse, I could have him for a night or two, but then so could *any* woman. Don't you understand?"

Tossing his boots aside, Sin laughed bitterly. "You ask a man who has never known love or kindness whether or not he understands your need to feel special? Of course I do. But while you condemn Braden for what he might do, let me ask you this. Have you ever really known him?"

Maggie sniffed and looked at him as if he were daft. "Of course. I've known him all my life."

Sin snorted. "No, you haven't. You may have seen him all your life, but you've never known the *real* him. If you had, you would know just how foolish your fears are."

"What do you mean?"

Sin's gaze intensified. "If you truly knew Braden, then you would know Braden would sooner gut himself than hurt someone he loves."

"What has that to do—"

"Think about it, Maggie."

She did, but at the moment, she felt completely stupid, for she had no idea what he was talking about.

"As the youngest of five headstrong boys," Sin continued, "Braden learned to negotiate peace between us. If you hit one of us, we'll hit back instantly, without thought. If you raise a fist or sword to Braden, what does he do?"

Maggie didn't hesitate with her answer. "He tries to talk you out of using it."

"Aye, but is he a coward?"

"Nay," she snapped defensively. "I've never known him to shirk from a fight."

"That's right. And do you know why he's like that?"

She shook her head.

"Unlike me, Braden doesn't like to hurt anyone."

Sin had yet to tell her anything she didn't already know, and none of that bore any importance on why she was angry at Braden. "What has this to do with his womanizing?"

Sin breathed as if exasperated with her. Although why he should be, she couldn't imagine. After all, he was the one being cryptic. She was merely trying to follow his logic.

"Tell me," he said, "how many women do you think he's been with?"

"By all accounts I've heard, nearly every woman in Kilgarigon, London, and pretty much any other place he's ever visited."

"By whose accounts?"

"The women who brag about him."

"Have you never thought about how odd it is that he has been with all these women yet there are no bastards of his roaming about?"

Maggie froze while smoothing her plaid over the straw. She'd never considered that. "But he has never denied it."

"Of course he hasn't. He's a man."

She ran through her mind all the years she'd

known him. The time she'd saved him from being mobbed by the girls of the village. Even today, the way Tara had gone after him.

Come to think of it, she seldom knew him to actively pursue a woman. Most of the time, he was running from them.

"Are you telling me he's had no women?" she asked suspiciously.

Sin laughed. "Nay. I'm sure he's had plenty, but I think some accounts are seriously exaggerated. Personally, I've only known him to take three women successfully."

"Successfully?"

"Aye, due to his reputation, I've noticed that most brothers and fathers tend to keep a close eye on him and whatever woman he's around. Most of his encounters were cut short before he could, shall we say, finish the transaction."

Now that she thought about it, she knew a number of such events herself. Indeed, some of the juicier interruptions had kept the village gossipmongers happy for weeks on end.

"Why are you telling me this?" she asked.

Sin averted his gaze as he unstrapped his sword from his hips and laid it down by his side. "Because Braden likes you. More than I've ever seen him like anyone else, and I can't stand to see him so misjudged. I think you owe it to both of you to give him a chance."

He met her gaze. "You know, Maggie, Braden can't help the way he looks, nor can he help the women who run after him. But he would sooner cut his arm off than hurt someone he loves."

At last she understood what he'd meant earlier. "You're saying he would never stray?"

"Not if he loved you. Believe me, I know my brother well enough to say, without doubt, that he would never leave a woman he truly loved for another."

"But he doesn't love *me*," she said, her voice breaking.

"Are you sure of that?"

Maggie's breath caught in her throat. Was he implying . . .

Surely not. Why on earth would Braden have any tender feelings for her?

"Are you saying he loves me?" she asked doubtfully.

"I'm not sure," he answered honestly. "But I do know he's a different man around you than he is other women."

"Different how?"

Sin shrugged. "It's hard to explain exactly. He's just more at ease with you. Teases you in ways I've never seen him tease anyone else."

"And how would *I* know if he loved me?"

Sin gave another bitter laugh.

He looked up as if addressing the Lord Himself. "Again, she asks a man who has never known love," he muttered. Then, louder, he said, "How does anyone ever know if they're truly loved or not? You just have to take a chance and see."

He seared her with the intensity of his gaze. "But I can tell you this: If someone were after something I wanted, I wouldn't stand in here weeping about it. I'd go take action on the matter."

His raked her with a cold stare. "I thought you were a fighter. Or are you willing to just give up on your dreams?"

"I'm willing to fight," she said.

Aye, that she was.

Stiffening her spine, she rose to her feet and went to find Braden and his strumpet.

Because if there was any truth to Sin's words, then she might actually have a chance at the man of her dreams. And if that was true, then she wouldn't stop until she had him at the altar.

Chapter 12

"Och, now, what a big, bonny man, you are," Tara purred as she took the platters and cups from Braden and set them inside the back door of her cottage.

Braden smiled at her as she closed the door and stepped out beneath the small overhang that protected the back door from the rain. It was a tight space, but it easily accommodated both of them.

The light from the cottage's window lit the area just enough that they could see each other.

A flash of lightning highlighted her face and the dark hunger in her blue eyes.

Aye, he'd be tasting a bit of heaven in a few minutes, and he couldn't wait to put an end to his celibacy.

Braden braced his arm above Tara's head, against the doorframe, and let his gaze roam her voluptuous body. She had one of those figures that could drive a man to distraction. Large, lush breasts where a man could bury his face and hands, among other things, and a tiny, inviting waist. Her hips flared gently, and by the way she was rubbing herself against him, he could tell she knew quite a few tricks to please a man.

And then the unimaginable happened as she glided her hand over his chest.

His body did nothing.

Nay, it couldn't be!

Instantly his smile faded.

Tara pressed her breasts against his chest and ran her arms about his neck. She breathed in his ear, stirring his wet hair, before she took his earlobe between her teeth and ran her tongue along the edge of it.

Normally, such actions would have his head reeling, and he'd be feverishly relieving her of her clothes.

But tonight . . .

Well, he couldn't say it wasn't pleasurable, because it was. Yet somehow, it wasn't satisfying to him. Worse, his body only stirred a bit. It was far from the fiery loins he'd been having the last few days.

And in that instant he knew why.

He wanted Maggie.

Dear saints in heaven! It was all he could do not to curse aloud as Tara ran her nails down his spine. And nothing happened. No chills, no . . .

Well, his body did perk up a bit as she rubbed her hand against his groin. Still, it wasn't the same reaction he'd had even last night when Maggie had teasingly displayed her more conservative, fully clothed cleavage at him.

Determined to prove himself wrong, Braden took Tara's chin in his hand, tilted her head back, and kissed her deeply.

She met his kiss fully and with the practiced ease of a woman who was well versed in the art of lovemaking. She could ride a man well, there was no doubt about it.

But still his body and mind remained painfully disinterested.

What he really wanted was the bold, innocent kiss of a redheaded hellion. This woman in his arms was nothing more than a poor substitute, and his body knew it.

Damn it straight to hell!

How could he want Maggie so? She made him insane. She was stubborn, opinionated and the last thing she wanted to do was please a man.

And yet . . .

I am a fool! A stupid, cursed fool who should have his head ripped from his shoulders.

Suddenly his and Tara's embrace seemed tawdry and vile. Despicable. And if Maggie should ever learn of it, it would crush her.

"I can't do this," he said, pulling back from Tara.

Nay, he couldn't, not while the true object of

his desire was waiting in the stable with his brother.

"Me da is already in bed," Tara said. "He'll never know." She reached for the laces of his shirt.

Braden caught her hands in his and took a step back. "You're a beautiful lass," he said. "But I'm afraid my mind is somewhere else tonight."

Tara licked her lips suggestively. "I could make you forget all about that one who holds your thoughts."

How he wished that were so.

"Good night, Tara," he said, releasing her and heading back to the stable. And with every step he took through the pouring rain, he cursed himself and Maggie.

What was he going to do?

Dear God, did he already love her?

Nay, his mind bellowed. He couldn't love her. He refused to allow himself to love a woman. Love made a man weak. It made him blind and foolish.

What if she one day asked him to forsake his blood as his mother had done his father? Or Isobail had done with Kieran and Ewan?

It was lust, he decided. He'd merely had a taste of Maggie and liked it.

Worse was the fact that he knew he couldn't even bed her to get her out of his system. He would never take that from her.

Throwing his head back, he wished the bloody

lightning would strike him dead where he stood. Because there was no way out for him, and no peace to be had.

Rain pelted Maggie's body, virtually blinding her, and soaking her clothes as she left the stable and started across the yard toward the house.

She was sure to find Braden there with one of the lasses. And she had a pretty good idea which one of them would be wrapped about him.

Her teeth clenched to stave off the pain, she rounded the edge of the stable.

A loud bleating caught her attention.

Squinting through the rain, she saw two shapes tussling nearby. It appeared to be two farm animals, no doubt doing something she shouldn't interrupt.

Maggie started to ignore them until a flash of lightning showed her the outline of a man's body.

Stunned, she froze, unable to believe her eyes.

Until another flash of lightning flared and she again saw the man pulling at the tiny beast.

Maggie smiled. She'd know that well-muscled form anywhere. Even when it was wringing wet and tugging at some poor, hapless animal.

Maggie rushed toward them to see a small sheep caught in the fence. Braden was kneeling in the mud, trying to free the little beastie.

Relief poured through her at the sight. He wasn't in another woman's arms! She felt like crying out in happiness. He had only stopped to free the animal.

She ran to his side.

"What are you doing out here?" he asked as she stopped beside him.

Unwilling to admit her suspicions, she changed the subject. "Can I do anything to help?"

"Aye, get back inside before you catch your death."

It was all she could do not to kiss him. At that moment, he was more beautiful to her than he had ever been before, and she felt terrible that she had so misjudged him. "Let me see if I can help." She knelt down and held on to the sheep.

"Keep her still," Braden said as he stood up, then leaned over the railing to free the animal's hind leg.

The sheep jerked and bleated again.

Lifting up a piece of wood that had fallen, Braden finally freed it.

The sheep took off running across the yard and vanished into the night.

"We need to get you inside," Braden said, taking her by the hand and running with her back into the stable.

Oh, how she wanted to shout! He was such a good, sweet man.

Sin had been right. Braden was her perfect hero.

Braden opened the door for her and the two of them entered the musky building.

"You're chilled to the bone," Braden snapped at her as she shivered just inside the doorway. "What were you thinking when you went out there?"

She responded by sneezing.

"Bless you," he said, retrieving a plaid and wrapping her up in it. He urged her toward the only empty stall, in the back by the four horses. "Now go get out of those clothes before you become ill."

Smiling up at him, Maggie nodded, then went behind the gate where she could have a bit of privacy. She heard Braden walking, but didn't look up to see where he was.

"Why didn't you stop her?" Braden demanded of Sin.

Maggie frowned at the rage she heard coming from Braden. It was so unlike him to be angry over anything, especially something as minute as a simple dousing.

"I didn't think anything of it," Sin said, his tone level and calm.

"Well, you should have."

"Ease off, little brother. I don't care for your tone." This time, she heard the note of warning in Sin's voice.

Braden growled at Sin.

Quickly she removed her wet plaid, binding and saffron shirt, then wrapped the dry plaid around her. She stood on her tiptoes to ask one of the men to bring her a new shirt, but the words died on her lips as she caught sight of Braden's back.

His *naked* back.

Her mouth went dry as her eyes feasted on the bare, tawny skin that gleamed in the candlelight. She'd known all her life that Braden was well formed, but never had she guessed exactly how fine a body he had.

A wealth of bronze flesh was stretched tight over muscles so toned that the sight made her burn.

Oblivious to her attention, he continued talking to Sin as he dropped his plaid and bared the whole length of his backside to her.

Her head light, she feared for a moment she might faint. He was gorgeous, absolutely gorgeous! And no matter how hard she tried, she couldn't tear her gaze away from his firm, golden buttocks that begged for a woman's caress.

She placed her hand on the stall to steady herself. White-hot desire shot through her as she imagined running her hand down his spine and feeling those tight muscles rippling beneath her palms. Touching those toned legs that were shadowed by short dark hairs.

Her breasts tightened as heat and longing swept through her.

Turn around, she begged silently, craving a look at the whole of him.

If his front looked half as good as his rear . . .

Braden turned his head and caught her staring at him. Maggie gasped in panic as his gaze held hers enthralled.

Instead of being embarrassed by his state of undress, Braden gave her a slow, wicked smile.

Maggie's face burst into flames and she quickly ducked back behind the stall. Oh, dear heaven, he had caught her!

She covered her face with her hands and wished she could vanish into the very floor.

Oh, good Lord, oh, good Lord!

"Did you need something?" Braden's taunting voice haunted her.

"I need a shirt," she called out, wishing that's what she'd done the first time. Why, oh, why had she stuck her head over the stall?

A few seconds later, Braden brought her one.

The roguish grin on his face horrified her. "Is there anything else you be needing?" he asked her.

Averting her gaze, Maggie shook her head. She would never be able to look him in the face again. " 'Tis all I require."

"You're sure about that?"

"Quite."

"If you're sure, then . . . I mean, I could—"

"I'm fine," she snapped, cutting him off. Then she made the mistake of looking up again.

The light, teasing look in his eyes took her breath away. The scoundrel was toying with her.

"You scurrilous knave," she said, but in spite of her best efforts, her own smile broke through.

"Scurrilous?" he asked playfully.

And as he ran his gaze over her body, she became all too keenly aware of the fact that she wore nothing save a thin red and black plaid draped over her shoulders. Good heavens, she was practically naked and he was right in front of her!

Flustered, she shifted. "Might I have a moment to dress?" she asked.

He cocked a brow at her. "I don't know about that. I rather enjoy the sight of you there."

She held the shirt up to cover her bare shoulder.

He laughed at her feeble attempt to cover herself. "Get dressed," he said, then turned his back to her.

Breathing a sigh of relief, Maggie quickly dressed, then left the stall.

Without a word or glance, Sin walked past her and climbed up to the stable's loft.

"What's he doing?" she asked Braden as she rejoined him.

"I'm leaving the two of you alone," Sin's muffled voice answered from above.

Braden tilted his head up to stare at the wooden beams above their heads. "Like it would matter, since we know you can hear everything we say?"

"Aye, well, I'm a pervert, not a voyeur."

Braden laughed. However, Maggie wasn't overly amused by Sin's blasé words.

She hung her wet plaid and shirt up on the stall door where the cows were.

Braden moved to stand behind her, so close that she could feel him. She turned to find him holding another plaid. His eyes dark and beguiling, he used it to dry her hair.

Maggie couldn't move as she felt his strong hands rub the cloth against her head in a sensual rhythm that stole her breath. Chills spread through her as she remembered the sight of his naked back.

At that moment, she wanted to kiss him. More so than ever before.

Until he spoke. "Now tell me why you were outside."

Her eyes flew open as his hands ceased drying her hair.

Unwilling to let him know she had suspected him of such knavery, she averted her gaze to the floor. "Nothing."

"Nothing?" he repeated in disbelief. "What, you just felt like taking a stroll during a torrential downpour?"

He dipped his head until he caught her gaze. "You went to spy on me, didn't you?"

How did he know?

Och, but the man picked a fine time to start being intuitive!

"What makes you think that?" she asked evasively.

"Instinct." A strange emotion darkened his eyes. One she couldn't fathom, but it looked surprisingly like guilt. "Did you think to find me with Tara?"

Her cheeks grew warm. She felt so foolish that she had ever doubted him. But she could see she wasn't going to get away without telling him exactly why she had gone outside in the rain.

Sighing, she nodded. "Well, you did intimate earlier today that you were interested in her."

"How? By talking to her?"

"Nay, by *flirting* with her."

He looked aghast. "Flirting?"

"Aye," she said defensively. After all, she had made the assumption based on his actions. "The way you look at a woman like she's the only thing in the world to you, like you see no other."

"Really?" he asked, his voice caught between pride and disbelief.

"Aye."

"You think this is something I always do?"

Maggie stiffened. "I know it is. Why do you think women are so mad for you?"

"My dashing good looks, of course."

Oh, the man was arrogant, and she couldn't believe she was catering to that ego of his. She should stop, and yet, for some reason, she couldn't. "Your brothers all have that, and yet they have never been as pursued as you."

"I always assumed it was because I was charming while they are all sour."

"What you call charming is flirting. And it is irresistible."

He laughed so hard, he choked.

"What?" Maggie asked, wondering what had struck him as so amusing.

He sobered to a degree. "I'm thinking you've always managed to resist it."

"That's because you've never used it with me. To you, I might as well be a stump."

He truly looked stricken by her words. A deep frown furrowed his brows. "I beg your pardon?"

"It's true," she said, her throat tight as she spilled out her observations to him. "You look at other women like you can already feel them in your arms, but when it comes to me, you look right past me. 'Tis an awful habit that has always hurt my feelings."

"Is that why you bit me when you were eleven?"

Shut up, Maggie.

But she didn't listen. Before she could stop herself or think better of it, the truth came spilling out. "Aye. All I ever wanted was for you to see *me.*"

She saw him pause and reflect on her words. When he looked back at her, his gaze was probing. Disturbing. "Perhaps I have misjudged you, but I wonder if you're not as guilty of that as I am."

"What do you mean?"

"Have you ever *really* looked at me and seen me? Or have you been as the others and all you've ever really seen are my looks? Because I guarantee it wasn't my personality you were ogling a minute ago, but rather my posterior."

Maggie opened her mouth in shock, then closed it hurriedly. Indignation ripped through her. How dare he accuse her of something so crass? She wasn't one of those shallow maids, to have her head turned by simple handsomeness. "That's absurd!"

"Is it? If you know me so well, then tell me my favorite color."

"Green," she answered without hesitation. "Dark green. The same color as your mother's eyes. The same dark green you have in most of the plaids you choose to wear."

By the look on his face, she could tell her answer took him completely by surprise. He couldn't believe she knew that about him.

But that wasn't all she knew. And before she could stop herself, she rattled off more things she knew about him. "Your favorite foods are roasted venison with stewed cabbage and elderberry tarts. You drink dark ale around other men, but in truth, you prefer mulled wine. When you're at home, you always have a cup of warm milk sprinkled with cinnamon before you go to bed. Your favorite tale is Dierdre of the Sorrows, and though you'd never admit it and you try to look disinterested when they play, you like to hear bards sing."

He looked completely baffled by her admission. "How do you know all that?"

"Because, I've loved you all my life."

Chapter 13

Braden didn't know which of them was more stunned by her confession. As soon as the words were out of her mouth, Maggie looked terrified.

He *felt* terrified.

Indeed, he couldn't move, couldn't breathe, as he stared at her while her words tore through him.

Eternity seemed to pass as they stood just a foot apart with her words hanging like a pall between them.

"Nay," he said at last. "You can't love me."

"Why not?" she asked, her voice filled with the same pain he saw reflected in her amber eyes.

"Because you can't."

Before she could move, he turned about and left the stable in search of a way to cope with the news she had given him.

But all he could focus on was the raw agony tearing through his soul. He didn't want her to love him. He didn't want any woman to love him, at least not for any longer than an hour or two.

Dear saints, how had this happened?

And why?

Braden paused at the edge of the stable and leaned back against the faded wood as he covered his eyes with his hand. The rain wasn't quite as bad as it had been earlier, but it still soaked him as he sought someplace safe from her clutches.

Over and over, her words echoed in his mind. She loved him. Loved him and knew things about him that he didn't think any woman had ever known. Not even his mother.

And all the while, he had ignored her. Had never paid a bit of attention to her.

He didn't know which made him feel worse.

Pain sliced through his heart. Emotions he couldn't define assailed him. Dear God, it felt as if someone were cleaving his chest in two.

"Braden?" he heard Maggie calling to him.

"Saints preserve me," he whispered, torn between the desire to make love to her and to run as fast as he could.

Before he could make his decision, she came rushing to his side.

Braden glared at her and cursed. "Woman, have you no sense, to be running back out into the rain?"

She arched a brow at him as she crossed her

arms over her chest in a feeble effort to keep herself warm. "I could say the same of you."

"One would think you'd know I wanted to be alone."

"Why?"

"Because I do. Now go back inside and dry off."

She lifted her chin stubbornly. "I'll go in when you do."

Exasperation filled him. "I canna believe you've made it to adulthood without one of your brothers choking the life out of your stubborn throat."

She took his angry words without flinching. "They have little room to talk since they were such good teachers on that account. Now I would have an answer from you."

Braden closed his eyes as he struggled for control of himself. He didn't know what to do or say. "Go back inside."

"Answer me."

Braden wished it were that simple. His feelings were complex and deep. All his life he had been loved. Every woman he'd ever known had whispered her undying devotion to him while they frolicked and played, and at the end of the day they had all married someone else.

At ten-and-six he had made the mistake of asking Nera ingen Alward to marry him. Two weeks later, she had sworn herself to Colum.

Her reason stung him to this day: *Braden, why*

would I marry you? You've a pretty face and are a hot tumble between my legs, but Colum has money the likes of which you canna fathom. Besides, he travels much, which will leave us time aplenty to play.

He ground his teeth. He had shown her in the end. His current assets made a mockery of Colum's puny home. Even so, it had never erased the pain in his youthful, broken heart.

Nay, women were fickle, faithless creatures. And unlike his brothers, he would never believe their honied lies.

But therein was the problem. When such words came from the lips of Maggie, he *wanted* to believe them.

Why that was so, he didn't know. He only knew that it would destroy what little was left of his heart to find out she was playing him falsely.

Maggie narrowed her gaze on him. "You call me stubborn, yet here you stand, more ready to drown yourself than answer a simple question."

Against his will, Braden reached out to her. He cupped her icy cheek in his hand. "You're freezing."

"I know."

He gave a half laugh at her matter-of-fact tone. "If you have loved me for so long, why have you never spoken of it?"

"Because I didn't think you'd want to hear it."

Maggie was far too astute. But then, she'd always been that way.

Her eyes turned dull. "Look, Braden, I'm not a

fool. I know I can never have you. I know you don't share my feelings and I wish I'd never spoken of them. Unfortunately, I can't take them back. Can we just forget what I said and go back inside before both of us catch our deaths?"

Braden nodded. Not because he was afraid for himself—he'd survived much worse conditions than this—but because he didn't want to see her sick. The depths to which he would go to keep her safe didn't bear investigating. In truth, that place in his heart where he found concern for her frightened him more than anything else ever had.

Reluctantly, he took her by the arm and led her inside.

When they entered the stable, Sin's voice rang out, "Guess you two will have to run around naked for a bit, since all your clothes are now wet."

"Actually," Braden said as he wrung the rain from his hair, "I was thinking of raiding your pack for some clothes."

"I somehow thought as much."

Braden handed Maggie one of Sin's plaids and his spare shirt.

Maggie took them and quickly changed in private, all the while her thoughts churning. Why had she ever spoken those words? And why did they torment Braden so?

The man had always been an enigma to her, but no more so than he was tonight. Shouldn't love make someone happy?

She scoffed at the thought. When had loving Braden *ever* made her happy? The sad truth of the matter was that loving Braden had only caused her misery. Nothing but misery.

Crestfallen, she belted the plaid.

When she returned to the center of the stable, she saw Braden wrapped only in a plaid, his chest bare and glistening in the low light. Her throat dried at the sight.

It was going to be a long, *long* night.

Before she could give the matter any more thought, Sin jumped to the floor. "Hope there's a way to bolt the doors."

Maggie frowned at his odd behavior and comment. "Why?"

"There's a sortie of women headed our way, and by the looks of them, we could be in for a nasty battle," Sin said as he made his way to the door.

Maggie's frown deepened. What was he talking about?

Braden cursed as he reached the door first and searched for a latch. "Wouldn't you know it," he said bitterly.

"There's nothing to bar it," Sin finished for him. "Well, doesn't this beat the devil?"

Even more perplexed, she stared at them. They looked as if the angel of death were upon them and they had forgotten to get last rites. "They're just women. Tell them you're not interested—"

"And they'll try and change our minds," Braden interrupted.

Maggie rolled her eyes at his dire tone. "No, they won't. You forget I'm a woman. I know how they think."

"And I know how they act," Braden said as he returned to her side. "They'll not leave until they get what they want."

Maggie laughed at his ego. "You're being ridiculous, Braden. You're not *that* irresistible."

His look bore into hers. "You think not? Then explain to me why Tara is on her way here after I already told her I had no interest in taking her."

Before she could think to respond, Seamus's three eldest daughters threw back the doors to the stable.

"Knock, knock, lads," Tara said, her hands on her hips as she surveyed them. "We've come to see to your comfort."

Chapter 14

Sin darted away from the women to the back of the stable.

The *I told you so* look from Braden was such that Maggie almost laughed. Until the youngest of the women headed straight toward her with a swing to her hips and a look in her eyes that told Maggie *exactly* what the woman was after.

Her.

Oh, bother me! She'd better move—fast.

Maggie started for the stall behind her, but tripped and fell.

"Och, now," the girl said as she bent over Maggie and pressed one pale hand to Maggie's forehead. "Do you have a boo-boo I need be kissing?"

The girl's lips were dangerously close to her own as the girl pressed her breasts against Maggie's arm.

Seeking a way to pry the hoyden off her, Maggie curled her lips in disgust.

"Uh, nay," Maggie said, dropping her voice an octave as she struggled to roll out from under the girl. "My boo-boo is just fine. Thanks."

"Now, ladies," Braden said as he sidestepped Tara's outstretched arms. "What would your da be saying if he caught you out here?"

Tara backed him against the wall.

Undaunted by Braden's evasive tactics, Tara laughed. "Oh, he'd be after the lot of you for sure. But he's off asleep already. Now," she said, grabbing his plaid and pulling his face closer to hers. "How bout another taste of those sweet lips of yours?"

Braden ducked and twisted out of her clutches.

Maggie was appalled. Never in her life had she seen such. Braden had been right about the women.

Mo chreach! They were in serious trouble.

Just as the girl reached to grope Maggie, strong arms pulled Maggie back.

In one fluid motion, Sin lifted her from the ground, tossed her up on a horse and smacked the rear of the beast. The horse shrieked, then bolted from the stable at a dead run.

Struggling to bring the horse under control, Maggie panicked.

The horse flew into the woods with the bit between its teeth. She pulled at the reins, but the horse paid her no heed as it dashed through limbs that clawed at her, threatening to knock her out of the saddle. Her heart pounding, she leaned forward and latched on to the horse's neck, praying she didn't fall off and kill herself.

It was probably a good five minutes before Sin and Braden caught up to her and brought her horse under control. Braden leaned over and took the bridle in his hand, then used his horse to slow hers. Her heart still pounded in her ears as she gave a quick prayer of thanks for the deliverance.

"Are you all right?" Braden asked her.

Still too terrified to speak, Maggie took deep breaths and nodded.

Braden patted her arm comfortingly, then turned on his brother with a furious glare. "Och, man, what have you done to us now?"

"I saved your bloody arse. What do you think would have happened had the women discovered Maggie wasn't a lad? Were you ready to explain?"

A tic started in Braden's jaw. "Now we'll be hanged for horse thievery!"

Sin shook his head. "I left more than enough gold for these nags. Their owners will be thrilled to have it."

Maggie watched as some of the tenseness faded from Braden. "My thanks, then."

Sin shifted in his saddle and cast a pitying glance to Braden. "You know, little brother, it seems to me you must live in eternal hell. I can't take you anywhere that the women don't seize upon you like the last morsel of their last supper."

Braden reached up and raked his hand over his own neck. "Aye, I just wished you'd acted sooner. That Tara had nails like a hawk. I swear, I think I'm bleeding."

It was then Maggie realized the truth of Braden. He wasn't a conscienceless rapscallion out to seduce any woman he found. Indeed, other than a little flirting, he hadn't really done anything to make Tara pursue him.

And though both he and Sin had tried to tell her that, it wasn't until this moment that she actually believed it.

"Where are we to sleep now?" she asked the men as they slowly picked their way through the dark woods on horseback and with their hastily gathered belongings. "And what are we going to do with the horses?"

It was Braden who answered her. "Since we have the horses, I say we ride them into the Mac-Douglas lands until we start to draw notice, then we leave them to graze. As for the night, anyone feel up to riding through it?"

Sin growled. "*Now* you think to ride? Where was that thought two days ago before I wore my legs out walking?"

Braden laughed. "You should be grateful. Better these nags be stolen than your warhorse or my Deamhan."

Sin grudgingly ceded the point.

"I would just as soon see this behind us," Maggie said quietly. In truth, too much had already happened on this journey and all she really wanted was to get this last confrontation over and done with.

So they rode in silence.

Long after midnight, and once the rain had ceased to fall, Maggie began to doze in the saddle.

Braden paused as he saw her nodding off. Afraid she might fall and hurt herself, he pulled her into his own saddle.

She awoke with a start.

"Shhh," he said. "I didn't want you to fall. Go back to sleep."

Instead of the argument he'd expected, she nodded once, rested her head against his chest and instantly renewed her sleeping.

Her trust amazed him. But not nearly as much as the strange tenderness he felt in his heart as he gazed down at her russet head leaning against his bare chest. Her breath tickled ever so slightly as she breathed against his shoulder. And it was all he could do not to cover her lips with his own and run his hand through her short curls.

His body roared to life, demanding her soft form.

For once, Braden took comfort in it. After what had transpired with Tara, he had begun to wonder foolishly if perhaps something were wrong with him. But the fire in his groin for her confirmed his earlier suspicion. It was Maggie he wanted. Maggie alone.

He shook his head.

Who would have ever thought that he, Braden MacAllister, would be pining away for plain little Maggie ingen Blar and her ugly shoes?

Marry her.

The words flitted across his mind so fast that he almost missed them. And for a minute, he allowed the thought to tempt him.

But it was impossible. He refused to marry a woman he might be in love with. 'Twould be suicide.

"What is on your mind?" Sin asked all of a sudden.

Startled, Braden looked up to see Sin turned around in the saddle, watching him. "What's that?"

"You're looking a bit pensive back there and I was wondering what thought you had tormenting you."

"Who says I'm being tormented?"

Sin reined his horse to where they could ride apace of each other. "Oh, I don't know. Perhaps that death grip you have on Maggie and the way you're looking at her as if you can't decide whether to cradle her or to toss her from your horse."

Braden hated the way Sin could read him so easily. "That is one uncanny ability you have there, brother. No wonder those English friends of yours swear you sold your soul to the devil."

Sin looked at him stoically. "A man has to have a soul before he can sell it."

Braden grew quiet. There was a lot hidden in those words. Years of pain and suffering. His brother had lived through the worst life had to offer and his strength was amazing. But more than that, Braden felt guilty for it. The other lairds had sent their youngest sons as hostages to the English. And by rights it should have been him who suffered in Sin's stead.

If he lived to be a thousand years old, he would never come to terms with the fact that Sin had gone while he had stayed.

"Is there any way you will ever forgive my mother for what she did?" Braden asked at last.

Even in the dark, Braden could feel Sin's hatred. "They tell me anything is possible. But since I can't forgive my own mother for what she did, why should I ever forgive yours?"

Braden said nothing. He remembered that fateful day every bit as well as Sin did. The day King David had come to their castle and demanded a son to help make peace with the English king after the war they had waged for northern England.

His father had turned a wary, thoughtful eye to each of his sons. The five of them had collectively held their breaths in fear, knowing one of them would have to go.

Lochlan had bravely taken a step forward when all of a sudden their mother grabbed him and pulled him back. She gathered her four sons to her side and left Sin standing alone. Isolated.

"You take a son of mine and I swear I'll kill myself," she had said.

His father, who had loved her with all his being, had offered no argument. And to this day, Braden could still see the horrified look on Sin's face as he realized his father was about to betray him.

And why.

"Go ahead, old man," Sin had snarled bravely, balling up his fists. "Send the mongrel bastard back to England while you coddle your Scottish whore."

Their father had answered Sin's angry words with a vicious backhand that had made the boy stagger. "No son of mine insults my wife."

"Then I'm no son of yours." His eyes filled with rage and loathing, Sin had straightened from the blow that had left blood trailing down his face.

Then he had spat his blood at his father.

Their father had raked the blood off his face, his lips curled in disgust. "You're nothing to me, boy," he had said coldly.

The pain on Sin's face at that moment was forever etched in Braden's memory. "Tell me something, old man, that I don't already know."

King David's men had taken Sin then, and only Braden and his brothers had screamed out in protest.

His father had merely turned his back and called for their nurse to take them to their room.

Not once had his father looked back at Sin, or even mentioned his name. From that day forward, his father had lived as if Sin had never existed.

Braden had never forgiven his father for that.

And it had been on that day when his eldest brother had left that Braden had sworn never to fall in love. He'd never allow a woman to mean more to him than his own blood. Never turn his back on a son because of a woman's vindictiveness.

It was for that reason alone he'd been careful over the years. Careful not to leave behind a child to suffer for his actions, for he knew of the nightmares Sin had lived through. And hell would surely freeze before Braden allowed a child of his to suffer in such a manner.

Maggie mumbled in her sleep.

Braden cuddled her closer. She was such a mystery to him. That she would traverse this path for the sake of her brothers and the lives of the clansmen spoke a lot for her.

And he found himself wondering what choice she would have made in his mother's place. Would she have given up the child not hers, or would she have stood to defend all of them equally?

Och, now, what does it matter?

Who wants the seriousness of a wife?

But deep in his heart, he knew there lived a tiny piece of himself that really did want a family. Maggie was right. He did love the fanciful tales bards sang of women who would defend their families with their lives. He wanted that dream. A dream of that one perfect soul mate who would never ask more of him than he could give. An unselfish woman who would never betray his trust or his love.

And to his immense shock, he found himself looking at Maggie and wondering if perhaps she could be the one . . .

You're a fool, Braden MacAllister. And a damned one, at that.

Aye, he was. Already he'd allowed her to lead him off against his common sense on a fool's errand that would most likely get them killed.

A lass such as Maggie was poison to a man such as he.

No woman was worth his life. Not now, not ever.

Not even Maggie.

Chapter 15

They traveled through the night and well into the next day before they finally stopped for a rest.

While the men led the horses to the side of the makeshift camp to rub them down, Maggie prepared a light meal of what was left of their bread and cheese.

The entire morning had passed in silence, though whether from stress or fatigue, she wasn't sure. Braden had been strangely distant from her all day, which was odd given how gentle he'd been while she slept in his arms.

Several times in the night, she had jerked awake to find his arms surrounding her with warmth, and one time in particular she had felt him leaning his cheek against the top of her head while he cupped her face gently with one hand. She'd felt so safe then, so strangely wanted.

But from the moment she had awakened completely and he had stopped to let her ride her own horse, she had sensed a wall between them. Almost as if he had shut himself completely off from her.

Maggie didn't like that feeling. Not one little bit.

What does it matter? she asked herself. *By tomorrow, one way or the other, all this will be over.*

Suddenly pain struck her dead in the chest. Aye, this journey would end on the morrow.

Tomorrow they could all be dead.

She, Sin *and* Braden.

Maggie went cold as the reality of it came crashing down on her, and she set her food aside. Robby MacDouglas was every bit as likely to kill her as he was to listen to her. More so, in fact.

It was a sobering thought, and for the first time since she had started this journey, the full reality of it hit her. This could very well be her last day on earth.

Struggling to breathe, she looked around as if seeing the world for the very first time. She saw the beauty of the pines and oaks, of all the trees surrounding her. The way their gray and brown bark contrasted with the lush green forest. She felt the crispness of the grass beneath her as she sat cross-legged on the ground. Heard the gentle lullaby of the birds and insects as they moved around her. She smelled the bright sunshine that warmed her skin, the dew on the heather.

The world was a truly beautiful place.

Dear Lord, she didn't want to die. Not yet. Not while she had so much left to do!

Unbidden, a thousand wishes whirled through her mind simultaneously. All the things she had wanted to do in her life but never had the chance to do. She'd wanted to see Ireland just once, to go south and visit Hadrian's Wall. She'd wanted to watch her children and grandchildren frolic across her yard as they hunted for dragon treasure and teased each other.

She'd looked forward to watching Anghus's infant son grow to manhood, teaching him to ride and pick berries. She'd even wanted to see Ian find a good lass and marry.

So many things she'd wanted to do, had always looked forward to doing.

Now her time for doing it might very well be up.

And then her gaze fell to Braden as he freed her horse to graze and started rubbing down his own. He lifted one strong hand up to brush a dark lock of hair from his damp brow.

Maggie froze. Of all the things she had wanted in her life, he was the one thing she regretted most not having. All the dreams she had dreamed of him, all the pretend kisses she had given her pillow—all that came rushing back to her.

And then she made a decision.

After all these years of living her life for others, there was one selfish act that she wanted.

If she did die on the morrow, there was one last thing she wanted to do. One regret she didn't want to have.

Braden left the horses to graze. He had started back toward Maggie when he noticed Sin sitting propped against a tree. He took two steps toward his brother before he realized Sin was sound asleep.

Smiling at the unusual event, Braden shook his head. So, his brother was human after all. There were times when even he had doubts.

Unwilling to disturb Sin, Braden tiptoed backward until he knew he wouldn't wake him.

As he drew closer to the camp, Braden forced himself not to look at Maggie. But it was difficult. He knew he had to keep distance between them, and yet it was the hardest thing he had ever tried to do in his life.

"While Sin is sleeping, I'm going to bathe," he said to her, retrieving his pack from the ground.

He had to give Sin credit. His brother had done a remarkable job of gathering most of their supplies before getting them out of Tara and her sisters' clutches. But then, speed of action and quick thinking under pressure were Sin's specialties.

When Maggie didn't speak to him, he glanced at her. She sat quietly alone, not paying him any heed.

No doubt I hurt her by ignoring her this morning. The pain of the thought sliced through him, and inwardly he cursed.

He should never have come on this trip. Never have volunteered to get the women out. If he hadn't spent so much time with Maggie the last two days, then he never would have known how much she meant to him. He could have lived out the whole of his life in blissful ignorance.

Sighing, he headed through the trees to the stream they'd been following.

He doffed his clothes and waded in, but not even the coldness of the water could squelch the fiery need he had for her. Any more than it could take her from his mind.

Braden dove under the water and did his best not to think of redheaded nymphs who were capable of stealing men's souls.

Maggie stared into the trees in the direction where Braden had vanished. Her hands shook as she debated what she should do.

Go on, her mind urged. *You already made the decision.*

Aye, she had made it, but she had yet to act upon it. It was the acting that gave her trouble. She knew Braden wouldn't turn her away.

But how would it change their relationship? Once she had carnal knowledge of him, they would never be able to go back to the way they had been before.

Of course, she really didn't want to go back to being invisible around him.

What do you want?

"I want a miracle," she whispered.

A full-blown, walk-on-water miracle. She wanted Braden to be hers. And if she survived the meeting with the MacDouglas, she didn't want to kiss him good-bye and watch him wander off with another woman.

And if you die?

She trembled even more.

Closing her eyes, she tried to decide what to do. As she concentrated, an image of Braden holding her drifted through her mind. She could feel him, smell him.

Taste him.

All her life, she had wanted him, and him alone.

And it was then she realized the full depth of her love for Braden. Nay, she couldn't go to her grave or even another day without knowing the man who had stolen her heart.

Even if it ultimately meant letting him go, she wanted to know what it truly felt like to love him completely as a woman.

Her entire body shaking, Maggie rose slowly to her feet, then headed off through the trees in search of the only man she would ever love.

Braden grunted as he ran his hands through his sleek wet hair. It felt good to be clean again.

He bent at the waist to rinse his face. And as he straightened, he heard a slight splash behind him.

Before he could move, two shapely wet arms encircled his waist and pulled him back against two perfectly round breasts that caressed the hollow of his back.

"Braden?"

He froze at the sound of Maggie's voice in his ear as her moist, bare breasts burned a hole in his spine. He wanted to say something to her, but his throat was so tight, he could barely breathe.

"Would you let me make love to you?" she asked.

Oh, this is a dream! It has to be a dream.

Surely his little blossom wouldn't . . .

His thoughts scattered as she loosened her hold on his waist and stepped around him.

Good Lord, she was beautiful. More so than she'd ever been before.

His gaze darted over her glistening body, taking her in all at once. Her damp russet hair curled around her impish, freckled face. Her creamy, bare shoulders sparkled from the droplets of water that caught the rays of the sun.

But most of all, he gazed at her bare breasts, at the tight, taut peaks that begged for a lover's kiss. A lover's touch.

And at that moment, he wished the water wasn't so deep, for it reached to her navel and he wanted to see more of her.

"Maggie," he breathed. "What—"

"Shhh," she said, placing a finger to his lips. "Don't say anything, lest I change my mind." Her gaze raked his body with a hungry, almost desperate look. "And I don't want to change my mind."

Braden knew he should turn her away. It would be the noble, decent thing to do. But then, he had never been noble or decent.

And before he could decide anything, she reached out and ran her hand over his chest, across his own taut nipple, dragging her nails ever so gently over his flesh. A thousand chills erupted through him as his body burned from the inside out.

Why was she doing this?

Why would she want a man like him? It made no sense to him whatsoever.

She moved her hand from his lips, then dipped her head to where she could draw his nipple into her mouth and suckle it ever so tenderly.

Braden moaned from the pleasure her tongue and lips gave him. And then she did the most unbelievable thing of all: She dipped her hand beneath the water and cupped him in her hand. That gentle, hesitant touch of her fingers against his shaft went deeper than the physical. It touched him all the way to his unrepentant soul.

Dizzy and on fire, he was past the point of rational thought. All he could think of was finally

sating the deep hunger that had incessantly
gnawed at him since the moment he'd seen her
defying him at the kirk's door.

How he wanted her. It was beyond his understanding and it was a desperation so profound
that it shook him all the way to his heart.

Cupping her face in his hands, he tilted her
head up to where he could claim her lips with
his own.

She sighed into his mouth as she continued to
stroke his swollen shaft with her hand.

Reflexively, Braden's body arched against her
palm and fingers, letting her have her way with
him as he tasted the pure heaven of her mouth.

Maggie feared she might faint as her head
swam from the taste of him, from the silken feel
of his rigidness under her fingertips. Never had
she imagined what a man would feel like. Braden
was so strangely soft and hard at the same time.
Like velvet stretched over steel.

Aye, she wanted this man. And if this was the
only way she could have him, then she would
take it.

For this moment in time, he was hers, and she
would love him the way she'd always dreamed of
loving him.

With the whole of her heart.

There would be no holding back. No timidity.

She would never want any other man to touch
her like this. To kiss her. Hold her. Braden was the

only man she would ever burn for. To the devil with her fears.

Braden picked her up in his arms and waded with her back to the shore. He placed her down on the plaid she had stretched out on the bank for them.

"You had this all planned, didn't you?" he asked with a light, humorous note in his voice.

Maggie nodded.

"And if I had turned you away?" he asked.

"I wouldn't let you," she whispered, then she wrapped her arms around his neck and pulled his head to hers for another long, deep and satisfying kiss.

Braden didn't disappoint her as he plundered her mouth like a Viking of old. She sighed in contentment and ran her hands down his lean, hard back.

He was the man of her dreams and she was going to enjoy this.

His muscles danced and flexed beneath her palms as his chest rubbed against hers. Exciting her, teasing her. Pleasing her.

Oh, but the man felt good. He tasted even better.

Her hero. Her love.

How she wished she could keep him like this forever. Lost in this moment where there were only the two of them. No past, no future. Nothing to separate them.

It was perfect.

He left her lips and trailed a scorching kiss to her neck where he suckled and teased her flesh with his tongue and teeth. Maggie arched her back, writhing in pleasure as his hands skimmed over her body. Down her freckled arms, over her waist to where he cupped her hips in his hands.

As he moved toward her breasts, she stopped him.

He looked up with a frown.

"This is my fantasy," Maggie said with a sheepish smile.

Then Maggie rolled him onto his back and straddled his waist.

She took a moment to savor the feel of his hard, taut muscles caressing the sensitive place between her legs. It felt so strange the way those muscles contracted as he breathed. Instinctively, she pressed herself against him, eliciting a quiver of expectation through her body and a deep growl from Braden.

All the feelings she had buried surfaced then, and she gave herself over to her dreams and fantasies. To all the times in her life when she had imagined him at her mercy.

And for the moment, he was all hers. She felt strangely empowered and invigorated. He might leave her come the morning, but he would never forget her.

Never.

Braden stared up in awe of her as he felt the

hairs at the juncture of her thighs gently tease his belly.

"And just what does this fantasy of yours include?" he asked as he watched her watch him.

Her smile grew wider. She dipped her head toward his and instead of giving him the kiss he expected, she lowered her mouth on to his throat.

Braden hissed in pleasure at the heat of her mouth as she seared him. Her tongue darted over the stubble of his neck, teasing and tormenting him with wave after wave of ecstasy.

It was so strange. He couldn't count the women who had done that to him in the past, and yet none of them had ever made him feel this odd sense of rightness. This sense of wholeness.

And what terrified him most was the fact he couldn't push her away. He needed this in a way that defied explanation.

She leaned forward so that her breasts were flattened against his chest and he shook all over.

"Maggie," he breathed raggedly, running his hands over the smooth, satiny skin of her back.

Then she moved her mouth lower.

Slowly, thoroughly, she covered his chest and arms with her scorching kisses. Her breasts pounded against him, flaying his chest with pleasure as her hands explored every inch of his skin.

Braden couldn't remember a woman ever being so bold with him. One who seemed to get her own pleasure from giving it to him. It was incredible.

And in that moment, he realized just how much his little blossom meant to him.

Saints have mercy on his soul. Whatever was he going to do?

Push her away.

He'd sooner die, and yet he knew that he would have to leave her.

Don't think about it.

Nay, he wouldn't. He would just savor the moment and the woman. Live it without thought of tomorrow. Right now there was just the two of them and he wouldn't let anyone, not even himself, separate what they were sharing.

Maggie reveled in the sounds of Braden's moans and growls filling her ears. She should probably be embarrassed by her actions, but she had made up her mind. If she was going to do this, then she was going to do it completely and without reservation.

Before this day ended, she wanted to know him from the top of his head all the way down to his toes.

That thought foremost in her mind, she dipped her mouth to the flesh of his hipbone. Braden sucked his breath in sharply between his teeth as he quivered beneath her.

Maggie laughed in her throat as she continued her relentless exploration of him.

Who would have thought that such a brave, strong man could be laid low by a simple caress?

That knowledge gave her power and excited her all the more.

He was hers.

Braden buried his hand in her hair as he fought the urge to take control of the situation. He would have his chance to fill her shortly. For the moment, he would content himself with letting her have her way with him.

But it was hard. And getting harder by the minute.

She moved her hand again to cup the pulsing ache between his legs. And then, to his utter amazement, she moved her head and took him full into her mouth.

Braden shook all over as her tongue toyed with him. He hissed as he stared in awe of her auburn head buried between his thighs.

She had no idea what that sight did to him. Her selflessness, her giving. She wasn't just taking pleasure from him like his other lovers. She was sharing the moment with him in a way no one ever had before.

And he loved her for it.

Unable to stand any more, he had to touch her. To taste her.

Maggie looked up as Braden shifted his body. "Braden?"

He flashed a dimpled smile as he stretched out

beside her with his head toward her feet. He positioned his hips even with her head.

"Don't stop," he said, his eyes warm and wicked.

Before she could respond, he nudged her thighs apart and buried his lips against her.

Maggie closed her eyes and moaned at the feel of his tongue delving deep inside her.

Oh, it was incredulous. Never had she experienced such unbridled pleasure. Wanting to feel more, she opened her legs wider. He took her invitation.

She bit her lip and groaned deep in her throat, then returned to the tender ministrations she had been giving him.

The mutualness of it touched her profoundly. This equal sharing, equal giving. It was splendid. Heavenly.

And if they survived the MacDouglas, she was going to find some way to keep this man with her. No matter what it took.

She was a fighter. Would always be a fighter, and she wouldn't give up on Braden. Never. Not until he belonged to her both heart and soul.

Braden's head spun as he again felt her mouth and tongue close around him. He cupped her hips to him as he ran his tongue over her and felt her shiver in his arms.

She was incredible. And to think, all these years he had never once given her a second glance.

You were a fool!

Aye, he surely was. But not anymore. He would never again be blind to her.

Never again ignore her.

And the possessiveness he felt toward her scared him even more. Because at this moment, she had captured his heart in a way no other woman ever had. In a way he knew no other woman ever could.

She alone could destroy him. She alone held power over his heart, and he trembled at the new-found knowledge.

Maggie couldn't believe what was happening. Where she found the courage to do these things with Braden, she didn't know. But oh, how wondrous. The mutualness of their union touched her all the way to her soul. It was so deep, so fulfilling, so incredible that she never wanted this moment to end.

The heat of his mouth seared her as he teased and suckled. And even more incredible was the feel of his fingers plunging inside her. In and out and around. Her body quivered and jerked as her head reeled from the sensations.

She closed her eyes. It was too much for her. And just as she was sure she would die from it, her body exploded.

Maggie threw her head back and screamed out in release as the world spiraled and careened around her.

Never, never had she experienced such a thing.

And still his tongue tormented her.

"Oh, Braden," she sighed.

He laughed almost evilly as he kissed her thigh. "I'm not through with you yet," he said, his tone warning and yet somehow playful.

He rose up between her legs and positioned his body over hers. Maggie reached up and buried her hands in his hair as he used his knees to spread her legs wider.

He brought his lips down upon hers, then plunged himself deep inside her body.

Maggie froze as pain overrode her pleasure. "Braden?"

"Shhh," he whispered against her lips. "Give it time."

He leaned back away from her ever so slightly and reached his hand down between their bodies until he found her nub. Maggie quickly forgot the pain as he gently toyed with her body, building her pleasure again.

He was so thoughtful and kind. From what she'd heard of other men, she knew most didn't care whether or not they hurt a woman her first time. But Braden did.

And it was what she loved most about him.

Instinctively, she rubbed herself against him, impaling herself even more deeply than before.

Braden bit his lip as he felt her moving against him. "Aye, my love," he said, closing his eyes to savor the warm, tight heat of her body around his. "That's it."

His breathing ragged, he let her take control of the moment as she milked his body with hers.

Never had he felt the like.

Opening his eyes, he saw the look of wonder on her face. Aye, she liked being in charge.

Ever one to please her, Braden rolled over without withdrawing from her.

Maggie sighed as she found herself on top of him again. She stared in awe of him and at the strange feel of his body inside hers and between her legs.

His eyes dark and gentle, he reached up and cupped her breasts in his hands. She covered his hands with her own, then lifted her body up, drawing herself down his shaft.

"Aye," he breathed. "That's it."

And then his hand returned to cup her between her legs as she rode him hard and fast.

And this time, when she came, he joined her.

Sated and exhausted, Maggie stretched out on his chest and simply enjoyed the feel of his arms around her as his breath stirred her hair.

Braden leaned his head back, shaken by what had occurred between them. He had known she would be a firebrand, but never had he guessed the full depth of her passion.

And worse, he was far from sated.

If anything, he wanted her more than ever before. Because now that he'd experienced her love, he knew she truly had no equal.

And that scared the devil out of him.

Maggie lifted her head up to look down at him.

"Is something wrong?" she asked, her brows drawn together with concern.

"Nay," he whispered as he ran his hands over her back. It wasn't really a lie.

In truth, things had never been more right.

And likewise, they had never been more wrong.

Chapter 16

As they dressed, Maggie could feel Braden's tenseness; it seeped into her very bones and made her ache. She didn't want to leave it at this.

"Braden," she said, drawing his attention. "I want you to know that I have no regrets."

His face was even more grim than before. And she could read the *I do* in his eyes.

Her heart heavy, she turned away from him.

So that was it. He truly had no feelings for her, and now he wished he could forget her.

At that moment, Maggie wished she had stayed at the camp. She should—

"Maggie," Braden said as he pulled her into his arms. "I'm not upset at you," he whispered. "I'm upset at myself. I should never have taken you. It was wrong of me."

He tilted her chin so that he could search her eyes. "Why did you come to me?"

"Because I wanted you." She reached up and touched his whiskered cheek. "I'm not asking anything from you, Braden. I don't expect you to treat me any differently than you did before. I was curious, and now I know."

Braden clenched his teeth at her words. The problem was now he knew, too. Already, his body stirred from her casual touch, from the scent of her freshly washed body.

He still wanted her.

In fact, he could take her again this instant.

And it scared him. Scared him more than anything else ever had. He would sooner walk naked into battle against a full English garrison than face her like this.

If only he knew he could trust her.

You could try.

How easy that sounded. But the consequences were too dire.

No woman was worth his life. It was the conviction he lived by, and it was the one truth he would never forsake.

Maggie saw the shadow fall over his eyes. He made a decision regarding her, she could feel it. And judging by the stiffness of his body, it didn't bode well for her or her heart.

You expected as much.

Indeed, she had. Now it was time for her to preserve her dignity. Rising up on the tip of her toes, she placed a tender kiss on his whiskered cheek.

"Thank you," she whispered in his ear, then she stepped out of his arms and walked back to the camp.

Braden closed his eyes as pain washed over him. He understood what she meant and it tore through him that he wasn't the man she deserved.

He stooped, picked up the plaid from the ground and folded it. Memories assailed him. Memories of her lying naked above him as she gave herself fully to their union.

She was magnificent.

And he was an ass. A giant, arrogant one who should be taken out and beaten by each of her brothers.

Sighing, he tried to put the matter out of his mind as he headed back to camp.

That night passed slowly for Maggie, who couldn't really sleep. All night long she tossed and turned as she tried her best to prepare her words for the MacDouglas.

Worse, dreams of Braden tormented and seduced her. But of all the dreams she had, the most terrifying was the one of the MacDouglas plunging his sword through Braden as she watched, helpless to stop it.

She woke in the morning with a prayer lodged in her throat and her hands trembling uncontrollably.

"Are you all right?" Braden and Sin asked as she sat straight up.

Her heart pounding, she could do nothing more than nod. But it was a lie and she knew it. She wasn't all right. She was terrified beyond her capacity.

Everything rested on her shoulders. If she failed, all three of them would pay with their lives.

Throughout the morning, her panic stayed close to her heart.

After breaking the fast, they rode through the morning and well into the afternoon, watching for anyone who might see them on horseback and offer a challenge. But their luck held and they passed no one at all.

In truth, it was eerie that they saw no one in the lush, green fields or along the road as they crossed MacDouglas lands and headed for the castle. In some ways it appeared as if the world had ended and they were the only survivors.

When they came within an easy walk of their destination, they left the horses to graze in a small meadow.

"Do you think the horses will be here when we return?" Maggie asked Braden while he turned the last horse free.

"We'll see," Braden said as he and Sin hid the saddles and bridles under a bush.

Maggie nodded, noting that he didn't mention what would become of them all if she didn't succeed.

It has to work, she assured herself as they gathered their packs and headed up the steep hill where the castle, and their fates, rested.

She couldn't fail. Not while Braden's life depended on her.

It was a couple of hours before dusk when they finally reached the old stone walls surrounding the MacDouglas stronghold.

Since William Rufus had ruled England, these walls had protected all the MacDouglases from their enemies. No one had ever breeched the fortress, laid a successful siege to the castle or held a MacDouglas laird hostage.

No one, that is, until Maggie had forged an alliance with the lady of the castle, and Ceana Mac-Douglas and her women had driven the men out.

In spite of herself, Maggie felt a little bit of pride at her accomplishment as she noted the large camp of men laying siege to the walls where women stood along the parapets taunting them. It was truly a miraculous sight. One she hoped to someday share with her grandchildren.

As the three travelers drew near the camp, Maggie saw the men had left their tents and were grouped around a single individual. From the looks of the camp, it appeared Ceana MacDouglas had wasted little time after Maggie's departure putting her husband and his men out. And by the dour looks on the men's faces, she could tell they didn't share Maggie's humor at their predicament.

Braden pulled her to a stop as he caught sight of the MacDouglas.

Barely a score and ten years of age, Robby Mac-Douglas was almost as handsome as the MacAllisters, and he was a feared laird in the prime fighting years of his life. Wide of shoulder and every bit as tall as Braden, the man could terrify a demon.

His reddish blond hair complimented his bright blue eyes. And by his carriage, it was obvious that he was a man who had been born to command others. He held his spine straight, his jaw stern.

Maggie felt her legs go weak in fear. Her moment at hand, she found herself seriously lacking in courage.

What an arrogant braggart I am, she thought ruefully as she watched the MacDouglas snarl at the men around him.

How on earth would she ever dare confront such a large, terrifying man?

But she must.

Run, her mind railed. *Run before it's too late.*

Still, she couldn't. She'd never in her life been a coward and this was not the time to become one.

Ha! Her mind argued. *This is the perfect time to learn cowardice!*

Maggie refused to listen. Taking a deep breath for courage, she stepped forward, then froze as she heard Robby MacDouglas's words to the crowd. "I'll give a king's ransom in gold to the man who brings me Maggie ingen Blar's head on a pike! I swear I'd rather break bread with the king of England than that horse-faced, toad-eating lickspittle!"

Maggie's heart pounded, and for a minute she feared she might run after all.

Sin bent down to whisper in her ear, "What are you waiting for? Go on and tell him how wrong he is not to end this."

Aghast, Maggie gaped at him. At the moment, she didn't find him funny. Not in the least.

Braden grimaced at his brother and pulled her aside. But before he could speak, the entire camp grew quiet as a horse came running from the castle walls and into the circle of tents.

The men broke apart enough that Maggie saw a rider slumped over the back of a white horse.

And he was covered in . . .

Or rather he was dripping . . . ?

Frowning, Maggie stepped forward, not quite sure if she could trust her own eyes and what she thought she saw.

The horse stopped and the rider looked at his leader as if he were sick to his stomach.

As the rider stood up in the stirrups, there was a strange sucking noise, and as he threw his leg over and dismounted, an odd, iridescent trail marked his descent. Then he slopped his way toward the MacDouglas as flies and other insects buzzed around his head.

"They honied me," the rider said to the group,

shaking his arms and sending trails of honey in all directions. Several men cursed as the honey landed on them.

His face grim, the rider snarled, "Them wenches done honied me from head to toe. Said they'd be throwing cabbages at the next one of us what comes near the gate."

Maggie covered her mouth with her hand to stifle her laughter.

Robby MacDouglas cursed. "Did you tell her you were there for a truce?"

"Aye, my lord. The lairdess said there would be no truce until she saw you and Lochlan MacAllister side by side at the gate."

The curse Robby MacDouglas let out shamed his former one.

"My lord," Braden said all of a sudden.

Maggie went cold as she gaped at him. What was he thinking?

Her heart pounding even more fiercely than before, she watched in stunned silence as Braden crossed the short distance between them and stopped directly in front of his family's mortal enemy.

How on earth could he appear so calm and un-shaken while it was all she could do not to faint?

Robby MacDouglas turned a hostile eye to Braden. "I don't know you."

The silence was deafening.

Braden nodded at Robby MacDouglas—the

man who had sworn to see him and his brothers in their graves.

Braden couldn't believe he was doing this. There must be a special corner of hell for a fool such as he. He only prayed it would be a few more years before he learned whether or not that was true.

In the meantime, Braden had to find some way to end this standoff before the three of them were slaughtered by the men or cabbaged by the women.

"Nay," Braden said in a good-natured tone, hoping to allay the laird's fear and mistrust. "You don't. I'm just a traveling bard, but I'm thinking I might be able to help you with this matter."

Braden resisted the urge to snort at himself.

How the hell did he keep getting himself into this?

Sweet Mother Mary, Braden thought, *can't you keep your mouth closed for a minute? Why must you always get yourself right into the thick of any fight?*

Robby's eyes reflected his own doubts over Braden's ability to handle the situation. "Can you, now, lad? And how do you figure that?"

"I'd like for me and my brothers to try and talk to the women."

The men broke out into laughter and several of them openly jeered.

Turning to face him, the man in honey raked Braden with a disbelieving stare. "Want to look like me, do you?"

Braden shrugged. "There are worse things than being covered in honey, and I've had harder things thrown at me than cabbage. But I think my brothers and I might be able to get the women to listen to reason."

Laughing, Robby MacDouglas put his hands on his hips and shook his head. "If you're of a mind to try, then I'm of a mood to see you harmed. Go ahead, lad, and God's favor upon you."

Braden nodded, then gathered Maggie and Sin.

"All right," Braden whispered to Maggie as they walked slowly toward the castle gate. "This is your one chance. You have to make the Lady MacDouglas listen to you."

"And if she doesn't?"

He exchanged a determined look with Sin. "Then I hope you'll forgive me for what I'm going to have to do to end this."

The stricken look on her face tore at his heart. He didn't want to add strife to her worries, but they had come too far to go back. She had to succeed.

As they drew near the gate to the castle walls, a cabbage came whirling straight at Braden's head. He barely had time to dodge it.

The old woman who had hurled it shouted down from her place on the wall, "We done told you men we'd—"

"Hold!"

Maggie recognized the voice of Ceana Mac-Douglas.

The lairdess peered down at them for what seemed like an eternity. After a long minute, the lairdess left the wall and Maggie could hear the clip-clopping of her shoes as she descended the wooden steps on the other side.

A few seconds later, a lock rattled and rasped, then the small door to the side of the main gate opened to show the head of a beautiful woman only a year or two older than Maggie. The Mac-Douglas lairdess looked like an angel, with her golden hair braided and wrapped about her head. The black and blue plaid she wore brought out the creaminess of her pale skin and made her blue eyes glow.

"Maggie, is that you?" Ceana MacDouglas asked.

"Aye," Maggie said. "May we come in?"

"Aye," Ceana said, then she stepped back into the safety of the bailey.

A woman of about two score, holding her broom like a sword, opened the door only enough to admit Maggie and her escorts, and as soon as they were through it, she slammed it shut and locked it.

Ceana stepped forward and took Maggie's hand in her own. Her cheeks were bright and her eyes shone with happiness. "Is it over?" she asked.

Maggie shook her head. "Nay, it has gotten worse. The men of my clan are ready to kill our laird if he doesn't settle this, and he refuses to settle unless your husband ceases to demand the life of his brother."

The lairdess dropped Maggie's hand and all the happiness fled from her face. "Oh, Sweet Mother Mary," Ceana breathed. "What are we to do, then?"

"I don't know," Maggie whispered. "I'm sick of the bloodshed, but I'm afraid the men have us this time."

"My lady?" Braden asked, drawing their attention to him. "Do you know of anything that can make your husband give up this feud?"

Ceana's face turned cold and angry. "Nay. He loved that she-devil to the exclusion of everything else."

"Then why did he marry you?" Maggie asked, then quickly regretted the bluntness of her question.

However, Ceana didn't seem the least bit taken aback by it. And when she answered, her voice was completely devoid of emotions. "For my money, and because his own mother insisted he take a wife."

"His mother?" Braden asked. "Is she here?"

"I'm standing right behind you, you whelp, with a broom to break across your hide if you make one move on any of us." She raked a look over him. "And don't you be thinking I'm so old that I don't remember what a young buck like you has on his mind."

Braden turned slowly to see the woman who had let them inside.

Agnes MacDouglas looked young for her age. Her strawberry blond hair held only the faintest traces of gray in it, and her blue eyes were searing in their intensity and filled with the vitality of a woman half her age.

She placed the broom handle on the ground and held it like a soldier would a spear as she placed her left hand on her hip and narrowed a probing stare at him. "I told my Robby-boy that woman was a snake when I first saw her and that wandering eye she had. I knew she was no good. But he wouldn't listen to me. He just had to have her, regardless of my warnings."

Maggie stepped forward. "Is there anything that could make him—"

Agnes shook her head before she finished. "She poisoned my babe with those practiced pouts."

Ceana's face turned to stone. "And now I carry his bairn and I will not give birth to this child until my husband stops pining for that she-devil!"

Sin snorted. "Should I point out, milady, that I doubt you'll have a choice as to when you birth your child?"

Ceana cast him a withering glare.

Sin just smiled in response.

"Wait!" Maggie said, interrupting them. "I think I have a plan."

Braden shivered at her words. God help them now, for he knew only too well about Maggie and her plans.

If he had any sense at all, he'd head back to England with Sin in tow.

He glanced around at the women surrounding them. All eyes were trained on Maggie, and his gut drew even tighter. They were actually going to listen to her.

Of course they are. They don't know what they're in for.

But he did.

"My brother Anghus used to have a saying," Maggie told them. "You don't know what you've got till it's gone."

The hair on the back of Braden's neck rose, and some inner premonition warned him to grab her and run back home as fast as his legs could carry him.

But damn fool he, he didn't move.

"Well," Maggie continued, "I think I know a way to show Robby MacDouglas exactly what he has, and to see if it means anything to him."

Chapter 17

Once the plans had been made for the following day, Agnes and Ceana led Maggie, Braden and Sin into the castle to feed them and to finalize their preparations. Maggie stayed only long enough to make sure everything would be ready, and then her nerves got the better of her.

Unlike the men, she didn't feel like eating. Not when her stomach was tied into so many knots, and so many doubts plagued her.

She needed a breath of fresh air and some time alone to think. Time alone where no one could see the numerous uncertainties that shredded her confidence and left her vulnerable and scared.

Heading out of the donjon, Maggie paused at the top of the stairs to glance about the bailey. Rushlights had been lit, and the women along the parapets had ceased their taunting of the men in order to eat their suppers and gossip with each other.

None of them paid her any heed as she descended the steps, then walked aimlessly around the dark yard.

What have I gotten myself into now? Maggie wondered.

True, the three of them were still alive, but there was a lot more to do before she would feel victorious. After all, everything hinged on the fact that the MacDouglas would care if something happened to his wife.

If he didn't . . .

Maggie trembled, then pulled her plaid shawl tighter around her shoulders.

As she rounded the side of the keep, a shadow drew her attention. She paused and turned her head to look at it.

At first she thought she might be seeing things, but the faint outline of a body was all too clear. Someone was skulking about, and unless her instincts were wrong, the shadowy figure was watching her.

Frowning, she took a step forward to peer a little more closely at her specter. The shadow stepped back, away from the moonlight and her ability to see it clearly. Maggie felt a moment's reservation, but the shadow didn't look very large or dangerous.

Ultimately, her curiosity overrode her trepidation.

Determined to learn who was watching her and why, Maggie closed in on the figure, only to find a lad of about seven years shirking away from her.

His face panicked, he glanced about for a way to escape.

"It's all right," Maggie said gently, relieved to find the lad and not a man bent on mischief.

No doubt the boy was only hungry and searching for food, or his mother. "I mean you no harm."

She still couldn't see his features plainly, but she could see the basic contours of a thin, narrow face. For several seconds, she stood completely still as he sized her up. By the shadowy curl of his lip, she could tell he found her lacking in some way.

"Are you that MacAllister lass?" he asked tentatively. "I was told ya had short hair."

"Aye, I am she."

Maggie heard his sigh of relief. And too late she remembered Robby MacDouglas's words about her head. And the value of it brought to him on a pike. Could the boy possibly be after that?

It seemed unlikely, but why else would he want to find her?

"And who are you?" she asked.

"Me name's Connor."

Maggie smiled. How sweet, it was the same name as Braden's horse. "And what is it you want with me, Connor?"

The boy stepped into the bright circle of moon-light to where Maggie could finally see him.

Her breath caught in her throat, for never had she seen a more perfect duplication of Braden. The lad's black hair was wild and in need of a trim. His long, lanky frame needed steady meals, but those eyes . . .

She'd know those greenish brown eyes any-where. But whereas Braden's were teasing and bright, the boy's were hard and jaded. Angry and harsh.

"I want you to take me home," he said.

Maggie's chest drew even tighter at the boy's request.

"Home?" she asked, praying it was all a coinci-dence. Perhaps he was a distant cousin to Braden. Perhaps one of the MacDouglases had kidnapped him thinking to use him against one of the other MacAllister clansmen.

Her mind grasped at any explanation other than the most obvious one.

"Aye," Connor said. "I'm one of their bastards. Me mother told me my da was a MacAllister and I want to go to their castle to meet my family."

Maggie's head swam at the confirmation of her worst fear. Braden had a son. One who had been seriously neglected, by the looks of him.

In that moment, she wanted to storm into the castle and ring the man's neck. How dare Braden take no responsibility for his actions!

Oh, just you wait, Braden, she thought. *I'm going to get you for this.*

"And where's your mother?" she asked.

Connor looked away and his eyes turned even angrier than before. "She died two summers back. I was staying with her sister, but she said she don't want no bastard who can't do what he's told. I was thinking since you were here that if I paid you, you'd take me back with you."

Connor moved forward then and held his little frail hand out to show her a glass bead, a shiny rock and a piece of charred, twisted silver that defied her abilities to identify it.

"I know it's not much," he said, "but it's all I got. If you take me home to them, you can have all of it, and I swear I'll find work and pay ya proper for putting up with me."

Tears gathered in her eyes as she stared at his extended hand.

How could anyone be so cold as to turn such a dear child out? And it was obvious he was a good lad. In spite of the anger in him, he was being respectful and honest.

Maggie knelt down by him and looked at his offering. "What fine treasure you have there."

He nodded solemnly as he fingered the glass bead. "This was in my mother's pin. It fell out and I was going to fix it for her, but she died before I could earn enough money to pay the smith to repair it."

Next he went to the rock. "This I took from outside our cottage when I was a little boy and they told me I couldn't live there anymore."

And lastly, he touched the silver piece. "That was the ring me father gave me mother. Me uncle tried to melt it down, but I grabbed it out of the fire when he wasn't looking and hid it."

He extended his hand to her and offered her all he had in the world.

Swallowing back tears, Maggie took his hand in both of hers and closed his hand over his payment. "This is far too valuable for me to take."

He looked confused.

She pulled the plaid shawl off her shoulders and wrapped it around him. "You don't have to pay me, Connor. I would be honored to take you away from here."

Happiness flared in his eyes for a full second before suspicion clouded his gaze. "What do you want from me, then?"

"Nothing."

He scoffed at her. "People don't do nice things for nothing. They all want something."

Goodness, but the boy sounded so much like Sin that it gave her chills. Just what had he experienced, to make him so distrustful at such a young age?

Reaching up, Maggie brushed a stray lock of ebony hair from his forehead, then cupped his cool cheek. "Not all people are like that."

Still, he looked suspicious.

Maggie rose and reached out to take his hand. "Have you eaten anything?"

Connor hesitated before he finally placed his hand in hers. "The women won't let me eat anything 'cause I'm a man."

She tightened her grip on his hand as they walked across the yard. The lad was far from a man, even though he acted as if he were ancient.

Oh, if she ever laid hands on his aunt and uncle, she'd give them both a sound tongue-lashing! How could anyone be so cruel when it was obvious the boy had a good heart?

"Come with me," she said gently, "and I'll see you fed."

Connor stopped dead in his tracks as she led him toward the castle.

"Nay," he said. "If me aunt sees me, she'll beat me for sure."

Let her try! In the mood Maggie was in, she was sure the woman stood no chance whatsoever. But it was obvious the boy had seen enough violence in his life.

What he needed now was protection, and she would keep him safe no matter what.

"Then I'll make sure she doesn't see you."

Maggie kept his icy hand inside hers as she changed directions and led him behind the castle and up the back stairs to the small room Ceana had given her for the night.

It was a very cool evening to be out, and poor Connor was barefoot and dressed in a tan and blue plaid that should have been tossed out as a rag.

It defied Maggie's best abilities to imagine the callousness of his aunt and uncle. She could never treat a child like this, and most especially not one related to her.

Maggie opened the door to her room. "Connor, did your mother ever tell your father about you?" she asked as she moved into the room to light the tallow candles on the small table before the fire.

He paused just inside the doorway.

Maggie watched as his eyes widened, then darted about the room to take in the glowing fire, large bed, small table and chair and warm furs. He blinked as if unable to believe she was allowing him into such luxury.

He quickly headed to the fire and stretched his little hands out toward it, seeking the warmth. "She said she went to him to tell him about me, but when she got to his castle, she saw him there with a beautiful lass."

Connor leaned toward her ever so slightly, and spoke his next words in a hushed whisper as if betraying some sort of secret. "She said they were kissing."

He straightened then, and recited the rest as if his mother had drilled it into his mind a thousand times over. "She said she knew then that all the words he'd said about loving her were false. She said all men were false and lowly, and that if God were truly merciful, I would have been born a daughter to her and not another man sent to break her heart."

Maggie's own heart lurched at his words, words he spoke with calm, quiet acceptance.

Unable to stand it, Maggie fell to her knees and drew the boy into a tight hug. At first he tensed and fought her hold, but she tightened her grip. She refused to let him go. The child needed love. He needed a hug, and she would not let another minute pass without giving it to him.

Then, to her surprise, he tentatively wrapped his thin, frail arms about her and laid his little head down on her shoulder.

"You know, Connor, God is merciful, and it is a wondrous thing to be born a son."

He said nothing, but she could feel his hot tears against her neck.

She cradled his head in her hand and just held him as tightly as she could as she rocked him slowly in her arms.

In that moment, Maggie knew what she would have done in Aisleen's place. She could never have let Sin stand by himself, let alone be taken by his father's enemies. Any more than she could let this child suffer another day.

She didn't know how Braden would react to Connor's presence, but she knew what she needed to do.

"You know, Connor," she whispered as she

rocked him, "if you don't want to stay with your family, I share a small farm with my sister-in-law, Kate. She has two wee bairns, a boy and a girl. I was thinking they might need a cousin to help keep watch over them."

He tilted his head back to frown at her.

Maggie smiled and brushed his hair off his face, then placed a hand to his soft cheek as she told him plainly what she meant. "I was thinking that if you prefer, you could come live with us."

His frown turned to disbelief, then his eyes sparkled. "I would have a family?"

Maggie nodded. "Aye. One that wanted you, and you would have a mother who loves you. Not to mention one who makes the best elder-berry tarts you've ever tasted."

For the first time, she saw him smile. Her eyes misting again, she reached up and touched the deep dimples that punctuated the gesture.

"I promise I'll be a good lad and only eat what you give me. I won't ask for any more, ever."

"You can eat as much as you can hold."

"Really?"

She nodded.

"Wahoo!" he shouted, then he quickly cringed and placed a hand over his mouth as he glanced about furtively. "I'm sorry about that."

"I don't mind noise," Maggie said. "I was raised with six boys and they were always shout-ing and screaming."

She rose to her feet and ruffled his hair with

her hand. "You wait here and I'll bring you some food."

Again that mistrust came into his eyes, but he said nothing as she left him.

A myriad of emotions whipped through her as she descended the stairs and quickly gathered a tray of food, telling the servants that she wanted to eat alone. No one questioned her.

Once Maggie had enough to fill Connor's belly, she headed back to him, cursing his callous family with every step she took.

Why hadn't Connor's mother told Braden anyway?

Maggie didn't know for sure, but she suspected Braden would have gladly taken the boy in. And even if he hadn't, Lochlan most assuredly would.

Don't judge his mother, Maggie, she told herself. *'Tis for God alone to do.*

But it was hard not to.

In fact, at that moment, she didn't know whom she wanted to thrash more, Connor's mother or Braden.

Laying the matter aside for the moment, she pushed open the door to her room to see Connor sitting on the bed. He jumped off as if terrified she would scold him, and when he saw the food in her hands, he wahooed again.

Maggie placed the tray on the small table by the fire and watched in delight as he crammed roasted beef, carrots, peas, onions and apples into his mouth.

Once he finished eating, she tucked him into her bed and left him there to dream of better days to come.

He fell asleep almost as soon as he closed his eyes.

Maggie listened to his gentle snore as she brushed her hand through his hair.

"Oh, Braden," she whispered, wondering how she was going to tell him he was a father.

On the one hand, she could kill him for leaving the boy, but on the other, she knew he had no way of knowing about Connor. Poor Connor's mother probably had no idea what she should do, and the sight of Braden kissing another had probably cut her all the way to her heart.

Had Maggie been in the woman's shoes, she would have marched herself across the yard and confronted Braden while he groped another.

But that was her, and not the poor woman who had been brokenhearted.

Suddenly a shiver went through her as she thought about herself. What if she carried his child already?

The answer was simple.

"I will love it as much as I love its father," she whispered. And she would. Just as she loved the little part of Braden that was snoring softly in her bed.

Like father, like son.

Leaning forward, she brushed her lips against

his forehead in a light kiss. "Happy dreams, sweeting."

She pulled the covers over him, then went to find his father.

Braden sat alone in the hall. Everyone else had long taken themselves to bed in preparation for what they would do on the morrow.

Even Sin had wandered off, making Braden wonder if his brother had finally found one of the Scottish lasses to his liking. And there had certainly been a number of them to choose from.

The bad part was that, for the first time in his life, none of them appealed to him in the least.

Braden cursed.

"She's turned me into a bloody eunuch," he muttered as he drained the last of his ale.

And then he thought of Maggie's words: *You prefer mulled wine . . .*

Cursing again, he set the tankard back on the table. How had she done it? How had she wormed her way into his carefully guarded heart?

Over and over, he could feel her against him. Hear her murmurs in his ear as her breath stirred against his skin. Closing his eyes, he savored the memory.

And then he cursed it.

He would banish her from his thoughts. Aye.

"Braden?"

He almost jumped out of his chair at the sound of her voice coming from behind him.

Turning, he saw her standing in the shadows. "I thought you would be in bed by now."

"I can't sleep," she said, moving closer. She paused at the table, turned to face him, then leaned her buttocks against the table's edge so that she could see him while they talked.

Braden kept his gaze on the tankard. He didn't dare look into those deep amber eyes, lest they captivate him and make him forget what he must—or, more to the point, must not—do to her.

"What is on your mind?" he asked with a nonchalance he didn't feel.

"I was thinking of something you said to me earlier."

She paused, and when it became apparent that she wasn't going to finish her thought, Braden made the mistake of looking up at her.

His heart ached at the confusion and sorrow he saw in her eyes. Her gaze on the floor beside his chair, she had her brows knitted.

"And what was that?" Braden prompted her, in spite of the voice in his head that told him to leave the matter be.

Maggie looked up and pinned him with a probing stare. "You said that you would love to have a family of your own. Did you mean that?"

His gut wrenched. So that was what was on her mind. She was now looking for him to marry her. And he couldn't do that. He mustn't.

"Now, Maggie, don't be thinking—"

"I'm not thinking of marrying you," she said sharply, cutting him off. "I am not the woman for you, and we both know it. I just wanted to know if you meant what you said. Do you want children?"

He couldn't imagine why she would ask such a thing.

Unbidden, an image of a child popped into his mind. One with her mother's curly russet hair and her father's bright hazel eyes. He could see the child so plainly in his mind, hear her gentle laughter as she ran, that one would think she was real.

And worse than the image was the sudden need he found within his heart to make that child a reality.

"Nay!" he roared, wanting to push the thought out of his mind as quickly as possible.

Maggie blanched.

"I see," she said quietly, then pushed herself away from the table. And him.

Braden reached out to take her hand and keep her at his side. "Maggie, wait, I didn't mean that."

"Aye, you did," she said, pulling her hand away from his. "I heard the passion of your denial all too plainly."

"It wasn't directed at your question." It had been directed at his own senseless need.

"Then what was it directed at?"

Braden opened his mouth to respond, then

quickly snapped it shut. He didn't dare tell her the truth. It would hurt her even more to know that what bothered him was the thought of the two of them being united eternally in the form of a child.

He would never hurt her that way.

"I . . ." He struggled to think of something. Anything he could tell her that would save her feelings but would not be a complete lie.

But he could think of nothing. Either he had to tell her the truth or lie. So, for the first time in his life, he lied to her. "Nay, I don't want children."

"Why?"

Again he saw the image of the little girl reaching out to him.

Closing his eyes, Braden blurted out the criticisms he had long chastised Lochlan over. "They're messy, and they smell."

Maggie gaped at him. "They're children, Braden. I daresay you weren't overly clean in those days either."

"But I never bit anyone."

Heat suffused her cheeks as she glared at him. " 'Tis a pity I didn't bite you harder."

She moved away.

Without thought, Braden caught her arm and pulled her back. "Don't go away angry at me."

"Give me one reason why I shouldn't."

He tried to think of one. But he couldn't. In truth, all he could do was stare at the moistness of her lips as he remembered the way they had tasted.

Without conscious thought, he reached out and cupped her face in his hand.

The anger fled her eyes as they turned a dark, deep brown. "Braden—"

She never got the chance to finish. Braden pulled her to him and claimed her lips for his own. Och, but she tasted so good to him. He could feel her breath against his tongue and he inhaled the sweet, feminine scent of her.

She had corrupted him in a way no woman ever had. She had made him noble. Caring. Kind.

Maggie saw in him things he had never known existed. Worse, he wanted to be the man she saw him as.

"Maggie," he murmured as he pulled her into his lap.

Maggie knew she should fight him. She should probably hate him. But she couldn't. Regardless of his faults and his past, she did love him. She would always love him.

And so she gave herself over to his magnetic power. She let him capture her and take her wherever he wanted to.

And right now, she needed him, wanted him more than she had ever wanted him before.

He ran his hands over her back, raising chills as he massaged and rubbed her skin beneath her shirt. Maggie deepened her kiss, biting and licking his lips as she fought the escalating heat of her body that craved his.

Braden stood with her then and leaned her back against the table. His touch scorched her as he unlaced her shirt and peeled it back to expose her right breast to his touch. His hand closed around the taut peak, tormenting it with pleasure as he laved her neck with his tongue.

Maggie buried her hands in his hair as she groaned in ecstasy.

And then he dipped his head to take her breast into his mouth. Maggie moaned as her body ignited. Her body was hotter than ever before.

Braden paused in his exquisite torture of her.

"Tell me what you want from me?" he asked, his voice deep and husky with need.

"You," she murmured, reaching for him. "I want you to make love to me, Braden."

Braden trembled at her request. Unable to deny either one of them, he lifted his plaid and buried himself inside her, all the way to the hilt.

They groaned simultaneously. Her breasts exposed by her unlaced shirt, Maggie writhed on the table before him. Braden dipped his head to take her lips with his own as he thrusted himself even deeper into her.

Maggie wrapped her arms around his neck and met him stroke for stroke. They rode each other hard and fast with a need built from years of longing.

Braden had waited his entire lifetime for a

woman who could see him as something more than just a pretty face or a rich pocket. In Maggie's eyes, he was a man. A human being with feelings and needs the same as hers.

And in that moment, he realized the most terrifying thing of all. He did love her.

Completely, fully and without reservation.

Only she had ever claimed his wayward heart. And he trembled from the fear and wonder filling him as he filled her. Saints preserve him, he was truly lost now.

Maggie arched herself against him, then froze and quivered in his arms as her release came.

Braden quickened his strokes, then quickly found his own piece of heaven as he released himself deep inside her.

Maggie lay on the table, her body still throbbing with pleasure. With Braden still trapped between her legs, she sat up and claimed his lips.

His kiss was deep and passionate, and to her amazement, she felt him start to harden all over again.

"I'm not through with you," he murmured against her throat. "Say you'll stay with me tonight."

"I'll stay with you."

Braden withdrew from her then and picked her up in his arms. He carried her to the stairs and up to his room.

He closed the door with the heel of his foot and didn't let her go until he reached the bed.

Tenderly, he laid her back against the furs and stripped her clothes from her body.

Maggie rose up on her knees as she quickly divested him of his own shirt, plaid and boots. She could only see him by the light of the fire, but it was enough to let her revel in the hunger he had for her.

She smiled. "You are so handsome," she said, running her hand over his bare, muscular chest. He shivered beneath her touch.

"And you, little blossom, you are so very beautiful."

She scoffed at his words. "What a liar you are."

He shook his head as he laid her back against the mattress. Mesmerized, Maggie watched the way the fire played across his tawny skin as he dipped his head to suckle her breasts. Again the inferno started deep inside as her as her body craved his touch.

He skimmed her hips and waist with his hands as he ran his tongue slowly, carefully over her right nipple.

Maggie's head swam.

"Like that, do you?" he asked.

"Aye," she breathed.

Her feelings of love and devotion washed over her as he moved his hand down to the center of her body and toyed with the sensitive flesh between her legs.

"And that?"

She couldn't speak; all she could do was writhe

to his touch, seeking those wonderful fingers that delved into her body over and over again.

Braden laughed, then dipped his head and replaced his fingers with his mouth.

Maggie reached down and buried her hands in his hair as he tortured her with pure bliss.

He cupped her bottom in his hands and lifted her hips so that he could gain greater access to her. Maggie obliged by pressing her feet against the mattress and lifting herself up to his questing, delving tongue.

Her entire body quivered and shook as pleasure assailed her. Finally, she could stand no more.

Maggie moved away from him then. He looked surprised as she sat up and eyed him.

"My turn," she said, wanting to give him the same pleasure he had given her.

Braden smiled in delight as she leaned forward on to all fours.

Oh, the sight she made in his bed, her short russet hair curling around her face as she rolled him over onto his back.

Instead of straddling his waist, she stayed to his right side. She took his hand into hers and brought it to her mouth. "Such wonderful hands you have," she breathed, running her fingers over his skin. "So strong and dark." Then she placed his forefinger into her mouth and ran her tongue over the pad of it.

Braden hissed in ecstasy as she nipped at the sensitive flesh. He watched in awe as she alternated his fingers one by one, giving each the same sensual attention with her tongue and teeth.

As she toyed with him, he reached out his other hand and cupped her breast.

She groaned and released his hand. Braden quickly closed it over her other breast. She smiled at him and placed her hands over his.

The sight of her hands over his as he touched her soft mounds delighted him. But not nearly as much as the sight of her eyes, dark and seductive, as she watched him watch her.

She was spectacular. The way she gave herself to him without shyness or reserve.

Never had he seen such. And he wanted more. He reached for her.

Maggie grabbed his hand and *tsk*ed at him. "Do I have to tie you up?"

He grinned evilly. "Would you?"

She laughed at him. "Do you want me to?"

"I must say I have never had that happen before. It might be interesting."

She arched a brow at him. "You would trust me to do that?"

"Only if you promise to untie me when you finish."

A wicked glint came into her eyes. Before he could reconsider, she pulled the laces from their shirts and set about tying his wrists to the bedposts.

Braden couldn't believe he had agreed to this,

and yet there was something so strangely erotic about it. He was completely vulnerable to her now. Something he had never been to anyone else in his entire life.

Maggie stared down at Braden lying against the white linen sheets. His dark skin contrasted sharply with the linen. The muscles on his arms flexed ever so slightly as she adjusted herself to sit by his side.

"Are you just going to look at me?" he asked.

"For the moment, aye." Because he looked scrumptious lying there, naked and warm, writhing on the sheets as his long, dark hair spilled across the pillows.

There were so many places on his body she longed to explore. The muscled curve of his neck. The ripples over his stomach that flexed as he breathed.

But first she decided to start with his thighs.

Aye, those strong, dark legs seemed to be the most delectable part of him. Well, them and his buttocks. Maggie smiled. She would taste him all before the night was over.

Moving to his feet, she placed herself between his spread legs and skimmed her hand up his calves and over his thighs.

Braden ground his teeth as her nails gently scraped his flesh. He stared down at her as she dipped her head and started biting the flesh of his inner thigh.

There was no pain, only a pleasure unimaginable. Never had he felt anything more exciting than her tongue gently dancing across his flesh as her hands explored him.

Laughing, she looked up at him. "Hmmm," she said thoughtfully, "where should I go next?"

She traced small circles with one fingertip over his thigh.

"Where would you like to go next?" he asked.

She bit her lip as if debating. Scooting to his side, she traced her finger over the contours of his ear. "Would you like that?"

"Aye," he breathed as fire coursed through his veins.

She leaned forward and gently stroked his ear with her tongue.

Braden hissed as his entire body jerked involuntarily. His body instantly sprang back to life, even harder than it had been before.

She trailed her mouth from his ear down his jaw, then buried her lips in his neck. Braden struggled against the laces holding him.

"I want to touch you," he said, his voice ragged with need.

"Where?" she asked.

"Everywhere."

She laughed again. "Sorry, love, you'll just have to wait."

She straddled him then. Braden arched his body as she skimmed herself from the center of his chest all the way down to his waist.

"You're killing me!" he growled, wanting to touch her so badly that he could barely stand it.

Maggie smiled wickedly at his agonized tone as she felt his stomach muscles contract beneath her thighs. The hunger in his eyes burned her.

He lifted his hips then and threw her forward onto his chest. "Kiss me, blossom," he demanded.

She did. Wrapping her arms around his neck, she lifted his lips to meet hers and she kissed him with all the strength she had.

Oh, but he tasted wonderful. And as their kiss deepened, she felt him harden even more against her bare thigh.

"You are a hungry one," she said as she pulled back from his lips to look down at his shaft standing out from his body.

"You have no idea," he said, his voice breathless.

Deciding she had tormented him enough, she turned and placed her hand against his rigid shaft. He shook all over.

"Like that, do you?" she asked.

"Aye."

She skimmed her fingers over his swollen manhood, gently toying with him while she used her other hand to brush the small trail of hairs that led from his navel to his groin. He hissed and growled as he writhed even more.

Maggie delighted in her power.

Braden couldn't think as he watched her staring at him. The look of love and desire on her face scorched him straight to his wicked soul. And just when he was sure he could stand no more, she finally took mercy on him.

Her eyes smoldering, she rose up above him, then impaled herself on his shaft.

He threw his head back and growled at the tight feel of her body enveloping him again. Lifting himself up, he drove himself deep inside her.

Never had he felt anything like her as she rode him hard. The feel of her body sliding against his as she moaned feverishly above him.

Unable to stand it, he fought against the ties that held his hands from her. He needed to feel her. Had to feel her.

Maggie must have decided she'd had enough as well, for she delivered one deeply satisfying stroke to him, then untied his wrists.

With a triumphant roar, Braden sat up.

"Now you're mine," he said playfully.

"I have always been yours," she whispered.

Before he could think on her words, he pressed her back against the mattress, separated her thighs with his knees and drove himself back into paradise.

She raked her nails over his back as he thrust against her. In and out, faster and faster, until he thought he would go mad.

She clasped him tight with her legs and arms, then threw her head back and screamed out his name as her release took her.

Braden laughed as he continued to fill her.

"That's it, Maggie," he breathed in her ear. "Hold me." Because, in truth, he never wanted her to let go of him.

She held him tight and when his own release came, it shook him all over.

Never had he met her equal. Braden lay there, still inside her, just listening to her breathe in his ear. Her breasts were flat against his chest, and for the first time in his life he didn't want to leave her. If he could, he would crawl inside her skin and stay there forever.

The peace inside him was indescribable. His body was fully sated and yet he still wanted more.

It was the strangest, most frightening thing he had ever encountered.

What was it about her? She was magical.

Rolling over, he pulled her to him. She curled against his right side with her head on his shoulder and one arm draped over him.

For hours they lay there, neither speaking, just feeling each other, grateful for the time in each other's embrace and terrified of what the morrow might bring.

In the wee hours of the morning, Maggie fell asleep.

Braden stayed awake, listening to her breathing as he held her close. It was such a miraculous sound.

"Maggie," he whispered against her hair, knowing he would have to leave her when this day was over.

Why? his mind demanded.

I have no choice!

She commanded him in ways no one ever had. Her touch made him weak, and he was helpless before her. Deep inside, he knew he would give her anything she wanted.

And that he could never do.

Nay, once this day was finished, so was their relationship. He must make sure of it.

Brushing his lips against her forehead, Braden allowed himself a moment to absorb the taste and smell of her. He closed his eyes and let those sensations wash over him. He would carry this memory for the rest of his life.

And it would haunt him throughout eternity.

"Good-bye, my love," he whispered.

Chapter 18

Maggie came awake slowly to the sound of Braden's gentle snore.

Not quite ready to rise, she snuggled closer against his side, until she recalled poor Connor waiting for her in her room.

Afraid the boy would think she had abandoned him, she quickly got up and dressed.

With a parting look at Braden's naked, slumbering form draped in furs, she rushed from the room and gathered apples, bread and a cup of milk for Connor.

She knew she should have told Braden about his son last night, but it just hadn't seemed the time. Especially not after the way Braden had reacted when she'd asked him about children.

Nay, she would have to wait until he was more open to the possibility. The last thing Connor needed was to know his father hated the very idea of having a child. The boy had been hurt enough; she would add no more pain to his damaged soul.

Still, that voice in her head nagged her to tell Braden about Connor. He had a right to know.

Clasping the food to her breasts, Maggie tried not to think about it lest she cry. And she had promised herself she wouldn't cry over what was necessary.

Braden would go his own way, and she . . .

She would care for Connor. The lad would be happy with her. Much happier than he would be with his uncles and father. After all, they were bachelors who had little knowledge of children. What Connor needed most was a mother's love.

If she couldn't give her love to Braden, then she would content herself with lavishing it on his child.

Maggie returned to her room just as the boy stirred.

Not fully conscious, Connor cringed from her as she stood over his bed. "I'll milk the cows," he whimpered, raising his arm to protect his head.

"It's just me, Connor," she said gently, placing the food and milk on the table. "And there are no cows to be milked."

He put his arm down and blinked as if unable to believe his eyes.

"I brought this for you," she said, handing him a slice of bread.

He ate it so fast, she half feared he would choke on it. "Slow down, lad, it'll make you sick."

He did, but only for a minute before he tore back into it, then reached for the milk and apples.

Smiling at his enthusiasm, Maggie ruffled his hair. "I want you to know that I have to go meet with the MacDouglas in a little bit, but as soon—"

"Nay," he gasped around a mouthful of apples. He swallowed hard and stared at her with wide, terrified eyes. "You can't be doing that. He'll kill you!"

"It's all right," she soothed, wishing her words could comfort her as well. "He won't harm me."

"Aye, he will."

"Nay," she reassured him, hoping it was true. "I can handle my own. But I want you to stay here until I return. Can you do that?"

His greenish brown eyes full of reticence, he nodded. "You will return, won't you?"

"Aye," she said, hoping it wasn't a lie.

Reluctantly, she left him and returned to his father. While she walked, she realized today was the day Ewan would free Lochlan. She only hoped Lochlan and her brothers were still safe and whole.

As gently as she could, she shook Braden awake.

"Braden," she whispered, brushing his hair back from his shoulders before she placed a tender kiss right where the tiny hairs covered the nape of his neck. She nipped his flesh with her teeth. " 'Tis morning."

Braden groaned and shifted ever so slightly, baring one tawny hip to her eager gaze. "It can't be morning," he mumbled, "I just went to sleep."

Maggie laughed as she lifted the fur and admired his naked backside. In her mind, she could see him again as he had been last night, unabashed and completely hers, his eyes narrowed on her as she rode him. She could feel his strong hands on her hips urging her on, feel his warm breath on her skin.

Even now her body burned for him.

And right then, it was all she could do to stay focused on the task ahead, as well as on those who waited below for them.

"It is morning," she repeated, "and we have a laird to meet."

Again he groaned before he rolled over, showing her his perfect male body.

"Fine," he said, rubbing his hands over his face. "Let us be about meeting our maker, shall we?"

Her cheeks burned as she saw his erection plainly in the morning light.

Braden laughed as he noticed where her gaze lingered. "What can I say? Even in dreams, you haunt me."

He sat up then and pulled her close. "Care to—"

A sudden pounding on the door interrupted him. "Braden?" Sin called from the other side.

"I'm up," Braden shouted at his brother, then mumbled beneath his breath, "and likely to stay that way if you keep pounding the damn door."

"We're waiting for you," Sin said.

"I'll meet you downstairs."

Maggie smiled bashfully at him. "They're waiting."

By his face she could tell Braden barely bit back some sarcastic retort. Grumbling under his breath, he reluctantly left his bed.

Maggie helped him to dress, then hand in hand they went down the stairs.

She knew she should tell him about Connor before they left, but for some reason she couldn't. The boy had been through enough rejection. She would take him home with her and in a few months or even years, when Braden was more ready for it, she would tell him.

As they reached the bottom of the stairs, she saw the women gathered in the great hall. In spite of the large number of them, it was so quiet, the only sound Maggie could hear was her heart pounding in her chest.

Sin rose from the table where he had been eating and met them just inside the door.

"Ceana is in position," he said. "I made sure she'll be comfortable for the rest of the day."

"Do you think this will work?" Braden asked his brother.

Sin shrugged. "Why not? I never thought we'd get this far. I guess in another hour we'll know for certain."

Braden looked at Maggie and tightened his grip on her hand. "Aye, we will."

It was then Maggie saw the uncertainty in his gaze. But it was only there for an instant before he concealed it.

Without another word, he led her from the hall.

Outside the door, Agnes stood at the bottom of the stairs, waiting for them in the inner bailey.

"Are you ready, my lady?" Braden asked her.

Agnes nodded, her eyes sharp and cunning. "We all are. And God help the lad if he doesn't react like he ought. I might be old, but I'm still spry enough to whack his bottom if he shames his upbringing."

Maggie smiled, even though she was terrified from the inside out.

With Braden standing between them, the three of them walked to the gate. Maggie crossed herself and whispered a quiet prayer for success.

Slowly, the women who had been manning the walls wrenched the gate open.

A sudden hush fell on the men as they gaped at the rising gates.

"I'll be a damned beggar in hell," Robby Mac-Douglas said. His face incredulous, he came forward to meet them at the entrance.

With a disbelieving smile, Robby held his hand out to Braden, who took it and shook it quickly. "How did you do it, man?"

Braden shrugged. "It wasn't hard."

"The devil you say," Robby said.

Robby met his mother's glare, then looked about behind them. "Where's Ceana?"

"She's gone," his mother said before Braden could deliver the deception they had planned.

Robby took the news like a king who had just found himself without a throne. The smile faded from his lips and the young laird's face flushed bright red.

Rage descended into his eyes. "What?" Robby roared. "What do you mean, gone? Gone where?"

Agnes put her hands on her hips as she faced her son with a *tsk*ing sound. "She couldn't take any more of your whining about Isobail. And who can blame her? I'm surprised she stayed with you as long as she did."

Robby glared at all three of them as if he couldn't decide who to cleave in twain first. His anger palpable, every muscle in his body stood taut. "When did she leave?"

"Last night," his mother said. "When I went to wake her this morning, I found this." She handed him the folded piece of vellum that they had prepared the night before.

Robby read it, his hands shaking.

With a fierce curse, he turned to his men. "Search the castle," he ordered them. "I want to make sure this isn't another one of Ceana's pranks."

"It's no prank," his mother said firmly. "She's left ya sorry hide."

It was then Maggie saw what they had wanted to see. The pain on Robby's brow, the concern and loss. Whether he admitted it or not, he cared for his wife.

She smiled.

"Gather the horses," Robby shouted to his men.

"Why?" Braden asked. "If you dinna care for her—"

The MacDouglas's eyes flared. "Why dinna you stop her?"

"She said you wouldn't even miss her," Braden answered with the very words Ceana had used to dissuade them from this plan. "She said you had never once seen her, for your eyes were filled with the image of Isobail ingen Kaid."

Robby winced as if he'd been struck. "I want my Ceana back!" he said, his voice ragged and agonized. "And I won't stop looking until I find her."

One of the young lads brought a saddled horse to Robby. As he moved to mount, Braden stopped him.

"It's not necessary."

Before Braden could explain, a shout rent the air.

Maggie turned to see smoke billowing out from one of the small buildings in the inner bailey. It took a full second more before it dawned on her which building it was.

The one where Ceana had gone to hide.

Her throat tight, Maggie watched in horror as the fire ravaged the building.

"Braden!" she shouted, but he was already on the run toward it.

"Dear God," Robby's mother breathed. "Ceana!"

"Ceana?" Robby repeated.

"She's in there," Maggie said, then ran for the building with Robby hot on her heels.

Maggie watched in horror as Braden started to run into the burning building, but one of the men pulled him back.

" 'Tis too late," the man shouted above the roar of the fire. "There's no way she could still be alive in that blaze."

Maggie stared at the orange and red flames twisting through the building and shooting up toward the blue morning sky. She couldn't believe what she was seeing.

How had this happened?

Oh, Lord, oh, Lord, oh, Lord, her mind reeled with terror and pain.

Ceana was dead!

And it was all her fault. It had been her plan. Her stupid, awful plan, and now poor Ceana was dead from it.

"Where's my brother?" Braden asked.

Covering her mouth with her hands, Maggie turned to look at Braden as he scanned the crowd for Sin.

A woman who stood beside her shook her

head. "The Englishman ran inside to save the lairdess as soon as the fire started." The young woman looked away, her eyes tormented and sad. "He didn't come back out."

Maggie's legs went weak, and for a moment she couldn't breathe.

Braden's agonized cry was only second to that of the MacDouglas. The two of them sank down to their knees while they watched helplessly as the fire engulfed the building where Sin and Ceana had been.

Tears filled Maggie's eyes. This hadn't been the plan. Ceana was only supposed to wait in there in case the MacDouglas searched the castle. She was to come out the minute her husband started to leave to pursue her.

It's all my fault!

Pain lacerated her chest. She'd never meant for anyone to get hurt. Never!

How would she ever live with herself after this?

"Braden," she whispered, placing her hand on his shoulder. "I'm so sorry."

Maggie saw the agony in his eyes as he looked up at her, and it tore through her. She had caused this. She had killed them both.

Why, oh, why had she started all this?

It was then the MacDouglas turned to them with a feral snarl curling his lips. Eyes narrowed, he looked at them as if he were seeing them for the first time.

"You spoke with a woman's voice," Robby said accusingly.

His breathing ragged, he slowly pushed himself up from the ground to his full towering height. The MacDouglas walked toward her like a lion stalking a hare. "You're that Maggie bitch, aren't you?"

Maggie couldn't speak as terror washed over her. Her eyes wide, she stumbled away from him.

With a practiced, deadly calm, Robby Mac-Douglas unsheathed his long sword. The murderous gleam in his eyes bespoke his intent loud and clear.

He was going to kill her.

Overwhelmed by grief, guilt and terror, Maggie backed away.

She'd only managed a step or two when her trembling legs buckled, and she found herself sitting on the ground, immobile. Completely paralyzed and stunned, she looked up helplessly at him.

His face deadly cold, the MacDouglas laird loomed above her like a mountain, his shoulders blocking the sun and the sky.

He raised the sword in both hands to plunge it down into her.

Just as Maggie was sure it would strike her belly, another sword flashed, deflecting the Mac-Douglas's sword away from her.

The MacDouglas cursed as he turned to face a furious Braden.

His eyes defiant and smoldering, Braden held his sword aimed at the MacDouglas's throat. "To get to her, you'll have to come through me."

"You want to die for her?" Robby asked.

"Aye," Braden said without hesitation. He glanced at her and for the first time she saw the love in his eyes. "I will die for her."

"Then die," Robby said before shoving Braden back and striking at him with his sword.

Braden skillfully met him stroke for stroke.

Maggie couldn't move, couldn't breathe as she watched the two of them. Worse was the fact it was obvious Braden held more skill. The Mac-Douglas fought bravely, but there was no doubt who would emerge the victor. And if Braden killed the MacDouglas, she and Braden were dead for sure.

The MacDouglas arced his sword for Braden's chest. Braden jumped back.

His reach overextended, the MacDouglas stumbled forward.

Braden bought his sword down toward the man's back.

"Hold!"

Maggie's eyes widened as she recognized Sin's voice.

But she didn't dare take her eyes off Braden as she watched in muted horror, anticipating his blow.

Somehow, Braden stopped his blade an inch from Robby's spine and brought it up and away from his opponent just in time to save Robby's back from the death blow.

Maggie released her breath in a rush as Braden turned away from her.

It was only then she looked to where Sin was walking toward them, cradling his left arm with his right hand, with Ceana by his side. The two of them were covered in soot, their clothes torn and faces red, but they were mercifully alive!

The MacDouglas pushed himself up from the ground with a happy shout as he rushed to his wife, calling her name.

Still shaking, Maggie smiled as the two of them embraced. It was a beautiful sight. The MacDouglas scooped his wife up in his arms and kissed her fiercely.

Maggie shifted her gaze back to Braden. To her amazement, he didn't run to Sin's side.

He came to hers.

His eyes filled with concern, Braden held his hand out to her and helped her up from the ground. Then, to her utter disbelief, he wrapped his arms around her so tightly that she feared he would break her ribs.

"Thank God," he murmured repeatedly in her ear as he just held her close to him.

It was then she understood the truth. Braden loved her. He truly, truly loved her. Even though he hadn't said it, she could feel it in the tightness of his hold, hear it in the relief of his voice as he whispered her name.

Tears gathered in her eyes as she wrapped her arms about his waist. This was so much more than she had ever hoped for. In all her foolish dreams, she had wanted this. And now . . .

She felt like shouting, or flying, or singing, or doing something miraculous to celebrate the joy she felt.

Braden let go of her and cupped her face in his hands, then he kissed her fiercely.

Maggie felt her tears flow down her cheeks.

"Fetch a healer!"

The cry of alarm broke them apart, and it was only then Braden looked to where Sin had been standing.

His brother had fallen.

Ceana held Sin's head in her lap as she called for help. The MacDouglas was kneeling by his side.

Braden ran to Sin, with Maggie one step behind.

Her heart pounding, terror filled her again as she looked down at Sin. He lay on his right side with his left arm bleeding and burned.

"What happened?" Braden asked as he knelt down by Sin.

"He saved me," Ceana explained. "One minute I was just standing there, moving things around, then the fire started. I think I might have knocked the candle over, maybe I bumped it with one of the sacks. I'm not sure."

Tears flowed down her cheeks as Ceana looked from Robby to Braden, then down to Sin's unconscious form. "I don't know what happened. I tried to get out, but my hem was caught. I couldn't move, and the fire was everywhere. I thought I was going to die, so I started screaming. The next thing I knew, Sin was there. He freed me, and just as we were leaving, a beam fell against him."

Her eyes wide, Ceana looked baffled by all that had happened. "He pushed the beam off and got us out. I thought he was fine," she said breathlessly. "He said he was fine. He looked to be fine."

"He just collapsed on the ground," Robby finished for her.

The healer came forward out of the crowd and pushed them away as she examined Sin's body.

"We need to get him inside."

Robby ordered his men to help Sin gently to a bed.

Braden watched helplessly as Sin was taken away. He glanced to Maggie and felt a horrendous tearing in his heart. Had he not been protecting her, he could have saved his brother.

He had chosen her safety over that of his own blood.

How could he have done such a thing?

Why had he not run to Sin first? Sin was his brother. He was the one Braden was supposed to protect.

Maggie reached out to touch him, but Braden shrugged her off. He didn't want to feel her hand on his arm. Not now. Not until he could come to terms with the decision he had made. And the possible cost of his actions.

"Braden?" she asked.

"I need to see to Sin," he said dismissively.

Maggie frowned as Braden left her standing alone in the yard. Something wasn't right. Braden had been so tender until he had seen Sin.

What had happened?

More discouraged than she had ever been before, she followed them inside.

When she reached Sin's room on the upper floor, Braden ordered her out.

"Let me help," she insisted.

"You've done enough," Braden said, his voice edged with an anger she didn't understand.

Her heart heavy, she turned and went below to check on Connor.

An hour later, Braden stood to the side of the bed as the healer reached into her clay jug for a leech. As she moved toward Sin, Sin's eyes snapped open, and he reached with his good arm to stop the old woman from placing the vile creature on his skin.

"You put that disgusting thing on me, old woman, and I'll cut your heart out."

"But you need to be—"

"I'm bleeding quite enough, and I personally like the poison in my blood and have no wish for it to leave me," Sin said tartly. "Braden, get her out of my sight."

Braden didn't argue. He did as his brother asked, then returned to the bed.

Sin's face was pale, but Braden could see the fire of life burning brightly in Sin's black eyes. Relief poured through him as Braden realized for the first time since his brother had fallen that Sin was no longer in any danger.

"Where's Maggie?" Sin asked.

"She's below."

Sin arched a brow at him. "Why is she below, alone?"

Braden blatantly ignored the question. "I thought you were going to die."

Sin scoffed as he shifted in the bed, then cursed as he drew rigid in pain. Hissing, he stared at his burned arm and curled his lip. "It takes more than a little fire to kill me."

"That wasn't a little fire."

Sin gave him a droll stare. "Trust me, brother, it was a little fire."

Unwilling to argue the matter, Braden shook his head. "I never should have left you."

Sin looked at him with a fierce frown. "What the devil are you talking about now?"

"I should have made you come outside with me."

Sin's look spoke loudly, *Are you mad?*

"I'm not some wench in need of my baby

brother to protect me, Braden. In case you haven't noticed, I happen to be one of the most feared knights in England and the Holy Land. It's not your banner that makes armies surrender on sight, but mine."

"Still, you are my blood."

That deep, probing stare of Sin's delved into him. "This has nothing to do with me, does it?"

"Of course it does," Braden insisted. "You are my blood, and I was protecting Maggie while I should have been protecting you."

"Nay, little brother. A man protects those who need it most. Those who cannot protect themselves."

"But I chose her life over yours."

Sin cocked his head to one side. "Since both she and I are alive and well, I fail to follow your logic."

"You're not well. You could have been killed."

Sin snorted. "I am merely singed. I assure you, I've suffered much worse than this. But what of Maggie? What happened to her?"

Braden clenched and unclenched his jaw as he thought over that morning's events. Over and over, he could see her on the ground as the Mac-Douglas plunged his sword down. The terror of the moment, and the fear in his heart for her life, were forever branded in his memory.

"Her plan worked," Braden whispered. "But when Robby saw the fire, he tried to kill her."

"And?"

"I saved her."

"You risked your life for her?" Sin asked in disbelief.

Braden nodded.

Sin laughed. "I'll be damned, little brother. You've finally succumbed to Cupid's arrow."

"It's not funny," Braden snapped. "I am powerless against her."

Again that probing stare delved into him. "Are you?"

"Aye," Braden said with a sigh. "One look from her and I am completely undone. What if she asks me one day to forsake my blood? Where would that leave me?"

"Wallowing in sweet bliss, I would imagine."

"You're not funny."

All the humor fled Sin's face. "And neither are you. You know, Braden, I learned not to trust out of necessity. But you . . ."

Sin didn't finish the sentence. He didn't have to. Braden knew what his brother meant.

Braden had never personally been betrayed. It was only by watching his brothers that he had learned the hardest of life's lessons.

"Do you think I can trust her?" Braden asked.

"That I cannot answer. The only way to find that out is to try it and see."

"And if she's not trustworthy?"

Sin sighed and shook his head as if exasperated

by him. "You're stronger than Kieran. You'll survive it. But I think, little brother, that you're missing the real question. What if she *is* trustworthy?"

"Then I'm a monkey's arse."

Sin smiled. "We seem to keep coming back to that, don't we?"

Braden laughed. Sin was right. It was time for him to stop being shortsighted and to take a chance.

All these years, he had been afraid. All the times he had thought himself so strong, when he was actually weak and too terrified to take a chance.

But Maggie . . .

She was worth it.

Worth his life, worth his heart. Worth everything. And he wouldn't let his stupid fears keep them apart another minute.

Braden was going to find her, and then he was going to marry her.

"Wish me luck."

Sin nodded. *"Bon chance, mon frère."*

Braden rushed from the room, needing to find Maggie.

He took the stairs two at a time as he ran into the crowded hall to find her. There were probably three score people there, who were laughing and catching up on all the events that had happened over the past few weeks.

Braden looked about, but nowhere did he see

Maggie's short russet hair or her laughing amber eyes.

Whcrc wao ohc?

Braden headed for the door.

"Braden MacAllister!"

The MacDouglas's shout brought instant silence to the hall as Braden froze dead in his tracks.

His entire body tense, Braden turned toward the laird, expecting the very worst.

His face unreadable, Robby MacDouglas crossed the hall with his hands on his hips. The laird narrowed his gaze on Braden.

Nothing and no one moved or made a sound as the two men sized each other up.

When Robby reached for him, Braden took a step back, ready to brawl. Then, to his utter surprise, the man threw his arms about him in a brotherly hug. Robby clapped him hard between his shoulder blades.

"I owe you and your brother, for the life of my wife and child. From this day forward, the Mac-Douglases will be allies to the MacAllisters."

Braden blinked in disbelief as loud shouts filled the hall, echoing off the stone walls.

The man wasn't trying to kill him? He could barely accept that reality.

Robby clapped him hard on the shoulder once more and stepped back. "You're a good lad, to brave my wrath and bring peace to our clans. You, truly, are a born negotiator."

It crossed Braden's mind that the credit didn't really belong to him. Maggie had done it. But now didn't seem like the time to contradict the MacDouglas. Not when peace was so newly formed.

"Thank you."

Robby nodded. "You're probably looking for Maggie?"

"Aye."

"She was outside earlier, headed toward the stable last I saw."

Braden went cold at the news.

Nay, surely she wouldn't . . .

Oh, who was he fooling? 'Twas Maggie he was dealing with.

Like as not she'd already left for home on her own. It was just the sort of thing she would do.

Terrified, he left Robby and ran as fast as his legs could carry him. If she had done something so foolish as to head back to MacAllister lands on her own where those thieves could find her, he would kill her himself.

His entire body quaking in fear, he threw open the door of the stable and nearly ran over a small child.

"My pardon," he said to the boy. "I'm looking for . . ."

Braden's voice trailed off as he looked to the lad and saw himself.

Chapter 19

Braden froze as reality crashed through him. He quickly calculated the last time he had been with a woman from the MacDouglas clan.

It had been right around the time when the feud began. Maybe seven or eight years ago. Right about the same age as this boy. He winced.

Maggie was going to kill him!

His mind numb, all he could think of was the look on her face when she found out, and the kick to the groin she was sure to give him the instant she saw the lad.

Oh, bother, he was in for it now.

The child eyed him warily.

"Hello," Braden said, trying not to scare the child, while inside he was shaking in horror from what he knew he had done. "What's your name?"

"Connor," the boy said. "Who are you?"

Braden didn't know what to answer.

I'm your father just didn't seem like the best way to introduce himself to the lad who, like as not, would hate his very soul.

So, instead, Braden switched the topic. "Where are your parents?"

The boy shrugged. "I don't have any. Oh, wait!" he said, his eyes shining instantly. "I do have a mother now." He placed his forefinger to his lips as if in deep thought and frowned. "But I can't remember her name."

"You don't know your mother's name?"

The boy scratched his nose. "My real mother was Fia, but she's with the angels now. And this other woman is taking me home to live with her."

Fia. Braden searched his memory. The name was so familiar to him, but for his life, he couldn't recall her. But the mere fact that he recalled the name as familiar said it all.

Dear Lord, this really was his son. He was sure of it.

He struggled to breathe as emotions swept through him: shame, happiness, guilt, terror. He ran the full gamut of human experience in the space of several heartbeats.

"What of your father?" Braden asked tentatively.

"I'm a bastard," the boy said, his voice laced with anger. "Me father didn't want me mother."

Braden winced as if the lad had struck him. "Maybe he did."

The boy shook his head. "Me mother said he loved other women, that he didn't want just her."

Braden closed his eyes as the words tore through him. He had never meant for a child to suffer for his actions. Oh, God, how could he make it up to the little fellow?

Somehow, he would. If it took the rest of his life, he would make sure this lad knew his father loved him, and that he would protect him.

Suddenly Braden heard a familiar tune from outside. And in an instant he knew the sweet sound of Maggie's voice.

Braden went cold. This wasn't good. Not good at all!

He had to hide the lad! Quickly. There was no telling what Maggie might do if she saw him.

Over and over, he recalled his mother's reaction to Sin. The scorn on her face.

He hadn't been able to protect the lad before, but he would protect him now.

He would explain it to Maggie once he'd arranged things so that the boy couldn't be hurt by her reaction.

"Connor," Braden said, placing a gentle hand on his thin shoulder. "Would you like to play a game?"

The boy's face lit up. "Aye!"

"This is called hiding. You find a place and stay there until I find you."

The boy looked skeptical.

Braden nudged him toward the back of the stable. "Go on and hide. I'll cover my eyes. Hurry."

The boy scampered off.

Braden heard him climb the ladder to the loft at the same moment the door opened and Maggie entered.

Braden swallowed as sweat beaded on his forehead.

She carried a large basket in her hands as she looked about the stalls. She froze the instant she saw him.

"Braden," she said coldly. "I didn't expect to see you here."

He swallowed as guilt and pain consumed him. He didn't want to hurt her any more than he wanted to hurt Connor.

Oh, but he had gotten himself into one fine mess. He just hoped he didn't lose Maggie over this.

"We need to talk," he said simply.

"Why?" she asked. "All has been said. I told you I would never ask anything of you. I meant it. Now, if you'll excuse me . . ."

He caught her arm as she started past him. "I'm not about to let you go home on your own."

She looked at him as if he were daft. "Think you I'm mad? I wouldn't dream of it."

"Then what are you doing here?"

" 'Tis no concern of yours." Then her eyes softened. She reached out and touched his arm. "I thought you needed to see to Sin."

"He's conscious now, but I wanted to see you."

"Why?"

Braden took the basket from her hands and set it on the ground. Taking her hand, he led her to the door.

"Braden, I—"

"Shhh," he said, cutting her off. "I need to speak with you, alone."

She looked about the empty stable. "Are we not alone?"

Braden glanced to the loft. He didn't want to chance Connor hearing whatever reaction Maggie might have to him.

"I would feel better if we were outside."

"Very well."

Braden led her just outside the door, to stand beside a large oak. "Maggie, I . . ." His voice trailed off.

For the first time in his life, he didn't know how to talk to her.

Should he just blurt out, *Maggie, I want to marry you, and while you're considering that, let me tell you about my illegitimate son?*

Nay, that wouldn't work.

Maggie, I love you. Would you mind taking care of my . . .

No wonder his father had withheld the news about Sin from his mother. This was a lot harder than he thought.

Maggie knew he'd never been a saint, but thinking him a lewdster and being presented with the evidence of his indiscretions were two entirely different things.

He just didn't want to lose her.

"Maggie," he began, speaking her name slowly. "I have some things I need to tell you, and I'm rather sure I'm going to make a mess of this. But could you please give me time to stumble through it?"

She nodded.

Braden took a deep breath. He didn't know an easy way to say what was in his heart, so he just blurted it out. "I love you and I want to marry you."

The shock on her face was almost comical. Her hands began trembling almost as soon as the words were out.

"Braden, I don't know what to say."

"Say, *Aye Braden I'd love to marry you.*"

"Braden, I would love to marry you, but it's not that simple."

His chest drew tight. "Why not?"

Her gaze went from him to the stable, then back to him. "I . . . I . . ."

"You?"

"I—"

The door to the stable burst open before she could finish her sentence.

Connor came bounding up to them.

Silently, Braden cursed the lad's timing and took a step back before Maggie had a chance to knee him where it would hurt most.

"Are those my sweet biscuits and jam?" Connor asked Maggie. "I hope they are, because they smell delicious."

"Aye, little bit, they're yours, and make sure you finish all the milk."

The lad wrinkled his nose. "I prefer ale."

"But you'll drink the milk."

His jaw slack, Braden glanced back and forth between them. "You know him?"

"Of course she does," Connor said. "She's my new mother."

Braden took another step back as he absorbed the news. "But how—"

"I met him last night," Maggie explained. "He wanted me to take him to the MacAllisters."

In an instant he understood why she had sought him out last night. "That's why you asked me about children?"

She nodded. "I didn't want you to hurt the lad's feelings."

Braden burst out laughing.

Connor scratched his head as he looked back and forth between them. "Can I go eat now?"

"Aye," Maggie said, "but before you leave, I want you to meet your father, Braden MacAllister."

"That ain't me father," the boy said. "Kieran MacAllister be my da."

They both stood stock-still as the lad's words rang in their ears.

"Fia ingen Bracken!" Braden said as he recalled

the name and the lass. Kieran had fawned over her for weeks before he met Isobail.

"You're Kieran's son?" Maggie asked Connor. "Are you sure?"

The boy looked at her as if she had gone mad. "Aye. Me aunt went to find him when my mother died, but she came back saying he was dead too and that she was stuck with me."

Braden sank down on his knees so that he could look more closely at the boy.

Now he could see the difference in the face. Kieran and he had shared the same eye color and hair.

He cupped the lad's face in his hands and stared at the living legacy Kieran had left them. "You have no idea how many people are going to love you where we're going."

"Really?" Connor asked, his voice high, his eyes gleaming.

"Aye," Maggie said as she knelt beside them. "Starting with Braden and myself."

Braden looked at her, his heart pounding. "You were going to raise him, thinking he was mine, and never tell me?"

"I would have told you when I thought you were ready."

He couldn't believe his ears. He had been so wrong about her. So very wrong. And he would spend the rest of his life making it up to her.

"You're amazing."

She looked away sheepishly.

He took her hand and placed a kiss on the back of her knuckles. "Thank you, Maggie. For everything."

This time, when she looked at him, he leaned forward and kissed her.

"Yuck!" Connor snorted. "Not that ickiness."

Braden broke away with a laugh. "Trust me, lad, one day it won't be icky to you."

"If that day ever comes, you can take me head and stick it on a pike."

"Go eat," Maggie said, her voice filled with laughter.

Connor didn't need any more encouragement. He bounded off at a dead run.

"You know," Braden said, tracing the contour of her cheek with his fingertips, "you never really did answer my proposal. Will you marry me?"

Maggie bit her lip, her brow furrowed. "Now, why should I be wanting to do that? All you've ever done is torment me. And now you thought I would be cold enough to just toss a boy out on his own."

"You thought I'd be so cold as not to want the child at all."

"That was your own fault. You're the one who said children smelled."

Braden laughed. "I did say that, but I didn't mean it." He cupped her cheek in his hand as he stared into those amber eyes that touched him all the way to his unrepentant soul. "In truth, there is nothing more on earth that I would ever want than to have a smelly, messy child with you."

"Truly?"

He nodded.

Maggie's bright smile lit her entire face. "Well, then, Braden MacAllister, I will gladly marry you, and have lots of smelly, messy children with you."

Epilogue

Two months later, Maggie stood in the midst of her wedding celebration with trembling hands. She still couldn't believe it was real!

All the years she had spent dreaming of this, and none could compare to the reality of it.

Pegeen, Merry and Ceana chattered around her, offering their congratulations.

But Maggie's attention was focused across the room where Braden stood with his brothers, her brothers, along with Connor and Robby MacDouglas, drinking ale and laughing.

Sin was again dressed as an Englishman and his left arm was no longer bandaged from the burn. If not for the very subtle way he favored it, no one would ever know he'd been injured.

Connor darted between the men as he basked

in their patient indulgence of his youthful exuberance.

Ewan stood above them all, his face grim, but every now and again, Maggie caught a twinkle in his eye as he traded insults with Braden or Lochlan, or brushed his hand through Connor's hair.

And Robby . . . It was still strange to see him standing with them. No one would ever guess that just a few weeks ago they had all been mortal enemies. She couldn't fathom the change Ceana and her babe had made in the rough laird. But then love was strange that way.

At this moment, all was right in the world and she was truly grateful for the miracle.

"Oh, Maggie," Pegeen exclaimed. "What beautiful shoes you have."

Maggie looked down to see her left shoe peeking out from beneath the hem of her skirt. The soft black leather slippers with tiny rose blossoms stitched into them had been a wedding gift from Braden.

Smiling, she remembered Braden's story of Enos and his words about her footwear, as well as her husband's vow that she would never again own a pair of ugly shoes.

"Thank you," she said to Pegeen.

Braden joined her then. Taking her hand in his, he placed a gentle kiss across her knuckles. "I wondered where you had wandered off to."

"I'll never be far away," she said. "I can't afford to be, since there's no telling whose bed I might find you in."

He laughed. "You know better than that, little blossom. There's only one woman who can satisfy me. And speaking of . . ." he bent and whispered a proposition in her ear that left her cheeks scalding.

"Braden!" she gasped in surprise. "Are you never sated?"

"Never," he said with a devilish gleam in his eyes. "But then, neither are you."

Maggie bit her lip as she glanced around to see if anyone else had heard his words. Luckily not, but in her heart, she knew the truth of it. She was never sated when it came to Braden.

It was then he handed her a small square package wrapped in kidskin. Maggie smiled as she unwrapped it.

Ever since they had returned from MacDouglas lands, Braden had lavished her with more gifts than she could fathom. Silver brooches, gold necklaces, a silver brush for her hair. He'd given her so much that she couldn't imagine what this newest gift could possibly be.

Frowning, she pulled back the wrapping to find the softest dark green fabric she had ever felt.

"It's silk," he said in her ear as he pulled her back against his chest and hugged her about the waist. Resting his chin on her shoulder, he rocked her ever so slightly in his arms. "I'm going to wrap you up in it tonight and devour you."

Her cheeks warmed even more.

Lochlan spoke up from across the room, and immediately everyone grew quiet. "You know, when I first heard my baby brother was traipsing over to MacDouglas lands, I thought he was a dead man for sure. Never did I expect him to return home to us, let alone actually succeed in stopping the feud. And if someone had told me he would return with a bride . . . Well, I'm quite sure the devil is currently cursing a blizzard as he tries to find warmth."

Everyone laughed.

Robby raised his tankard toward them. "To Braden MacAllister, the best peacemaker e'er born."

Maggie's jaw dropped as everyone cheered *Braden's* accomplishment.

Braden laughed and whispered in her ear. "Don't contradict him, little blossom, not unless you want to start another feud. You and I know the truth."

Maggie turned her head to look at him and smiled. There was a lot more to that comment than Braden had meant.

For the first time, she did know the truth. She loved Braden, he loved her, and he would never leave her as her father had done her mother. And she would never ask more of him than he could give.

There was just one more truth they needed to share. "Braden?" she asked sweetly. "When it comes to children, do you prefer a boy or a girl?"

"As long as it comes with its mother's fiery spirit and russet hair, I couldn't care less. Why?"

She stood up on her tiptoes and whispered softly in his ear, "Well, I guess come next summer we'll know exactly what he or she looks like."

Braden's entire face lit up at the news. With a triumphant shout, he lifted her up in his arms and kissed her deeply. The crowd carried his shout as they cheered his kiss.

"Long live Braden and Maggie!"

And long live their love.